ACKNOWLEDGMENTS

I am one of those people who can sit down and write a book with only a few tears shed and a little teeth-gnashing. But write a thank-you note, a letter explaining my kid's absence, or anything that resembles a message of sympathy and I'm at a loss. I'll do my best to thank the people who are instrumental in helping me create and write about the life of Alison Bergeron and the mysteries she solves. I consider myself very lucky to be surrounded by the people who make writing, working, and living very easy tasks for me. I'll try to do my best to let them know here.

Thank you to Deborah Schneider and Cathy Gleason at Gelfman Schneider for their unfailing support and good humor when I turn into "needy author."

Thank you to Andy Martin, Kelley Ragland, Matt Martz, and Sarah Melnyk at Minotaur Books for embracing both my story and Alison Bergeron's.

We used to be a "writer's group," but now we're just a duo. Thank you to Alison Hendrie, without whose encouragement and wise counsel I would not be able to do what I do with any confidence whatsoever.

The posse at NYU remains true and committed to making sure I stay healthy and sane. Thank you to Anna, Rosie, Queen, Kathy, Rajni, Caroline, Crystal, Norma, Nelson, and Nurse Joanne; words will never be able to express what you mean to me. You're doing great on the "healthy" part. The "sane" part? Not so much.

Thank you to Lucy Zahray, the "Poison Lady," who taught me more than I ever thought I would need to know about arsenic.

Thank you to Jim, Dea, and Patrick. I couldn't have dreamed up a more wonderful family.

One

Meeting your boyfriend's parents for the first time shouldn't involve wearing bathing suits.

Is it just me or should that be a hard and fast rule?

My best friend, Max, didn't agree. Anytime she gets to wear a bikini is a good day. But she's a size two with six-pack abs. Me? I like to think that at five ten I resemble one of those hard-bodied beach volleyball players, but in actuality, I'm less gazelle and more stork. With a potbelly.

I was headed to meet my boyfriend's clan, the Crawfords. And frankly, I'm a little uncomfortable, at my age, with the "boyfriend" designation; sounds a little juvenile to me but I hadn't come up with anything better. This soiree was being hosted by Bobby's brother, Jimmy, whom I had met under less than ideal circumstances — let's just say that it was an "unfortunate incarceration" and he's a really good lawyer — and his wife, Mary Pat, and I had been told that it would take place around the swimming pool. And that Mary Pat had a "banging body," according to her husband, who was completely in her thrall. Hence, my dilemma.

Max said that I needed to get a sarong.

I spoke slowly. "But that would mean that I would have to go to Bali and I don't have time for that. We need to be there by two."

"They sell sarongs in America," she reminded me.

"Yes, but that would mean I would have to go to a mall, and in case you didn't hear me, we need to be there by two." Anyway, I was still in bed, talking to Max on the phone.

"I wish you had told me sooner. I would have lent you one of mine." I didn't ask why she had a sarong — or more than one, for that matter — nor did I remind her that I outweighed her by fifty pounds and would look stupid with her sarong tied around one leg. "As fascinating as this problem is, I have to go. The Hooters waitresses are threatening to strike if I don't give them a real case to work on."

Max is the head of a cable network called Crime TV and is working on a reality show that combines Hooters waitresses and private investigation. (Don't say it. I already know.) I had no idea how that was considered "entertainment" but Max had the golden touch and every reality show she produced was a ratings blockbuster. She was considered something akin to lightning in a bottle in the world of reality television combined with crime, so who was I to judge? I'm a college professor who teaches creative writing to disaffected college freshmen, along with a few upper-level courses to juniors and seniors, and Max thinks that it's a miracle I can stay awake while giving lectures to my classes, which I take as more of an insult to my teaching ability than to the attention span of my students. I like my job, even if when I use a three-syllable word, the students look at me with the same quizzical look my dog gives me when I say anything besides her name and the word "cocktails."

I had described the show to Crawford, and his eyebrows rose. "You've got to admit," he said, his cheeks turning slightly red at the thought, "there's something to be said for women with big boobs in bikini tops following philandering husbands around." And then, because he'd spent his formative years as an altar boy and knew that he was going to hell for saying "boobs" in mixed company, he wisely shut up. And probably did a silent Act of Contrition.

My eyes lighted on the cherry Ring Pop sitting on my nightstand that was, ostensibly, my engagement ring. It had all happened so fast; we had just left City Hall after Max and her husband, Fred, had gotten married — and Crawford had sprung a proposal on me, shocking me with his spontaneity. Crawford's not a spontaneous guy; everything he does is thought out and measured, wood burning in that gorgeous head of his. But this was completely out of the blue and I hadn't really given him an answer. The pool party and the meeting of the entire family, though? That made me think that he assumed that I had said "yes." I probably would at some point, but for right now, I was on the fence. Everything was great between us. But having been married to a serial philanderer, who was now six feet under, I was a little gun-shy. It was going to take me a while to sort this whole thing out.

After staring at the Ring Pop for an inordinately long period of time, I went back to staring at my old bathing suit. I chided myself for not having done what most normal people would do in this situation: gone to the mall and tried on every bathing suit in the store. However, since it was August, I was sure that fall clothes were already on the racks, and I would be destined to take one of the last suits in the store, either a string bikini or a flowered muumuu with matching leggings.

Crawford said that "everyone swims" at Jimmy's parties; that was a direct quote. Apparently, Jimmy had spent a boatload of money on a pool and hot tub and the family was a bunch of waterlogged Irish Americans who couldn't be dragged out. And they loved to play Marco Polo, according to Crawford. I lay back on my bed, considering my options. I could tell Crawford's family that I had just had liposuction on my abdomen and I couldn't get my stitches wet. Nobody would believe that. Even in a prone position, my stomach was visible over the waistband of my pants. I could tell them that I almost drowned as a kid and was afraid of the water, which was true. Or, I could just tell them the truth, which is that I can't swim and avoid water and all related sports. One thing I've found is that if you tell someone you can't do math, they're fine with it. Can't read? No problem. We'll teach you! Can't swim? Admitting that is akin to admitting you've been in the pen. Nobody believes you and then, after they've stopped laughing, everybody eyes you suspiciously.

I have a lot of other admirable qualities but didn't feel like I could share them with the Crawfords without sounding like a braggart. One of them is that I exaggerate everything to the point of paralysis at the thought of certain situations.

Like meeting your future in-laws. And revealing a character flaw like not being able to swim.

I got off the bed and looked at my bathing suit on the floor next to the bed. It was the same one I had had since my honeymoon with my late ex-husband. I had forgotten to pack a bathing suit for the trip (which gives you a little insight into my preoccupied, postwedding state — paging Dr. Freud . . .) even though we were headed to Aruba, and had been forced to buy a two-hundred-dollar Speedo in the hotel gift shop that was now more than ten years old and missing some important expanses of elastic.

I threw the bathing suit on the bed and decided that I wasn't going to do anything I didn't want to do. But I also decided that I needed a big iced coffee to steel my resolve. I put Trixie, my golden retriever, on her leash and started into town, a short walk from my house.

I live in a little village in tony Westchester County, where, years before, with a small inheritance from my parents, I was smart enough to buy a tiny house perfectly situated due to its proximity to both my work and New York City. After my divorce from the aforementioned late ex-husband, it turned out the house was just the right size for me, my dog, and Crawford when he visited. Crawford lives in Manhattan and commutes to the Bronx to the detective squad at the Fiftieth Precinct. I wondered what would happen if we did marry. Would he move here? Would I move there? How would two people who had lived on their own for a while adjust to living with other people again? We had been dating for a little over a year and Crawford was clearly perfect, but he also had two teenage daughters, an ex-wife who was getting remarried in a few months, a really intense job, and his own way of doing things after living alone for a long time. We had a lot to finagle if we were going to make this work.

Most important, how would Trixie feel?

I grabbed my coffee cup from the dish drainer before I left; my village was going green and I was going right along for the ride. Before leaving, I took a quick look at the calendar that hung on the side of the refrigerator. Yep, still August. I find August to be a tough time for me, something that never changes from year to year. My mother's birthday had been in August. She had also died in August. Every year, I expect it to get better, but here we were, a decade later, and I still feel like I can't catch my breath. Was that ever going to change? Was I being unrealistic to expect that it would?

I didn't feel the same way about my father's death, even though at the time, it had been just as difficult. The difference was that he hadn't suffered like my mother had. He had just gone to work one day and dropped dead, too young, at the UPS office where he picked up his truck and deliveries every day. His friends said he was dead before he hit the ground, and for some reason, that gave me some measure of comfort. I was only a teenager when that happened but still, I could deal with his absence in a way that I couldn't when it came to my mother.

Maybe it was all those years we had together, just the two of us. Or maybe it was because of how much she had suffered. Every year, I tried to sort it out, and every year, I just marked the days down until August was over and it was no longer an issue.

When I got outside, I was not surprised by the weather: hot and steamy, a typical August day in New York. The humidity would have me looking like Gene Wilder in no time. I reconsidered the jeans and T-shirt that I had put on before I left and decided that an ensemble a little less sweat-producing would be appropriate for the pool party. At which I decided I would definitely not be swimming. Trixie tugged at the leash, delighted that we were heading into town, even though she would be sitting outside the coffee shop while I had my iced coffee in the air-conditioned comfort of Beans, Beans. (I know — my mind goes there, too, but who am I to tell the hippie owner, Greg, that "beans, beans" is the start of a not-so-nice childhood rhyme of a scatological nature?) Greg is a lovely guy with a messy, gray Afro who loves coffee and calls everyone "dude" regardless of their sex. He often has on a T-shirt that says JESUS IS MY HOMEBOY and thinks that Beans, Beans is the most clever name for a coffee shop. Who was I to disabuse him of that notion? The store is decorated with thrift-store finds and has a funky, neighborhood vibe that I love. So what if the coffee isn't great? Greg is a nice guy, he needs the business, and I need the coffee. It worked for me. Crawford, on the other hand, thinks it is overpriced and a little precious. He likes his coffee in a paper cup with a plastic lid and Greek-looking decorations on the side. And he likes his muffins like he likes his women — hard on the outside, soft on the inside, and without any adornment. I only fit that bill about sixty percent of the time, but he's accepted that. That's the way he's been drinking his coffee and eating his muffins for years and nothing is going to change him. And he really doesn't like being called "dude."

I wrapped Trixie's leash around a parking meter and gave her a kiss, thinking about my soon-to-be-consumed iced coffee and what I would wear once I peeled these jeans off. The bathing suit with the missing elastic was looking better and better.

The village was hopping on this Saturday morning and I took in the building traffic in the center of town. Almost every parking space was filled and people milled about, waiting until ten o'clock when the boutiques and other stores opened. I was glad that I had walked.

I thought about the impending party. I was friends with Crawford's Aunt Bea and she had made a few comments about his mother being a "piece of work." I had heard the expression before and knew that it connoted a lot of different things in different people's minds. Was she an eccentric? A little bit loony? That I could handle. I came from a long line of French-Canadian whackos. Or was she mean and nasty? I never could get Bea to commit, and what was I going to do? Ask Crawford? "Hey, what's the deal with your mother? Is she a bitch on wheels or just a little crazy?" That wasn't going to work. I had myself kind of worked up about the whole thing. Meeting the parents was stressful enough, but when you had a wild card in the mix — one Kathleen Crawford — it was enough to induce a seizure.

I was lost in thought as I approached Beans, Beans and put my hand on the handle to the outer door, not really paying attention, lost in the reverie of thinking about what items resided in my closet. I thought about a pink shirt that made me look thinner than I actually was but then remembered that it had a huge chocolate ice-cream stain on the right breast area. Trixie made a sound and I turned to tell her that I would be right out and that I would probably bring her a treat. While my head was turned, the door to the coffee shop swung open, my hand still gripping the handle, the edge of the door catching the side of my nose and the right side of my face as I was pushed backward onto the sidewalk. Two men spilled past me, locked in some kind of pugilistic fox trot. They tumbled onto the sidewalk a few feet away from me, punching and kicking each other. As I hit the ground, I saw that one of them had a bloody nose, and that the other one was missing a shoe. I focused on the fact that his tan stopped at his ankle and I thought that was really weird. All I could think was "socks and boat shoes?" This floated through my mind in the seconds before the pain in my face flooded like a tsunami into my consciousness.

My head landed next to Trixie's front paws. She immediately set up a howl, barking as though she were rabid. In between barking, she licked my face. I must have looked pretty bad if she was that concerned. She started circling the parking meter and uttered a few low moans. I heard strains of Sly and the Family Stone's "Everyday People" coming from inside Beans, Beans, a lot of cursing, and finally, a loud and booming "Dudes!"

I'm going to have much bigger problems than wearing a bathing suit to a pool party, I thought, as I touched the welt growing under my eye. I struggled to my feet with a little help from Greg, who was wearing a T-shirt that said DON'T NEED A PERMIT FOR THESE GUNS with arrows pointing to either arm. Greg is big, but he's not fit, and despite the pain I was in, I was feeling a little punchy. I burst out laughing, which turned to crying in mere seconds.

"Dude," he said, taking my elbow. "Come inside. I've already called the police." He took in the two men and shook his head sadly. Jesus, Greg's homeboy, would not be pleased. The two men were still rolling around on the sidewalk, and nobody was trying to intervene now that they were out of Greg's shop; the crowd obviously ascribed to the "don't get involved" line of reasoning or else they just enjoyed watching a good donnybrook. I heard sirens as the police raced down Main Street and pulled to a stop in front of the store. The two men separated and I recognized one of the fighters: George Miller, the head of the Department of Public Works, who stood against the plate-glass window of Beans, Beans, panting heavily and pointing at the other man. The only reason I knew George was that I handed him a fat envelope of cash every year for his crew because, God knows, they had taken many a garbage collection from outside my house that wasn't really on the Monday "approved" garbage list. Like a sleeper sofa. And a few paint cans that weren't exactly clean. And more dog waste disguised as regular garbage than I could tally. I loved those guys and felt compelled to show my love once a year. I didn't recognize the other guy and couldn't imagine what had brought him to blows with the head of the DPW.

A group of people who had been in the coffee shop had come out onto the street and were clustered a few feet away, mumbling quietly about what had happened. A couple of other patrons were still inside the store, their noses pressed up against the other side of the glass window. Miller said nothing because he couldn't catch his breath. He bent over at the waist and put his hands on his knees.

The other man, the one without the shoe and the tan that stopped at his ankle, rested against a parking meter. "You'll be sorry, Miller," he said, much too calmly for someone who had just engaged in such strenuous fisticuffs. He was in his mid-forties, with a crew cut and horn-rimmed glasses that sat askew on his face. Unlike Miller, who was a rough-hewn kind of guy with a ruddy complexion, he didn't seem like the type who engaged in these kinds of shenanigans on any kind of regular basis. Having seen Miller around town, dealing with the townsfolk and his crew with a demeanor that could only be described as "impatient," I was not entirely surprised to see him as one half of the brawling duo. The other guy, however, seemed like he would be more comfortable at the local country club — the one that cost a quarter of a million dollars just to *apply* to — than rolling around Main Street with the head of the DPW.

Two policemen approached the men. Greg knew both of them. "Hi, Larry. Joe," he said, his meaty hand still gripping my elbow. "I'll be inside. These two are up to their usual b.s., but this time, they've hurt someone else," he said, pointing to me. I'm hurt? I thought. That wasn't good news. I kind of suspected it but I didn't like getting confirmation from an outside source.

Larry, I presumed, motioned to me. "Do we need an ambulance, Greg?"

"Oh, good God, no!" I said, more forcefully than I intended. Larry gave me a curious look. The last thing I needed was to be taken away by ambulance. I'm kind of famous around these parts, and not for anything good, so I just wanted to go home and put a package of frozen peas to my face and forget that I'd ever ventured into town that morning.

"You might want to get that looked at," Larry said, hitching up his pants while studying my face. He turned to George Miller, who was fidgeting by the window and looking as if he were considering taking flight. "You're not going anywhere, George, so stay put," he said. Larry pointed at my face. "You know, you really might want to get that looked at," he repeated.

I didn't know what "that" was and I was afraid to find out. I put my fingers gingerly to the place next to my nose and felt a lump. However, when I pulled them away, there was no blood and I took that as a good sign.

Greg spoke up. "I'll be inside when you want to talk to me." He let go of my elbow and untied Trixie from the parking meter. "Under these circumstances, Trixie can come inside. It's hot. She probably needs some water." Joe made a grunt of protest at the dog being inside a food establishment but Greg shot him a look. "You take care of these morons, Joe, and I'll take care of Alison."

We made our way into the shop and the crowd of gawkers parted to let us pass. Greg asked anyone who was just rubbernecking to take it outside as he was going to close up shop to straighten what had been upended in the fight. I took in the usually tidy space: two tables were turned over, as were a few chairs. The fighters had also broken the glass that fronted the muffin case. I took Trixie's leash from Greg and walked her around the damage and to the back of the coffee shop, where everything was just as it should be, tables and chairs completely upright with a few empty coffee cups left behind.

Greg tossed me a cold, wet rag from behind the counter. "Here. Put this on your eye."

"How bad is it?" I asked.

"You have a welt. I saw the whole thing. If you hadn't turned around to talk to Trixie, you would've lost an eye."

Jeez. Life with an eye patch. Or a glass eye. I had never considered that. "Thanks, Greg," I said, holding up the wet rag. It wasn't the cleanest first aid I had ever seen and it smelled like coffee, but beggars can't be choosers. I put it on the welt and immediately felt better. "What's going on with those two idiots?" I asked, hooking a thumb toward the sidewalk.

Greg grabbed a broom from behind the counter and began sweeping up the glass in front of the muffin case. "Miller has a real problem with Wilmott."

"Wilmott?"

"The guy without the shoe."

"Oh," I said, and pulled Trixie closer to me as Greg bent down to pick up a few shards of glass from the floor. I now knew exactly who he was talking about. Carter Wilmott was from an old village family, independently wealthy, and considered himself something of a whistle-blower when it came to the village. I had never met him so hadn't realized it was him. But my assessment of the ankle tan was correct; the Wilmotts kept a large sailboat in the marina next to the train station and were known for being avid sailors. Carter had a lot of time on his hands, what with the independently wealthy part, so he spent his days posting on a blog dedicated to the village and its goings-on. The blog was called "Our Village Matters" and he was merciless in his criticism of local politicians, national figures (particularly Republican ones), and apparently, the DPW. I had been living on campus during the last few weeks of the spring semester, and reading the blog — a guilty pleasure — was one of the ways I kept up on what was happening in the village. Apparently, I had missed the DPW screed. But knowing Wilmott's MO, I am sure it was yellow journalism at best. I think I even remember a sarcastic post about Greg and his novelty T-shirts; it was a wonder Greg still let him come into Beans, Beans. Then again, Greg was a peace-loving man and I could see him forgiving Wilmott his rants.

Greg finished cleaning up the glass and brought Trixie a bowl of ice-cold water, just as he had promised. She dove in as if she had been in the desert and lapped up the water, spilling most of it over the sides with her enthusiastic slurping. He pulled up a chair. "Let me see," he said, and held out his hand.

I handed him the towel. "I should go check this out in the bathroom," I said and got up.

Greg gave me a look that indicated that might not be such a good idea. But what was I going to do? Walk around avoiding mirrors? No time like the present. I went back to the unisex bathroom and turned on the forty-watt bare bulb that hung over the toilet and took a good look at myself in the ancient mirror.

"That'll leave a mark," I said to myself and the red welt on my face. I washed up and dried my face on some scratchy paper towels and returned to the coffee shop, where Greg was continuing to clean up the debris that was littered around the front counter. I offered to give him a hand but he declined.

"The place will be fine once I get it cleaned up," he said. The bell on the door jingled and we turned to find Carter Wilmott making his way back into the shop. Greg shook his head. "You know what, Wilmott? You're not welcome here anymore. You are banned from Beans, Beans," he said, albeit in the kindest way one could communicate another's persona non grata status.

Wilmott swayed a bit on his feet, and grabbed his throat. He looked at me and I could see a thick sheen of sweat on his brow. "I just wanted to say . . ." he started, but began coughing violently. Even Greg, who was as mad as I had ever seen him, stopped what he was doing and leaned across the counter.

"Do you need some water, Carter?" Greg asked.

Before Wilmott could answer, George Miller burst through the door of the shop, his feet falling heavily on the broken glass, making a noise not unlike my cereal makes when I pour in the milk. Miller drew a fist back, and with a forceful roundhouse punch, landed a blow to Wilmott's head. I cried out just as the police followed Miller inside.

Wilmott went to his knees. I got up from my seat, in that weird position of feeling as if I should do something yet not knowing what that might be. I took one step toward Wilmott as Greg made his way from around the counter, moving faster than I was.

Wilmott rocked from one side to the other, and caught my eye once more. ". . . to say that I am sorry," he said, and fell face-first into the pile of dirt and glass that Greg had swept into a tidy mound. I made a tiny sound while Trixie moved behind the counter, terrified of what had just transpired.

Greg knelt beside Wilmott, Larry the cop doing the same. The other cop grabbed Miller in a chokehold, using his free hand to handcuff him. Greg moved to the side, worriedly knitting his hands together in front of the counter, while Larry the cop expertly flipped Carter's body over and began CPR. He pounded on the man's chest, sweat beginning to roll down his cheeks. He continued for two or three minutes and then checked Wilmott's neck for a pulse.

He rocked back on his heels, his face a mask of sadness and incomprehension. For some reason, he looked at me and said, "He's dead."

Two

"If I had to guess, and guessing certainly isn't encouraged in our profession, I would say that Mr. Wilmott expired from . . ."

The Westchester County Medical Examiner, one John "call me Mac" McVeigh, paused in mid-sentence, leaving me and Greg and all other interested parties on the proverbial edge of our seats. Having spent the last two hours in the company of the ME, I knew that he was prone to these little lapses in conversational fluidity. In the space of the last few hours, he had gone into one of these semicomas at least four or five times, looking up to the heavens with his pale blue eyes, searching for the right word or the answer to his own question. Finally, he brought his eyes back down and finished his sentence.

". . . blunt force trauma to the head."

The group — comprised of me, Greg, a bunch of cops, and a couple of crime scene technicians — let out a collective sigh, all relieved that the question had been answered even if we had all come to the same conclusion long ago. It was almost as if the ME were a magician and we were waiting for the "reveal," the suspense was so great. I thought it was a bit unorthodox for the county medical examiner to determine cause of death without an examination, but McVeigh struck me as an inordinately unorthodox kind of guy.

Larry the cop whispered to me, "They call him 'Mac the knife,' you know."

Of course they do, I thought.

It was close to two o'clock, the time that Crawford and I were to leave for the family gathering. I checked the clock on the wall behind the counter nervously, knowing that I had just gotten involved in something that wasn't going to end any time soon. Instead of having a problem like what bathing suit to wear, I now had the problem of appearing to stand up the entire Crawford clan, swimmers all. I also had the problem of being one of two witnesses who had seen a man clock a guy in the head, presumably causing his death. George Miller was long gone, having been put in handcuffs and transported off to the police station. There was no doubt in my mind as to what had happened, nor for any of the other witnesses, including Greg and the officers who had responded. He was protesting his innocence vehemently, but we had all seen and heard the ruckus and knew the outcome. Carter Wilmott was dead after having been punched in the head by George Miller. Case closed.

The ME sat down at the table across from me and pulled out a notepad. "Once more," he said, adding, "with feeling."

In spite of myself and the situation, I laughed. Ever since he had arrived, the mood had lightened considerably, despite the fact that we were all still in the presence of a dead body. He kindly positioned himself so that I couldn't see Carter's body or the assistant ME and his associates roll the body into a black zippered bag, which they placed on top of the gurney. I knew what they were doing, but Mac's bald pate obstructed my view.

"What would you like to know?" I asked.

"Just the facts, ma'am." He laughed. "I've been dying to say that."

I went over everything that I had seen. Again. I've learned that that's the way these things go.

"So you saw Mr. Miller punch Mr. Wilmott, our deceased, in the head?"

I nodded.

Mac regarded me, his kindly hound-dog face telegraphing his discomfort with my having witnessed what was probably a murder. "Not exactly how you thought your day would turn out, huh?" He leaned over to pet Trixie. "Nice dog. I used to have a beagle. Horrible animal, but great pet. Ate everything in sight but would go to the mat for me and my wife."

"What was her name?"

"My wife or the dog?"

"Both," I said, laughing again.

"Wife is Marie but I call her 'Reezie.' Dog was Daisy." He pulled a card from his lab coat pocket. "Here's my card. If you need anything, or want to add anything else, please feel free to call me." He turned around, and confident that the gurney was gone, stood. "You'll probably have to go to the police station. You know that, right?"

"I figured as much."

"You have someone to pick you up afterward?"

I didn't know if he was just concerned or offering his services. "I'll probably call a friend."

He nodded solemnly. "You shouldn't be alone tonight. This was a terrible thing that you saw."

I blinked back tears. It was. So how come everyone was walking around the coffee shop as if it were a regular morning and business as usual? One cop was even eating a muffin that had survived the wreckage and another had whipped a latte for himself. Why was the medical examiner — the person with the most experience dealing with death and dead bodies and who should have been the most inured to the whole thing — the most sensitive one in the bunch?

Before I had a chance to dissolve into a tear-filled puddle, the door to Beans, Beans opened and an attractive woman in a crisp white blouse and expensive tailored jeans walked in, her eyes covered by giant black sunglasses, the kind Max refers to as "Jackie O's." She stepped in and spoke to one of the uniformed officers, careful not to step on any of the broken glass that littered the coffee shop floor. From the murmurings of the officers around me, I gathered that she was Lydia Wilmott, Carter's wife, and that she had come to see his body before it was carted off to the ME's office.

Greg gave me a meaningful look. "You know who that is, right?" he whispered from his perch on the counter, hooking a thumb in Lydia's direction.

"I can venture a guess," I whispered back.

Lydia stood over the gurney where Carter's body lay, and bent over slightly, giving all of us a nice shot of milky white breast encapsulated in white lace. I looked away discreetly, as did Mac, the only gentleman in the room, it seemed. He unzipped the body bag a few inches and pulled it aside. Though an unorthodox viewing and identification at best, I guessed that everyone figured that now was as good a time as any.

She nodded slowly. "Yes. That's him."

It seemed curious to me that she was alone but it appeared that was the case; I didn't see anyone else around who was a civilian. She asked one of the detectives in the shop if she could have Carter's personal effects. A whispered exchange took place, but by the looks of it the detective was not supposed to give her Carter's possessions. He finally relented and gave her his car keys. I heard him say that there was no use in the police taking the car but they would need everything else for the time being.

Greg slid off the countertop and pulled out a chair beside me to get a better look at the action. He leaned in close, his "guns" resting on the table. "She gives them about twenty grand a year for their annual fund drive, so I'm not surprised that they'll do exactly what she says."

"Why do they need to take all of his stuff, though?" I whispered back.

"Don't you watch *CSI*?" Greg asked rhetorically.

I don't. I watch cooking shows and the shows where they kidnap people and make them throw out their wardrobes. Oh, and CNN. That's it. And *Brady Bunch* repeats. But no *CSI*. *CSI* is definitely out. If I want to see a close-up of someone's esophagus with something foreign stuck in it — also known as "cause of death" — I'll just look in my dog's mouth.

Lydia spent a few more minutes talking with the rest of the police officers and crime scene officials, remarkably composed for someone whose husband was wrapped up like a mummy in a plastic bag on the floor. She stepped out onto the sidewalk and started down the street, presumably to find Carter's car. I wasn't sure how she was going to get it home given that she had arrived alone, but it seemed important to her that she drive it home herself and nobody involved was giving her any grief about that.

Mac and his staff finished up. He started for the door, but before leaving for good, he turned back around and gave me a little wave. He and the rest of the ME staff boarded a windowless white van and headed back to the office, Carter's bagged-up body in tow. I stood and tried to find the detective in charge to learn what my next steps in this process would be. I found Larry, one of the original cops on the scene, and touched his arm to get his attention. But before I could get the words out of my mouth, I was interrupted by a loud explosion somewhere outside of the restaurant. The remaining windows shook with the force, but didn't break. Larry grabbed my arm and pulled me to the ground, where I lay, facedown, for a few seconds, waiting for a second explosion that never came.

Greg let out his fortieth or so "Dudes!" of the day. Seemed that that was his go-to expletive in tense situations.

Once it seemed clear that the blast was a one-time event, Larry rushed outside to join his colleagues who had congregated on the street. Curiosity got the best of me and I followed them. Something had indeed exploded and it was Carter's car, which by the looks of its flaming remains had been a very expensive Mercedes-Benz.

Most of the inferno generated from under the hood. The blast had dislodged a parking meter from its home on the sidewalk and the front paned-glass window of the local gift shop was broken. Passersby seemed dazed but unhurt, surprisingly, with the exception of one lady who had a gash over her right eye that was bleeding profusely. One uniformed officer radioed for an ambulance as well as the fire department to respond. Traffic was snarled on the usually busy main thoroughfare and another officer went to dislodge the bottleneck.

My eyes were fixed on Lydia Wilmott, a good twenty feet from the car, a few feet from me, Carter's key fob jingling in her shaking hands, her arm still extended, her finger still on the unlock button.

She turned and looked at me, the closest person to her. "That was a close call," she said.

And with that, she fainted.

Three

I was acquainted with Detectives Hardin and Madden but knew they weren't fans of what I considered my best comedic material so I decided to play it straight. I was in one of the interrogation rooms in the local police department, being one of the four who had witnessed the untimely demise of Carter Wilmott. Trixie didn't count. She was sitting next to me, at the station, occasionally licking my hand when she felt that I was getting nervous, which was just about every ten seconds or so. I didn't have anything to be nervous about — I hadn't actually killed the guy — but I didn't enjoy being in police stations and I especially didn't enjoy the harsh glare coming from Detective Madden. I noticed that she was wearing the same navy blue pantsuit that she had had on the first time we had met. Perhaps it was part of a collection of navy blue pantsuits that inhabited her very orderly closet? Or was it just a coincidence? Who knew? Actually, who cared?

I did, that's who. When I'm nervous, I focus on things like Detective Madden's imaginary closet and whether or not she had a boyfriend, girlfriend, husband, or wife. And if she thought the coffee at Beans, Beans was as terrible as I did. And if she ate doughnuts with Detective Hardin when I wasn't around.

"Well, did you?" she was asking me, breaking directly into my musings about her personal life.

"Did I what?" I asked, trying to refocus my attention. I sat up a little straighter in my chair. Trixie licked my hand with mucho gusto.

"Did you notice anything about Mr. Wilmott's physical appearance prior to his death?" She folded her hands on a file in front of her. Of course she already had a file on the case; she was a terrible dresser but extremely organized.

I thought back to what had transpired just a few hours previous. "Well, he was red in the face, sweating, and grabbing his throat at one point," I said. "But I attributed all of that to his having been in a fight." I picked up the soggy washcloth in front of me that had once held ice for my nose and pressed it against my forehead. It was still cold and a lot damp and did alleviate the pounding behind my eyes for a few seconds.

She wrote something in her tiny, squiggly penmanship on the pad in front of her. She looked up again, and boy, if she didn't look just like one of the nuns at St. Thomas. I then set about on a mental journey whereby Detective Madden entered the convent as a young girl, decided she didn't like it, and left it to pursue a career in law enforcement. Only when she cleared her throat loudly did I snap to again. "How long had you known Mr. Wilmott?"

"About forty seconds," I said. We had been through this before. That's the thing about cops: they like to ask the same question over and over again maybe hoping you'll crack and tell them something they want to hear instead of something you've just made up. I don't know. It's a tiresome routine to me.

She stared at me again. Detective Madden didn't like me for some reason — maybe it was a leftover feeling from her investigation into my ex-husband's murder — and was making that painfully obvious during our chat. I looked at the clock behind her head. It was now three hours past the time I was supposed to meet

Crawford at my house to go the pool party. I was hoping that he had passed irate and was now worried about my whereabouts.

"Can I please call my boy . . . Crawford?" I'm still not comfortable calling him my boyfriend, let alone fiancé. I had been at the stationhouse for three hours now and Detective Madden had been reluctant to let me use the phone. Who did she think I was going to call? And what difference did it make? I had left the house with only enough money to buy coffee and without my cell phone, and now I was at the mercy of a detective with an axe to grind.

I decided that she didn't have a boyfriend, girlfriend, husband, or wife, nor was she sleeping with Detective Joe Hardin. It's not a myth that the lack of regular sexual activity makes you grumpy. Just ask Crawford.

She begrudgingly handed me her cell phone, a fancy-looking operation with a keyboard. My cell phone is the size of a man's loafer and has an antenna. "Yes, you may call your boy, Crawford." That was what I had said but not what I had meant, but I let it go. Did I look like someone who used rapspeak to talk about their significant other? I examined the phone and decided that I wouldn't be able to figure out how to dial it let alone make sure the call went through successfully. I looked at her pleadingly and asked her to dial Crawford's number; although I had tried, my attempts at dialing had resulted in some vowels, the pound key, and some completely unrelated numbers. She obliged and handed the phone back to me.

Crawford sounded a bit wary when he answered, clearly not sure who was calling him. "Crawford," he said.

"Hi. It's me."

"Where the heck are you? And whose phone is that?" he asked, sounding a little mad but not enough to use the word "hell" in his question. "You know we were supposed to leave three hours ago."

I dropped my voice to a whisper even though the detective and I were mere inches from each other. "I'm at the police station."

"Which one?" he asked. I was surprised that he didn't ask why I was in a police station, or what had happened, or why he didn't just assume it was the one in my town. I guess I had been in a few police stations during our time together so asking which one was a better opener for this conversation.

"Mine." I looked over at Madden and gave her a weak smile. She continued to stare back at me. Nope, she didn't find me funny, or appealing as a human being, at all.

"What happened? Are you okay?"

Actually, that should have been the first question, but I gave him the benefit of the doubt. He was obviously flustered by my disappearance, or so I hoped. "I was in the coffee shop and a man died."

"Died? As in . . . died?" Clearly, there was no "as in."

"Died." The look on Madden's face told me that this phone call had gone on longer than was allowed. "Listen, where are you? Can you get over here?"

"I'm at your house. I was worried sick." He left out "after I was furious that you had left town at the thought of meeting my family." "I've been listening to your cell phone ringing in the house this whole time. You have to start carrying that thing." He paused. "I'll be right over."

I handed Madden back her phone. "He'll be right over," I said, but she didn't care. She put the phone back in her pocket and picked up her pen. "Can I go?" I asked.

She considered that for a few minutes and then stood. "Yes. When your friend gets here, you can go. But please stay in town. I think we'll have more questions to ask you," she said, glaring at me a little bit. She started for the door and then stopped, something on her mind. "What's with you and the dead bodies?"

I stood, my hand wrapped tightly around Trixie's leash. It wasn't the first time I had been asked that question, nor would it be the last, I supposed. "Pardon?"

"You. Dead bodies. What's the deal?"

I shrugged. "I don't know. Just lucky?" I ventured.

She exited the room with a sigh. Not only did she not find me funny, she obviously found me tedious as well. I was batting a thousand. I should have stayed in bed. "Come on, Trix," I said, and led the dog out of the room, down a long hallway, and into the front of the police station. We didn't have to wait too long until Crawford showed up. I saw him loping up the front walk toward the door; Crawford doesn't move very quickly unless necessary. I, however, rush everywhere whether or not I'm late or the situation calls for it, so I ran toward the front door, putting us in the uncomfortable position of trying to open the door at the same time. After a few seconds of battling each other on either side of the door, he stepped back and put his hands up in surrender. "Ladies first," he called through the door.

I pulled at the door and ran outside

without saying good-bye to the desk sergeant and threw myself into Crawford, finally letting out the tension that had been bottled inside of me since I watched Carter Wilmott lose his breath and then collapse to the floor. "Get me out of here," I said, handing over Trixie's leash and doing an accelerated perp walk down the front walk toward the street. Crawford followed behind me. Once I was at the sidewalk and off police property, I turned to him. "We don't have to go to the pool party today, do we?"

Crawford's sad face almost made an appearance and got me thinking that I didn't get a pass on pool parties or family meetings. If watching a man die didn't qualify as a "pass," I didn't know what did. But he shook his head. "I sent our regrets." He took my face in his hands. "You know you have the beginnings of a black eye, right?"

"Of course I do," I said. "That's where the story begins." I touched my nose right below my eye and felt the bump there. "How bad is it?"

Crawford's a terrible liar. "Not bad." There was a bench in front of the police station and he sat down. Trixie sat next to him, her head on his thigh. "Pretty bad." He reached up to touch it, thought better of that idea, and let his hand drop. "Horrible."

I looked out at the street and everyone going merrily about their business in the town. "Thank you for being honest." I started down the street again, Crawford and Trixie by my side. "What's with me and dead bodies, Crawford?"

He took my hand. "You're shaking."

"Have you ever seen anyone die?" I asked. It was a rhetorical question but he answered anyway.

"They're usually dead by the time I get to them." He pulled me back to the bench and patted the space next to him. "Sit down."

Instead, I paced nervously up and down the sidewalk. It was hot and humid, and in the short time I had been outside, my shirt was plastered against my back. "I'm serious. What's up with this? Nobody I know finds dead bodies or sees people die like I do." I felt a tear roll down my cheek. I plopped onto the bench and put my face in my hands. The whole day came crashing down on me and I let out a few muffled sobs. I could feel Crawford's hand on my soggy back; eventually, it made its way around my shoulders and he pulled me close. I sobbed into his polo shirt for a few minutes before pulling myself together.

He leaned in and kissed me above the ear. "What happened?"

I started to explain but was interrupted by a loud "Dudes!" coming from the walk in front of the police station. I drew the bottom of my shirt across my face and turned to face Greg. "Hi, Greg," I said.

Greg lumbered toward us, looking a little worse for wear. "Did they give you the third degree, too?" he asked. He stuck a huge, meaty hand out to Crawford. "Greg Weinstein."

That made Jesus as Greg's homeboy even more curious, but I decided not to go there. "This is my boy . . ." I started. "This is Crawford."

Crawford gave me a look that indicated that if I hadn't watched a man die that day, we'd be having a very long talk about Ring Pops, engagements, and various and sundry other topics related to matrimony. He then gave Greg the once-over, something that he did with most people upon introduction. It was a cop thing, I gathered.

"Your boy Crawford? That's pretty hip, Alison. Nice to meet you, Crawford," Greg said. "Jeez, I thought I'd never get out of there. What else is there to say besides 'he came in, he grabbed his throat, he stopped breathing'? How many times can you say that?"

I nodded. "Same story, different detective," I said. I thought of Detective Madden and decided that I was going to go through my closet, find anything that was navy blue, and throw it out. It is not a flattering color.

"I had that Hardin guy. He finally ran out of steam a few minutes ago and let me go." Greg wiped his hands on his jeans. "I gotta get back to the store. Do you think it would be in bad taste to open tomorrow?" he asked, genuinely concerned.

I didn't think it would be in bad taste but I wondered how many people would actually show up. Or how many would show up just to say that they had been in the store where Carter Wilmott had died. I didn't have time to answer. Crawford jumped in. "If I were you," he said, "I would open again on Monday. That'll give you a chance to process what happened today and let things settle down a bit."

I looked at him, a little stunned. "A chance to process what happened"? That wasn't Crawfordspeak. But obviously, he was adapting to the situation at hand and to Greg's vibe. Good job, Detective Crawford, I thought.

Greg mulled this over for a minute and

decided that Crawford was correct. "Good call, dude."

I saw Crawford flinch slightly; I knew the "dude" business wouldn't go over well, but he took it like a champ. He held out his hand again. "Good luck with everything."

Greg nodded and looked at me. "Alison, can I give you a hug?"

With those "guns"? I thought. Of course. I let myself be enveloped by Greg's big, giant, sweaty, flabby guns and let out a sob that I had been holding in. He hugged me tight for longer than I was comfortable with and finally let go. "See you Monday?" he asked.

"Most definitely," I lied.

I watched Greg walk away, my mind going through a mental spin cycle of the events. What would be the aftermath of Wilmott's demise? Would Greg have to close, the stench of death forever washing over his little business? Selfishly and without compassion, I wondered if I could now break free of the hold that Beans, Beans and Greg had over me, forcing me to drink really terrible coffee on a regular basis. I blushed at that thought. It was very unkind and, hopefully, not characteristic, but I wasn't willing to "explore" that, as one of the professors in the psych department at school would say.

Greg was a guy who had devoted himself to this little village and who participated vigorously and without a thought for himself or his income at all of the local events. Need free coffee for the PTA event? Greg would provide. Kids want to have a bake sale? They could use Beans, Beans anytime they wanted and for however long they needed the space. Want to have an open mic night and play your guitar for the locals? Greg would provide the store, after closing, for your performance. I guess, in spite of the bad coffee, I wanted the store to stay open. I looked up at Crawford.

He knew what I was thinking. "Nope. Count me out. I don't want anything to do with this."

"How do you even know what I'm going to say before I say it?"

He took my hand and led me down the street. "Because I know you too well. And I've been down this road before. You," he said, stopping me from crossing into traffic, "are on your own."

"This could ruin Greg," I said.

"How?" he asked. "It was an accident. A fight. You think everyone's going to stay away from the store because some guy died in there?"

I reminded him that where he worked, it

was a different story. Sure, people died in public places all the time, and if he was involved, chances were good that they had been murdered. Still, people frequented the little bodegas where someone had been shot, or the diner where someone was found dead in a bathroom stall, or worse, with their head in a plate of eggs. (It had happened. Crawford had told me.) Here, it's not like that. The people of my sleepy village weren't used to death being so close and might have a problem with it. I voiced my concerns aloud.

He threw his hands up. "Do what you want. You're going to anyway."

On that point, we definitely could agree.

Four

"You sure you don't want to get that looked at?" Crawford asked from his position on a lounge chair next to mine. He held a sweating bottle of beer in his hand as I balanced a vodka martini on the armrest of my chair. Despite the day that I had had, I was enjoying the fading light in my backyard, the light breeze after an unbearably hot day, and my two favorite beings beside me: Crawford and Trixie.

I shook my head. "Most certainly not."

He looked at his watch and downed his beer quickly. "I've got to go."

I had advance warning that he'd be leaving but I was still disappointed. His girls were at the pool party and needed to be picked up so that they could spend the night with him in the city as they did every Saturday night. "See you tomorrow?" We had left my concern about the future of Beans, Beans back by the police station and hadn't discussed it again.

He nodded before leaning in and giving me a kiss. He studied the black eye. "Got any frozen peas?" He thought for a moment and reconsidered that request; I had iced the eye when I had first arrived home but had tired of the sensation on my face and the feeling of melting ice. "Of course you don't. Want to hold a frozen bottle of vodka against your eye? Because that's the only item in your freezer."

"You've got that right," I said. "I'll be fine. It's a black eye. No big deal."

But it was a big deal, which I found out when I was awakened after being asleep for only about a half hour. I turned and looked at the clock and saw that it was just past midnight and my face was throbbing, pain emanating from my nose up to my forehead and reaching around to the back of my head as if my whole cranium were encased in a vise. I sat up and didn't know which part of my face to rub first to relieve the ache, so I decided to go into the bathroom, rummage around in the cabinet for anything stronger than an Advil, and chase it with a big glass of water. I had had a prescription for Vicodin at one time but I enjoyed the opiate so much that I had decided to flush the remainder down the toilet, a decision I came to rue at that moment. I settled on three aspirin and a half dose of NyQuil to help me sleep.

An hour later, after taking another, full dose of NyQuil, I was still wide awake, staring at the shadow pattern the tree branches outside my window were making on my ceiling. I looked around the room, Trixie sleeping peacefully on the floor beside me, and spied my briefcase, my laptop resting on top of it. I got out of bed, trying not to wake the dog, who opened one eye and regarded me warily. When she saw that I only had word processing in mind, she went back to sleep.

I crawled back into bed with my laptop. A year earlier, Max had implored me to get a wireless router, even though I'm a cheapskate at heart and couldn't stomach the expense of what seemed, at the time, to be a useless purchase. I usually sit at my desk when I do work, so why I had to be mobile with my laptop confounded me. Tonight, I thanked her, because I could get back under the covers, look up every fact I wanted about Carter Wilmott, and not have to sit in the steaming heat of the guest bedroom where I kept my desktop. I opened the computer and turned it on, listening to Trixie's noisy exhalations as I waited for it to warm up. I was searching the Internet for Carter facts before she had snored four times.

I started by reading the latest entries on the blog. Wilmott had a cadre of regular posters: HappyVillager201; Old Timer; Coffee Lover; BadgeGal; the prolific Wonder Woman. And the intellectual FancyPantz who could quote sections of the village building code with alarming accuracy and ease. That was someone I wanted to meet. He also had his fair share of detractors, led by RepubVoter and his sidekick, MuchAdo. These two were vociferous in their rants about Wilmott's political leanings, and being as the village was in the hands of a Democratic majority at the moment, they were none too happy about anything. Conversely, posters such as Crazee About Cats, Straight A, and Law School Val were completely in love with him and his unabashed support of the village mayor and trustees. It was like an online Dodge City, with a post by Wilmott, and then a multitude of comments, some referencing earlier comments on a post or even comments on earlier posts; these people clearly had a history.

I scrolled through various posts and accessed the archive, where I read more of Wilmott's reporting about various members of the town. It was fairly sleazy and one-sided, and while he obviously thought of himself as a purveyor of truth in a town of dishonest officials, he was quite plaintive and biased in his reporting. There were no photos of Carter except for those that accompanied his restaurant reviews, reviews that I hadn't read prior to tonight's online reconnaissance mission. I read the reviews dispassionately; this was a guy who clearly had a high opinion of himself and his culinary expertise. Then, I got to a post about my favorite restaurant, Sadie's, and my unbiased opinion of him turned definitely sour. Sadie's was the first place that Crawford had taken me and I had warm feelings toward it. To read that Wilmott had called it "a dive — at best" got my hackles up and I must have let out a little sound because Trixie picked her head up from the floor and growled at me in agreement. He continued: ". . . the ambiance is poor, the service even worse, and the food abysmal. The only good thing I can say is that I got drunk on the rotgut house wine but only because the owner bought me a carafe in the hopes of getting a good review." I hadn't realized that Wilmott was also a restaurant reviewer, but he took on every restaurant and eating establishment in town.

Even delis.

I clicked on the link that was titled "Tony's — I'd Rather Eat a Can of Worms Than His Chicken Salad" — a most unoriginal title written by a guy with a limited knowledge of adjectives. Again, we returned to "abysmal," "poor," and "worst." The commenters who weighed in below the post were split between outrage — "Tony's is a village institution" — to complete agreement with Wilmott's assessement. Me? I loved Tony's, but since Tony loved me, in the romantic sense, I didn't go there very often anymore. Add in the crazy, jealous wife he had recently acquired and I was staying away for good. But he didn't deserve to be lambasted on this hack's Web site, that was certain. Tony was a kind man with a good heart, and a wife I was pretty sure had created the torture technique we had all come to know as "waterboarding." She was that mean. And she didn't like me.

But Tony's chicken salad was the best. I knew that for sure.

There was a picture of Wilmott standing outside of Tony's; he was making a face that conveyed his disdain for the place. In his hand was a wrapped sub — chicken salad, I presumed — which he was in the process of pitching into a garbage can. I looked closely at the picture. Although he was dressed similarly to how he had been dressed that morning in his oxford shirt and khakis, they were clearly one or two sizes larger than the ones he had been wearing when I saw him. He was a husky and robust man in the picture, not the thin, almost frail-looking guy that I had met and watched die. I wondered if his wife had put him on a diet, because no man would want to go from the way he had looked in the picture to a ninety-eight-pound weakling. From the looks of things, he should have eaten that sub. He had obviously been wasting away.

Or maybe Tony's wife, Lucia, had been poisoning him. I wouldn't put it past her.

One of the most recent, and as it turned out, last entries was about the DPW and, specifically, George Miller. I could see why Miller might have a problem with Wilmott after he was described as having a "bulbous nose — one that could only belong to a full-blown alcoholic" and a "less than stellar record on environmentally sound methods of waste disposal." Wilmott also took issue with Miller's wife, saying that she was the most flagrant scofflaw in town when it came to recycling or lack thereof. Pictures taken of an unsuspecting Ginny Miller were posted on the blog in various stages of scofflawness. In the photos, she was shown throwing beer cans into the regular garbage and shoving plastic shopping bags down into the sewer grate at the side of her house. Besides getting joy from posting extremely unflattering photos of the rather hefty Mrs. Miller, what purpose did dragging her into this serve? I had already decided that Carter Wilmott was a jaded, cynical, angry man with too much time on his hands. But last time I checked, besides being not good for the environment, you could still throw beer cans into the garbage and put anything you wanted down the sewer with the only punishment being a stern talking-to from the head of the DPW or a passing cop. And if you're married to the guy who runs the garbage removal in town, you can basically do whatever you want.

But now at least I had an idea of what had precipitated the fight that morning. I think if Wilmott had posted shots of me lugging out the garbage in spandex leggings and a too tight Syracuse University T-shirt, like he had of Mrs. Miller, I would have beaten the crap out of him myself.

Before turning in for the night, I found something on the blog that piqued my interest: Lydia Wilmott's advice column. Having met Lydia earlier and watched her identify the remains of her husband calmly and coolly, I was drawn to her column to see what might be in there that would give me insight into a woman who was extremely composed in the face of death. I read a couple of the "Ask Lydia" columns that appeared under the masthead. Lydia, it turned out, answered questions from the community on everything from getting your grout clean, to Botox, to setting up a book club, to marriage. It was the marriage postings that were of most interest to me, because from the sound of it, Lydia and Carter's marriage was like Jean and Billy Graham's crossed with Pamela Anderson and Tommy Lee. Solid, holy, steamy, and full of great sex. Lucky Lydia. A sampling to a poster with doubts about his or her upcoming nuptials: "The first time Carter kissed me, it was like the ground moved. My loins trembled. And that, ColdFeet, is what it should be like. No doubts. If you don't feel overwhelming love for this person you'll be marrying — if you wouldn't DIE for this person — or them for you — don't get married." I groaned. That was way too much information. Especially for a town blog that focused on the irregular holiday schedule of the garbage department and the not-green ways of the DPW head's wife.

I, for one, had no idea where my loins were and if they trembled. I would have to ask Crawford. I bet he knew. He knows stuff like that.

But I had to admit that it wasn't bad advice, except for the dying part. Lydia was extremely descriptive about her love, but she was right about her counsel to Cold-Feet. Where had Lydia Wilmott been when I was in the process of marrying Ray Stark, the man with the golden penis? Had I had the luxury of posting anonymously to a blog lo all those years ago and gotten Lydia's sage advice, I might have avoided nine years of heartache and humiliation.

One more thing crossed my mind, and although I was starting to feel the effects of the NyQuil, or was slowly dying from a NyQuil overdose, I searched for "bomb-making." After getting hits for about three million pages on how to make a bomb — and I'm exaggerating only slightly — I concluded that one wouldn't necessarily have to be a munitions expert to create a car bomb that one could attach to a car engine. It wouldn't hurt, though. I'm the kind of person who gives up on preparing a dish if I don't recognize an ingredient listed early in the recipe; same would be true for making a bomb. While it looked like most of the things you would need to create said bomb would be found in the hardware store, some wouldn't. And that's where I'd be out of the bomb-making business.

I had read enough. I was just about to turn off the computer when the phone rang. And when the phone rings at two o'clock in the morning, it can only be one person.

The music was loud and thumping and I had to strain to hear Max, who sounded as if she were inside an amp. "Hi, Max!" I shouted, even though I was sure she could hear me.

"Hear you have a black eye!" she hollered back into the phone. "How did that happen?" To someone in the club, she yelled, "Ketel One! Up! With three olives!"

"I didn't know you drank martinis," I said.

"I don't. Queen does."

"Queen who?"

"Queen Martinez."

As usual, we were off topic the minute we had gotten on one. Was it worth it to ask who Queen Martinez was? Or why Max was with this person in a club on a Saturday night? Probably not, so I returned to the subject of my black eye. I could only assume that Queen was a Hooters waitress. "So, my black eye . . ."

"Yeah! I'm coming over tomorrow to see

it," she said and promptly hung up. I rolled over on my side and grabbed a pen and paper next to my bed and wrote, "Find out who Queen Martinez is. Max coming over on Sunday." I knew that when I woke up in the morning, I would have forgotten all about this phone call and to ask about the identity of this royal friend of Max's.

Trixie was now wide awake and standing next to the bed. Rather than give her a complimentary middle-of-the-night walk, I pulled my comforter aside and patted the bed next to me. "Come on in," I said. She wasn't Crawford, but she would have to do.

Five

I was right. I had no recollection of my phone call with Max until I looked at the paper next to my bed that said "Queen Martinez." And then it all came back to me. I looked at the clock and saw that it was almost nine; I had no idea what time Max was coming over, but figured it wouldn't be before noon. I had a little time to get provisions for her, her caveman husband, and Crawford, who always showed up around two on Sundays.

While I was showering, I reviewed the previous day's unpleasantness. A year or so ago, I had found my ex-husband's dead body, but I hadn't seen him die. I decided that watching Carter Wilmott die was much more unpleasant. To see someone have life, and then lose it, was completely disconcerting, and I cried a little bit while the hot water beat down on my face. For about the hundredth time, I wondered how Crawford did what he did for a living. Although he didn't see people die, he certainly examined his share of dead bodies. Besides being gross, it had to take its toll on you emotionally. How could it not? I wondered if that was why Fred, Max's husband and Crawford's partner, was as distant and crabby as he always seemed or if his personality was just a congenital birth defect. I decided to give him the benefit of the doubt.

Definitely a birth defect.

One of my birth defects, discovered later in my life than most, was that I had become extremely nosy. I knew when it had started — right after I had almost been accused of murder — but it was something that I thought would go away with some introspection and self-reflection. Alas, it was still present and it revealed itself to be quite chronic. So, it was when I was sitting on my bed, drying my hair in a nice fluffy towel, that I realized that I needed to pay my respects to Mrs. Wilmott. After all, I had been there when her husband died. It was only polite.

Truth was, I wanted to know what it looked like when a presumably happily married woman, or so proclaimed Lydia Wilmott in her blog postings on Carter's site, lost a husband. She had looked extremely composed yesterday when she had come to Beans, Beans to identify the body, but her eyes had been covered with sunglasses so I wasn't sure if they were red-rimmed from crying. Maybe she had been in shock. Or maybe her blog posts covered a more serious problem, which was that while she was crazy about him, he wasn't crazy about her. But after seeing both of them for the first time yesterday, it wasn't hard to tell that he had gotten quite a good deal. The lady was a looker and Carter . . . not so much. If I were Carter — and right now, I was very glad that I wasn't — I would have been thrilled to be married to such a gorgeous woman.

I took a circuitous route to the Wilmotts', driving through town to take a gander at the spot where this whole mess began. Beans, Beans was closed up tight, but Greg had a sign on the door indicating that he would be open for business the next morning. There was still some yellow crime scene tape flapping in the wind, particularly around the area where the car had blown up. I shuddered when I thought about the damage that the explosion could have wrought and thanked God that nobody had been killed.

After my side trip, I arrived at the Wilmotts' considerable Colonial, high on a hill, with a panoramic view of the Hudson River, and was let in by someone I later came to find out was Lydia's sister, Elaine, who didn't offer an introduction. The house was a beehive of activity; it seemed that every member of Lydia's extended family had come to be with her during her time of mourning; they seemed to be scattered throughout the immense house, and I could hear conversations going on all around me in muffled tones.

After what I had read on the blog and from what I could gather from being in the house, there were two children but they were college aged and presumably away at school, somewhere I'd be in the next few days. Pictures of them — a boy and a girl — dotted every wall and flat surface that I could see from my vantage point in the foyer. I wondered where they were and how long it would take them to get back. I stood awkwardly in the doorway explaining to the sister that I was a fellow villager and that I had been present when Carter had died. I wanted to pay my respects. But I must have been a sight, the giant bruised eye and all.

Elaine, as she grudgingly offered after I asked, was a dour-looking middle-aged woman with a sparse sprinkling of mousy brown hair atop her head, clad completely in blue cotton sweats that did nothing to accentuate any good aspects of the doughy body beneath. She regarded me with suspicion for a few minutes and rightfully so: outside their beautiful house on their very quiet street was a news van from our local Westchester station, News47 Westchester, and a reporter just dying to get inside the house. Apparently, a man dying as precipitously as Carter was a story of major interest to the county residents.

As soon as Elaine was convinced of my good intentions, she ushered me into the house and back to the kitchen, where a grief-stricken Lydia Wilmott stood, washing a large glass pitcher at the sink. From where she stood, Lydia had a full view of the river, stretching out beyond the treetops in her backyard, but she clearly didn't notice it at that moment. I wondered if she ever did. I knew that if I lived there, I would stare at it every day, the beauty of the river being something I never tired of. The house was tastefully decorated in period 1920s furnishings and light fixtures and would be exactly the kind of house I would love to live in, if I had three million dollars lying around. Lydia continued washing the pitcher, avoiding my gaze, her eyes fixated on the water rushing out of the faucet and down into the drain. Elaine explained to her who I was and why I had come.

"Are you feeling better?" I asked, thinking that she had hit the ground pretty hard when she had fainted the day before.

"I'm fine," she said. "Thank you for asking."

"I am very, very sorry about your husband's passing," I said, moving the potted plant that I had brought closer to the counter where she stood. I placed the condolence card underneath the plant. "You can read that later," I said unnecessarily.

Elaine, who was close in age to Lydia but not as attractive, lurked around the corner of the kitchen, either trying to eavesdrop or make sure her sister was holding up, considering who I was and my relation to her husband. Lydia didn't speak but continued to wash the pitcher, which was already clean by my estimation. I took in her pale complexion, beautifully coiffed auburn hair, and in particular, the impressive diamond tennis bracelet dangling from one delicate wrist. She was dressed casually in jeans and a white oxford but I could tell both articles of clothing were very expensive. They didn't have the look and feel of my similar attire, both items purchased at T.J. Maxx. It was a few uncomfortable minutes before she spoke. I thought that maybe I had made a mistake by coming here.

"Tell me," she said, finally finishing up the pitcher and putting it on a stainless-steel dish drainer. "Did he suffer much?" It was at that point that I heard her throat hitch and saw tears fill her eyes. She grabbed a Williams-Sonoma dish towel and pressed it to her face. Out of the corner of my eye, I saw Elaine lurch forward but Lydia held up a hand. "Elaine, please excuse us."

Elaine looked none too happy about Lydia's request but she also looked like she had been taking orders from Lydia for years. Like the little mousy woman that she was, she scurried away and took refuge in another room, where I could hear a muted conversation begin.

"I'm sorry," Lydia said after taking the towel away from her face. "She worries about me." She wiped the counter unnecessarily with the towel; the granite gleamed in the morning sun. "She's my older sister so she's used to taking care of me." She let out a sigh. "Right now? I'd just like to be left alone."

I understood. I noticed that the water was still running in the sink even though she had finished washing up. I leaned across the counter and pushed the handle down. "He didn't suffer," I lied. Not if you don't count the massive blow to the head. "Maybe it was a heart attack," I said, hoping that just one punch to the head couldn't kill someone. And that was coming from a literature professor, an excellent source for cause of death if there ever was one. "He just fell to his knees and . . ." I thought of a more appropriate word. "Took his last breath. It was very fast." More than I wanted to say but it would have to do.

"Did he say anything?" she asked.

I searched my memory. Although I thought the experience and every detail of it would be seared in my memory forever, I found myself losing pieces of it already. Was he wearing his glasses when he came back in? Did he ever retrieve the missing shoe? What color was his shirt? It was all a blur. I couldn't remember if he said anything and I didn't want to lie and say something like "tell Lydia I love her" because that would just sound too made up. But I couldn't help myself. "He said, 'Lydia.' " If she ever caught me in the lie, by trying to confirm this detail with Greg or the police officer, I would say that everyone was in a state of shock at the time and that their memories were betraying them.

"But he didn't suffer," she said, more of a statement than a question.

"No," I replied. "He didn't suffer. It happened very quickly."

"Because I don't know what I would do if I thought that he had suffered greatly." Her gaze returned to the sink.

"I'm very sorry for your loss." It was a sentiment that didn't bear repeating but I had nothing else to contribute.

She smiled politely, but briefly, and leaned onto the edge of the sink, her sizable bracelet clanging against the side. "What happened to your eye?"

Again, a lie seemed better than the truth. "A door. Actually, a doorknob." I shrugged as a way of conveying my klutziness. "Should have turned on the light when I got up in the middle of the night."

She looked at me pityingly and pursed her lips, beginning to say something but thinking better of it. It was clear that she wasn't buying my story, but she obviously hadn't put two and two together about how I had ended up looking like this and I was glad for that. I wondered if the police had told her that because of her husband's major brawl with George Miller, I was going to look like Rocky Balboa for the better part of a week. I'm guessing that they had but I was also guessing that she had decided to put that somewhere else in her brain where she wouldn't have to think about it.

"The ME still doesn't know for sure what he died of." She was concerned obviously about that fact. "They suspect blunt force trauma to the head but they won't be sure until the autopsy is done."

"It was quick." I decided that after adding that little repeated gem, I wouldn't speak unless spoken to.

"What were you doing there?"

"Where?"

"Beans, Beans."

Wasn't that obvious? Maybe not. The coffee was horrendous. "Getting coffee." I let go of the counter. I don't know why I felt compelled to offer my unsubstantiated opinion, but I did. "Maybe it was a heart attack. Or an aneurysm. Something major and fatal. A stroke, maybe. There was no time." I found myself choking up, something that I shouldn't be doing in front of a dead man's wife. "And they tried," I said, a tear falling onto the counter. "I was there. They tried."

Lydia came over to me and graciously put her arms around me. "It must have been horrible for you," she whispered.

It was! I wanted to cry, but I gently

disengaged from her hug and wiped a hand across my face. "I need to go," I said. "I just wanted to say I was sorry."

Lydia called out to me as I passed the powder room in the hallway. "Alison. One more thing."

I went back into the kitchen, once again astounded by the view from their French doors. I went back to my place at the counter.

"It doesn't matter how he died," she said. "He would have died eventually." She saw my face and quickly amended, "We all do."

I thought about George Miller and his involvement in all of this. Was he the one who had attached the device to the car engine, sending pieces of it sailing through town? Or was the fight completely unrelated to what would have been the eventual murder of Carter Wilmott? I didn't know, but I did know that I had spent way too much time in his house and I had to get out. I didn't even think about asking the question that was on my mind but for which I already had something of an answer: who wanted your husband dead? Short answer? Everyone. I bid good-bye to Lydia again and left the kitchen. I went into the hallway and was just about at the door when I heard Elaine's voice behind me.

"He was as healthy as a horse, you know."

I turned and looked at her. "Pardon me?"

"Carter. Healthy as a horse. He just had a checkup last week."

That's great, I thought. That hadn't helped him when he keeled over in front of me in Beans, Beans from maybe an aneurysm, maybe blunt force trauma to his head. I wondered if his doctor was hiding under his desk, his malpractice insurance policy clenched in his trembling hands. Elaine looked at me, waiting to hear my response.

"Well, that's interesting," I said, for lack of anything else to contribute. I felt as if I had stumbled into one of those real-life mystery parties where there is a dead guy, lots of suspects, and one person who can figure the whole thing out.

"Don't you think it's strange?" she asked.

"People die of mysterious causes all the time," I said. Or they die from getting punched in the head. If they don't die of that, they get in their car and get blown up, particularly if they are Carter Wilmott, seemingly the most unlucky man ever to have lived. I didn't say anything else because I didn't want to incriminate George Miller any more than he had already incriminated himself. Although the ME suspected the blow to the head as the culprit, Carter looked way too winded and sick for someone who had only been in a fight. "He probably had an aneurysm. A stroke." Brought on by getting boxed in the head. I was back to my old script. Who knew? I had no experience with people dying suddenly and of seemingly natural causes. Everybody around me lately seemed to die a violent, untimely death. What was I supposed to do? Assume that he was murdered by George Miller? From a punch to the head? Or was I supposed to sit around and wonder who had the means and motive to create a car bomb and attach it to his engine? Not much of a mystery concerning the punch to the head; the ME would be all over that in a matter of days if that was the case. The car bomb, however, was definitely a more interesting twist in the case.

Elaine raised an eyebrow. "I just think it's weird," she said cryptically. I decided that Elaine was the sister that they kept locked in the attic; all that time alone had given her a flair for the dramatic. She had probably been constructing this mystery in her head for years after reading the Nancy Drew book *The Secret of the Old Clock.*

"I don't know what you're getting at," I said, "but I just came to say I was sorry." She pulled at a loose thread hanging from the waistband of her sweat suit and I got nervous. What if she unraveled the thread and her pants fell down? I was getting out of there as quickly as I could. "I'm sorry," I repeated for what seemed like the hundredth time. "I just wanted to say that."

But as I walked down the street, I admitted to myself that I hadn't been there to say I was sorry. I had been there to nose around. Nobody just drops dead for no good reason in a coffee shop. At least I didn't think so. George Miller, in my opinion, would have to have fists of steel to have killed Carter with one blow. But now, having met the grieving woman in person, I realized that going there was just a horrible, selfish thing to do. I got into my car, gave the news van the finger, and drove back to my house.

Six

I was in a black mood by the time I got home, still in a tizzy about what I had witnessed the day before, and angry at myself for going to the Wilmotts'. I was even angrier at myself for buying into Elaine's conspiracy theory, whatever that was. He was a healthy guy. So what? That wasn't a guarantee that his heart would suddenly stop working, or his aorta would explode after the fight he had had with the DPW guy, or that a vein in his head would begin to bleed and would kill him almost instantly. But I couldn't stop thinking about her beady eyes and the thread on her sweatpants and her insistence that Carter had been healthy. And about the fact that Carter would have been blown to smithereens had he not died in front of the muffin case of Beans, Beans. He was a healthy guy with a car about to blow up, and a lot of enemies, I suspected.

Although I had locked the house up before I left, Max and Fred were sitting inside, at the kitchen table, Trixie by Fred's side. Max gave me a cheery "Hello!" while Fred just grunted. That was the best I was going to get.

The torn screen over my sink indicated Max's point of entry. She saw me looking at it and offered a weak, "Sorry." Max has a history of jumping in and out of windows; she's a regular break-in artist. Given that she's petite and wiry and has some experience at it, she'd be a perfect second-story man. Fred didn't look contrite at all considering I knew that he had hoisted her up to the window, in, and over the sink right below it.

I pointed at the screen. "You're paying for that." I went to the refrigerator, opened it, and peered inside. Unless I wanted a caper, pickle, and mayonnaise sandwich on stale bread, there was nothing to eat. I looked at the clock; it was twelve-thirty. I had a little breathing room before Crawford appeared. "And you're getting it fixed today, so I hope you can find a hardware store that's open."

"Where were you?" Max asked. "And have you been crying?"

I closed the refrigerator with a loud thud; I wasn't in the mood to explain. "What do you guys want to eat?" I asked. I pointed at the screen again but was at a loss for words. Surely Fred could have found a better way to gain entrance to the house.

Max and Fred stared at me; it's the rare occasion that I call them out on their venial sins, but today was one of those times. My meeting with Lydia Wilmott, while seemingly uneventful, had left me rattled. I was mad at myself for having insinuated myself in her life under the pretense of compassion. It was just plain wrong. And I was going to make myself, and everyone around me, pay.

Even the sight of Crawford coming through the front door earlier than I had expected him did nothing to dampen my feelings of shame and self-loathing. He sauntered down the hallway toward the kitchen, took in the faces on the three of us, and whistled through his teeth. "What am I walking into here?"

"What do you want for lunch?" I asked. "These two have gone dumb," I added, hooking a thumb in Max and Fred's direction.

Crawford leaned down and let Trixie nuzzle his neck. "Turkey. Ham. Tuna. Whatever."

"That's not helpful," I said. "And what

are you doing here so early?"

He gave me a steely look; Crawford does not enjoy crankiness, particularly mine. He turned and walked back down the hall toward the front door. "Let's start over." He let himself out, and then back in, calling, "Honey! I'm home!"

I couldn't help but smile. When he came back into the kitchen, I put my arms around him and buried my head in his chest. "They broke my screen." I didn't have to mention that I had seen a man die and subsequently, his dead body, and that was the reason for my sullenness; telling Crawford that would be a little ridiculous. He had probably seen a dozen dead bodies in as many days in the past month.

He looked over my head and saw the damage. "Have I taught you nothing?" he asked Fred. "You've got better skills than that."

"I was hungry," Fred said. Oh, that explains it.

I asked Crawford to come with me to the grocery store. Before we left, I asked Max to walk the dog. When I saw that she was going to object, citing her hatred of anything on four legs, I shot her a look and pointed at her. "Not a word. The leash is hanging right there," I said, pointing to the hook that Crawford had installed by the back door.

We went outside and I heard someone call my name. Across the street, my neighbor and friend, Jane Farnsworth, was jogging across her lawn and making her way toward mine. "Alison!" she called, waving as she ran. She joined us on the driveway and caught her breath. "Did you hear what happened?" she asked and then, taking in my appearance, revised her question. "What happened to you?"

"Long story," I said.

She stared at the black eye for a few seconds and that reminded me of just how bad I looked. I needed a big pair of sunglasses. "Did you hear about Carter Wilmott?" she asked, starting to cry.

"I did," I said. "Did you know him?"

She nodded. "Lydia is a friend of mine," she said. "We met in playgroup when Brendan and her son, Tyler, were two."

Small town, I thought. Everyone knows everyone. Except for me. I don't know anyone except for Jane, her two sons, and her partner, Kathy. I had never laid eyes on Carter or Lydia before the past two days. "I just saw Lydia," I said, and could sense Crawford's surprise; I knew there would be questions to answer on that front. "I was there when he died."

Jane grabbed her chest and gasped. "You were?"

"I was. He died quickly," I assured her, this becoming my mantra. I suspected it wouldn't be the last time I recited that fact about Carter's death.

"Lydia is devastated." She wiped her hands across her eyes. "She hasn't made arrangements yet. There's going to be an autopsy. He was as healthy as a horse." Clearly, Jane didn't know the exact details of what had happened, the blow to the head, or the fact that Carter was in distress before that happened. She also didn't mention the car exploding and I wondered if Lydia left that little tidbit out of the conversation. Seemed likely. A lot had happened that day.

"Would you let me know when the arrangements are finalized?" I asked.

Jane seemed a little surprised that I would want that information but she assured me that she would. "I'll call you later." She broke down and I put my arms around her, happy to be comforting her and not the one being comforted. I'm in that position far too often and felt as though I were using up all of the good will I had in the comfort bank. When she composed herself, she kissed my cheek and started back toward her house.

Inside the house, I heard Max calling to Trixie. I knew the dog wouldn't come. She finds Max exhausting and hides under the dining room table every time she's around. I took that into account when I had asked Max to walk her; it would take at least a half hour to track the dog down and get her on the leash, which would hopefully keep Max occupied during my absence. Leaving Max without a task is akin to giving a toddler a roll of toilet paper: there won't be too much of a mess but you'll still have a lot to clean up. "Will there be a murder investigation?" I asked as we walked to the car.

He opened the passenger side door for me. "Sounds like they've already got the guy."

I slid in and waited for him to get into the car. "George Miller."

"They'll probably get him on manslaughter. The fight, the big blow to the head, it's all there." He looked over at me and could tell that I was dubious. "Whatever you're thinking, Inspector Clouseau, forget about it. The police will investigate, and hopefully find out, who put the device on the engine, and that person will go away for attempted murder along with George Miller," he said, stressing "attempted." "But if you want more information, call my brother, the hotshot lawyer, and have at it." He backed down the driveway, our conversation obviously over. There's nothing worse than a hungry Crawford.

He drove us to the Stop & Shop at the corner of Route 9, but thankfully, he didn't ask me about my visit to Lydia Wilmott's house. That didn't mean we wouldn't be discussing it later. I grabbed a cart and wheeled it inside, happy to be doing something normal and ordinary, like looking at fruit and deciding between potato salad and cole slaw. He followed behind me, admiring the big selection of fruits and vegetables; Crawford lives on the Upper West Side and gets most of his groceries from the Korean grocer two doors down from his apartment. Suburban grocery stores never ceased to amaze him with their size and selection. I turned to hand him a bag of limes but instead found myself staring at Lydia Wilmott, an Hermès kerchief on her head, giant black sunglasses hiding her presumably red, tear-filled eyes. I stuttered out her name, careful not to alert the other shoppers that the newly widowed woman walked among us in the grocery store.

Crawford dropped the kiwi he was holding and waited for an introduction. "Lydia

Wilmott, Bobby Crawford," I said, and she took his hand tentatively. I didn't go into the whole, "he's my boyfriend even though we're too old for that terminology but I haven't decided whether or not to mess up a good thing by marrying him" spiel.

"I'm very sorry for your loss," Crawford said, good former altar boy that he was.

Lydia stood, straight-backed, her hands gripping the handle of her shopping cart. Her lips were set in a grim horizontal line and she stared at Crawford from behind her very expensive designer sunglasses, ignoring his condolences. "I appreciated your visit this morning, Alison." She plucked a kiwi from the stack next to Crawford and threw it into her cart. "I had to get out of the house. There are too many people there and I just need to be doing something normal."

"I understand," I said. I handed her a bunch of bananas that she was too far away to reach and she thanked me.

She turned to Crawford and addressed him. "What did you say your name was?"

"Crawford," he said. "Bobby Crawford."

She nodded slowly. She continued to appraise him from behind her dark glasses, and while I was used to Crawford getting admiring glances from the opposite sex, I sensed that this wasn't one of those occasions. She was studying him for some other reason, its nature indeterminate to me. "And what is it that you do for a living, Mr. Crawford?"

I didn't know what that had to do with anything, besides her curiosity, but Crawford answered that he was a police detective. Lydia nodded slowly. "Here?" she asked.

"No. New York City," he said.

She nodded again, and by the grim set of her mouth, I could tell that she wasn't impressed. In fact, she seemed disgusted. Maybe she had had a run-in with a cop? Unpaid parking tickets? A jaywalking fine? All I knew was that she was not pleased to meet Crawford, even though she said so as she started off down the apple aisle, careful to avoid the glances of any other shoppers who were rubbernecking with gusto. The Hermès scarf and sunglasses notwithstanding, everyone knew exactly who she was.

Crawford looked at me and mouthed, "What was that?"

I shrugged and went with a full-blown lie. "You're handsome. You're going to get looks." I pushed the cart down the aisle and toward the deli counter, Crawford following behind me.

"That wasn't what that was," he said,

looking over his shoulder to see where Lydia had gone, but she had disappeared into one of the vast aisles in another part of the store. When he determined that she wasn't in earshot, he turned back toward the deli counter. "Is it our turn?"

I showed him our number. Nine hundred and seven. The number on the neon counter read "three." There were four other people ahead of us, waiting for cold cuts. "We're going to be here a while," I said.

The deli man approached and moved the number ahead. "Four!"

When no one answered, the woman at the head of the line interrupted. "I have forty-eight," she said, proffering her ticket.

"Five!"

The man behind her offered his input. "I have ninety."

"Six!"

Crawford let out a loud exhale.

"Seven!"

I looked at my ticket again. "I have nine hundred and seven," I offered weakly.

"Eight!" The counter guy was more exasperated than the customers were but clearly couldn't find his way toward waiting on the lady who was first on line. "Eight?"

Crawford steered the cart away from the counter and me out of the store. "Hey, what are we doing?" I asked as he grabbed my elbow and pushed me toward the car, leaving the cart behind.

"We're getting out of here, that's what we're doing," he said. "We're going to Tony's."

My heart sank. Did we need cold cuts that badly? Couldn't we have pizza instead? The last time I had been to Tony's, his new wife, Lucia, had hurled an invective at me from the kitchen, suspicious that I wanted in on Tony's sexagenarian deliciousness. Trust me — I don't. I've got a guy who's all that and more. Okay, so Crawford doesn't have unlimited access to Boar's Head cold cuts, but he's got a lot of other things going for him. Not being in his sixties is one of them. And being taller than me is the other. Tony is pushing seventy, bald, fat, and short. Sure, he's loaded, but that's not going to cut the mustard with me. Lucia can have all two hundred and fifty pounds of him stretched across his five-foot-four frame.

I had never actually laid eyes on Lucia, but I had incurred her wrath so much that once she had thrown a pot of meatballs at my head from her hiding place in the kitchen. Fortunately, it had missed me but it would have left a mark had it not. Tony seemed terrified of her, too; clearly, she was as dangerous as she seemed. My heart was racing as we pulled up in front of the deli, my hands clammy. Crawford jumped out of the car. This was a man in need of a sandwich. I was still in the car when he pressed his face to the passenger side window and asked, "Are you coming?"

I wasn't going to and then I thought about Wilmott's blog and review of Tony's deli. It wouldn't hurt to go in, smile a little at Tony, flash a little boob, and ask some questions about how he felt about the blog. Crawford saw the change in my demeanor and immediately asked what I was up to. I feigned ignorance. "What are you talking about?"

He threw a look over his shoulder; he didn't know exactly what I was up to but he knew I was up to something. I followed him into the deli, resisting the urge to shudder when the bell rang over the door, announcing our arrival. That bell always reminded me of Tony and his love for me, along with flying pots of meatballs. I couldn't help it. Tony looked up at the sound, took in my face, and broke out into a smile so wide I feared his face would crack.

"Mi amore!" he called, and then realizing he was married to a character from Dante's *Inferno,* he dropped his voice. "My love," he whispered.

I looked at Crawford, who rolled his eyes.

"Hi, Tony," I said, maintaining a decent distance from the counter so that he wouldn't grab me in a sweaty, cold-cut-smelling embrace. "We need some cold cuts."

"You need some cold cuts," he repeated. "You need some cold cuts! Is that how you greet me after all this time?" He threw his arms open, expecting me to reach over the counter and lean into them.

I started coughing; there had been a nasty strain of the flu traveling about the county and I begged off, citing some general malaise. "I'm sorry, Tony," I said. "I wouldn't want to get you sick." I fake-sneezed for extra effect.

He leaned over the counter. "For you?" he asked dramatically. "I would die."

And you just might, I thought, if Lucia gets wind of this. I wondered where she was and why I still didn't have spaghetti sauce all over the front of my shirt; I decided not to tempt fate and kept my voice low. I heard Crawford let out a loud and impatient sigh.

Tony studied my face. "What happened to you?"

I went with my old standby: "Long story."

He didn't really accept that as an answer but I wasn't going to elaborate. He continued to stare at me. And then at Crawford. And then back at me. "Right. So back to the cold cuts," I said. "Crawford? What would you like?"

Crawford can't order a cup of coffee in a fancy coffee shop because he gets too confused by sizes that are listed in other languages and descriptions that aren't in his lexicon. He still hasn't figured out that foam is regular old milk all frothed up. But order cold cuts the man can do. He rattled off an array of cold cuts, some of which I had never heard of, but all of which Tony had. Tony set about slicing meat through the big slicer and putting thin cuts of meat onto paper. When he was done, we had about six packages, along with several bags of chips, a couple of loaves of Italian bread, and a six-pack of beer, which Crawford had set about amassing as we waited for our order.

Tony looked at me forlornly. "You never come here anymore."

I shrugged. "I'm sorry, Tony. I'll come by soon," I said, even though I had no intention of doing so. I heard some pots and pans rattling around in the back of the store and knew I had only a minute or two to find out what I had come in for: just how much Tony and Lucia hated Carter. "Tony, did you know Carter Wilmott?"

He blessed himself, Father, Son, and Holy Spirit, kissed the Jesus head around his neck, and then spat on the floor in fury. "Son of a bitch," he said, quickly adding, "God rest his soul."

Crawford had his hand on the door handle and was anxious to leave. "You didn't like him?" I asked, feigning ignorance. I didn't like him, either, and that was just from reading his blog; I had no personal experience with the guy. Oh, right, except for the dying-in-front-of-me part. That's about as personal as it gets.

Tony leaned across the counter and was close enough to grab my hand and bring me close. My midsection hit the ice-cream case fronting the counter with a thud, and with an indelicate "oof," the breath left my lungs. "He was a very bad man."

I struggled to catch my breath and listen to Tony at the same time, which wasn't easy.

"He said very bad things about my store," he whispered conspiratorially, looking over his shoulder to see if Lucia was in sight. I had never seen her, but that didn't mean she wasn't somewhere else in the store. "I thought Lucia was going to kill him."

I was feeling faint. Between the heat of the kitchen, the lack of oxygen, my growing hunger, and the pungent odor of roast beef combined with mayonnaise wafting off Tony, I knew I wasn't going to last long. I decided to ask the question I had come in to ask. "Does Lucia know anything about explosives?" I could almost read Crawford's mind: way to cut to the chase, Alison. Whether or not Carter had died from a blow to the head was irrelevant in my mind. Someone wanted to kill him, and for some unknown reason, I wanted to find out. That, coupled with a misguided allegiance to Greg and bad coffee, was enough for me to poke around.

Tony smiled proudly. "No, but I was a cook in Korea," he said. "Learned a lot about blowing things up from the guys we fed. Once we blew up a whole pig!"

I was aware of Crawford's hand gripping my elbow as I slid down in front of the ice-cream case. "That's interesting," I said before I passed out, thinking about how good a roast beef on Italian bread would taste when I finally woke up.

Seven

I'm a fainter. Always have been. Even worse, I'm a puker. Fortunately, when I awoke, propped against the counter with a dirty dish towel pressed to my head, I was free of puke. I had slid down the counter into a sitting position before I had really conked out completely. The bag of cold cuts was on the floor where Crawford had dropped it; he knew I was going to faint even before I did.

Crawford asked me if I could get to my feet and I tried to put them under me. After a few tries, I managed to get into a standing position. Tony handed me a cold bottle of water, and the genuine concern on his face made me forget that he was more attracted to me than my first husband had been, a thought that gave me pause. Crawford thanked Tony for his help and helped me out of the store and into the car. He turned it on and put the air conditioner on full blast.

"Are you okay?" he asked, directing the vents toward my face.

"I don't know what happened," I said, truly at a loss. "I think it was when he pulled me into the counter. I lost my breath."

"You looked queasy long before that," Crawford said, taking a handkerchief out of his pocket and wiping my brow. "You haven't looked well since I picked you up yesterday."

"Do you blame me?" I asked. "I saw a dead body."

"Not your first."

"No. Not my first. But hopefully my last." I leaned my head on the air-conditioning vent closest to me and sighed. "Take me home."

Crawford kept an eye on me most of the way home, but he also kept looking in his rearview mirror quite a bit, raising my hackles. "What are you doing?" I asked.

"Who do you know who drives a beat-up blue Subaru Outback?"

I scanned my memory. "No one." I swallowed again, hoping that the taste of bile in my throat would dissipate with each gulp. "But does the Tony thing give you pause?"

"What Tony thing?"

"Korea. The pig. The explosives."

Crawford kept an eye on the rearview mirror. “No.”

“No?” I was incredulous.

“No,” he repeated. “He’s an old man with a cranky wife who he might someday kill, but for the Wilmott murder? I don’t see it.”

“Carter Wilmott wrote some really nasty things about him on his blog.”

“I just don’t think Tony would have shared an anecdote about blowing up a pig in Korea if he was the one who put the explosive on the car engine. Doesn’t make sense. Too obvious.”

“Sure, it’s obvious, but Tony . . .” I started. He took a hard right down a one-way street and I banged into my door. “Hey!” I straightened up after he slowed down. “What are you doing? If that’s your way to get me to stop talking about this, a polite ‘shut up’ would have sufficed.”

“Someone’s been following us since we left Tony’s.” He threw the car in park, and jumped out. I turned and saw that the car was behind us but now backing up, dangerously, down the one-way street. Crawford began running after the car, yelling at the driver to stop, who continued driving backward until they were down the narrow residential street and back out onto the main drag.

Crawford jumped back in the car and

went into reverse.

"No! Not the backward car chase!" I said. "I'm already ready to throw up."

"I have to see who that is," he said, his head facing the back of the car, his foot pressing the accelerator down almost to the floor. He swung out onto the main street and drove into the traffic, only managing to cut two cars off in the process. The Subaru was nowhere to be found and he dejectedly pulled over to see if I was still in one piece. I hit him with a salami that I had pulled from the bag from Tony's.

"What are you trying to do? Kill me?" I asked, my breath short after holding it during a very brief, but very tense, car chase in reverse.

"No, I'm not trying to kill you," he said. "But I wonder why someone would be following us. Aren't you the least bit curious?"

"No. Not curious. Not interested in the least." I leaned my head against the seat rest. "About the same level of curiosity as you have for Tony and explosives. Can we please just go home now?"

Max was her usual caring self when I walked in through the back door. "You look like shit." Sometimes I wondered why we were friends.

Fred grunted in agreement. They were still

at the kitchen table in exactly the same positions as when I left. The screen was still torn, but the window was closed and locked. I guess I was going to be calling my friend Hernan to fix it during the week. It appeared that they were waiting for food and hadn't moved since Crawford and I had set off on our grocery journey.

"Did you take my dog out?" I asked.

"I can't find her," Max said. She slid something into her pocketbook.

"Was that a tape measure?" I asked.

She smiled insincerely. "Can't fix the screen if I don't know how big the window is."

I didn't believe a word of that. "But you didn't know that the screen would be broken when you left for here. Or do you just carry a tape measure around in your Marc Jacobs bag?"

"It's a Michael Kors," she said.

"Whatever." I waited. "Well?"

"Yes, I do. I do carry a tape measure around in my pocketbook. It comes in handy when I want to measure something."

The conversation could have gone on indefinitely but I let it go. I grabbed the dog's leash from the hook by the back door.

Crawford put the bag of deli products on the counter. "Do you want me to go with you?" he asked, knowing that I was going to walk the dog in the absence of any responsible dog walkers in the house. He came over and took my cheeks in his hands. "Are you feeling better?"

I nodded. "I just need some air," I said. I felt like Lydia Wilmott all of a sudden; I just wanted to be alone. Walking Trixie by myself was just the ticket. "You guys eat. I don't have much of an appetite." I knew I wouldn't be two minutes out of the house before those scavengers had eaten everything but the wrappers the cold cuts had come in. Max is as voracious an eater as her six-foot-five husband and my tall drink of water of a boyfriend; she can pack it away with the best of them despite her diminutive stature.

I put Trixie on the leash and headed down toward the river. This route would lead me away from the village and away from anything that brought up bad memories. I would avoid Beans, Beans and the police station, and be able to enjoy the peace and serenity that walking with my dog along a beautiful waterway would bring. I had made it halfway down the street and was almost to the river when a pickup truck pulled around the corner and screeched to a stop in front of me. A woman with short spiky hair and a better body than her blog pictures would suggest jumped out of the truck and came toward me. Trixie let out a low growl, assuming that this wasn't a friend.

"You Bergeron?"

I recognized her as the lovely Mrs. Miller from the blog. "I am." This woman had obviously spent some time in the gym since Carter or one of his blog staff had taken those pictures of her. Her upper arms were toned and tight, jutting out from a fitted tank top that accentuated a large, but impressively perky, set of boobs. Her stomach was flat. Her workouts, however, hadn't seemed to do much about chunky thighs and a rather comprehensive bottom; I assumed she would get to those parts now that the upper body was such a specimen of fitness.

"Come with me," she commanded, getting back into her truck cab.

I stood by the side of the road without moving, curling Trixie's leash into my hand, drawing the dog closer to me. Mrs. Miller waited expectantly in her car. Finally, when she saw that I wasn't getting in, she rolled down the passenger side window. "I said to get in!" She stared at me with big round blue eyes, unadorned by makeup but with the longest, darkest lashes I had ever seen.

Mrs. Miller had probably been a looker before she had fallen prey to the physical horrors of middle age. Once she got the thighs and the butt worked out, she would be a fine-looking lady.

She was obviously used to people listening to her but she had never met me. I decided that just walking away would be the best course of action, so I pulled Trixie to my side and began to amble down the street, even though my instincts told me to run like the dickens. Behind me, I heard Mrs. Miller make a sharp U-turn, knocking over a garbage can that had been set out for Monday morning pickup, and follow behind me at a slow pace.

"You know they've got my husband in jail, right?" she called from her truck window. Her tone had a faint overtone of accusation.

I kept staring straight ahead. The woman was scaring the crap out of me although I wasn't sure why. She wasn't trying to run me down, but she was clearly agitated and she had the "guns" that Greg could only dream of. And that could probably crush my trachea with one chop. "No, I didn't know," I said. That was certainly an interesting turn of events, though.

"Manslaughter," she spat out.

Just as Crawford had predicted. I wondered how the police could arrest Miller without the ME's report, but Crawford had seemed pretty sure that this was the way it would go down. "I'm sorry?" I said, not convinced that I should be.

"You were there. You tell the cops that he had nothing to do with it," she continued, now parallel to me and close enough to touch. Riding in a pickup gave her the advantage of being at eye level, something a car wouldn't.

"I can't do that. I *was* there."

"Yeah, but they had a fight. Instigated by that louse Wilmott."

"Your husband punched him in the head. Hard. He died. Draw your own conclusions." Although I still wasn't convinced that was the cause of death, I wanted Mrs. Miller to consider the fact that it could possibly be.

She thought about that for a minute, resting her head on the steering wheel. When she picked her head up, her face had gone slack. "Oh, and sorry about the black eye." Something in her now nonthreatening tone made me stop walking. I turned toward her. "Eat a lot of papaya and pineapple and mix two tablespoons of salt with two tablespoons of lard or vegetable oil and spread it over your eye. Make sure it's closed." She saw the look on my face; I wasn't a lard type of girl. Vaseline was the closest I got to anything moisturizing. "Trust me. It helps with blood circulation. And the papaya and the pineapple make the discoloration go away faster." Her tone was rough but her suggestions kind. I wondered if Mrs. Miller was a Gemini. The abrupt change in her demeanor surely hinted at two sides of the astrological coin.

"Thanks."

"No problem. I'm a nurse," she said, gripping the steering wheel of her idling truck; she was my second nurse of the day, counting Elaine. "Do you want to help me or not? They've got George in lockup and it's only a matter of time before he's shipped off to stay with the general population in White Plains." She set her mouth in a grim line. "That's not going to be good for him."

That was probably an understatement. I commanded Trixie to sit because this was obviously going to take a while. "Listen, there's nothing I can do to help you. I told the police everything I know. Your husband and Wilmott had a fight and then Wilmott died. I don't know what he died from —"

"Blunt force trauma to the head," she said, interrupting me. "From a punch.

That's what they're saying. That's the coroner's best guess. The Wilmotts are very powerful in this town and the cops want to close this case fast."

Talk about the wheels of justice turning quickly. "I still don't know what I can do." I wanted to mention that there were two cops on the scene — as well as Greg — who could also verify that George had hit him in the head but I didn't mention that. She was pretty agitated already.

"Tell the cops it was just a fight. Tell them that you never saw George hit Wilmott in the head. Tell them that Wilmott fell and hit his head and that my husband's fist did not come in contact with Carter Wilmott's head. Case closed." She dropped her hands into her lap and looked up at the interior roof of her car. "Tell them anything that will help me get George out of there."

"I can't do that, Mrs. Miller."

"Ginny."

"I told them what I saw, Ginny. That's exactly what I saw. To me, that's exactly what happened."

And that's when she cracked. I don't know why I was surprised, but when the tears started falling, I saw the softer side of Mrs. Miller. "They're going to at least get him on manslaughter. You're not going to press charges, too, are you?"

I shook my head. "It was an accident."

Her lips quivered as a tear fell onto her tank top. "Thank you." She rested her head on the steering wheel. "I don't know why I tracked you down. I don't even know you. I should have assumed that you had already told them everything you know. I'm just grasping at straws."

I didn't know what to say. Her tough façade gone, I now saw a woman who would do anything to help her husband and who loved him deeply. Not unlike Lydia Wilmott. "Where are you a nurse?" I asked.

"Phelps," she said, referencing a hospital in Tarrytown, where I grew up. It was about ten minutes north of where we stood. "I've been there for twenty years. I'm the head nurse in oncology."

I always wonder why I can't move on and why, for me, August is the cruelest month. Now I knew. Everywhere I turned were reminders of my mother, her life and her death. I knew Phelps well. My mother had died there after a long battle with a rare but deadly form of cancer. I searched my memory to see if I recalled ever having seen Ginny Miller, but I came up blank. But if she was as wonderful, professionally, as all of the nurses there had been to me and my mother, I now had newfound respect for her. And I certainly didn't find her frightening.

I remembered Tony's Korean War adventures and the pig explosion. "Your husband ever been to war, Ginny?"

"No. Why?"

This lying thing was coming easier and easier as the weekend wore on. I figured if I had gotten information out of Tony so easily about his war exploits, finding out if George had had any similar ones would be a piece of cake. I was right. She had answered immediately. "Because if they get him for manslaughter, he's in for the battle of a lifetime." Okay, so it was overly dramatic, but it was the only thing I could come up with on such short notice.

The tough façade returned and Ginny gave me a hard look, even though what she had to say was kind. "I'm sorry I came on so strong," she said, throwing the truck into drive and peeling off down the street.

I looked at Trixie. "What was that?" I asked her, but as usual, she didn't have a response. I did know one thing: the bizarre nature of the weekend was making me look forward to going back to school and working freshman orientation, something that I normally dreaded. I guess something positive had come out of this big, giant, tragic mess.

EIGHT

Crawford was whispering in my ear as I tried to go to sleep that night.

"Not tonight, Crawford. I don't feel well," I said, and pulled the comforter up closer to my ears; I had the air conditioner on high and the bedroom was a cool fifty-nine degrees, just the way I liked it. I had filled Crawford in on my conversation with Ginny Miller after Max and Fred had left. He had been interested, but not intrigued, as I thought he might be. Actually, he had been singularly unimpressed hearing that I had been accosted by a woman who would do anything to save her husband from the clink. He had seen suspects and their loved ones go to much further lengths to avoid jail time. "I think I have that cow flu that was all the rage a few months ago."

"Swine."

"What?"

"It's the swine flu. Mad cow disease, swine

flu. Two different things."

"Thanks for the clarification. We're still not having sex."

"If you don't feel well again tomorrow, you should call a doctor."

"I only have a gynecologist. And my lady parts feel just fine. I don't have a regular doctor."

"Then get one."

I took a deep breath; I didn't feel congested but I didn't feel uncongested, either. Somewhere in between. "Who do you think put that explosive device on Carter's engine?"

"Who cares?"

"I care," I said.

"Well, you shouldn't," he said, rolling over to face the window, his back to me.

"Don't you think it's weird?"

"Yes, it's weird," he said. "But I just don't care. I didn't know the guy, but he's responsible for you having a black eye, so as far as I'm concerned, good riddance."

"Crawford!"

"Seriously. You witnessed a horrible thing. Let's move on. We have bigger things to discuss than who put an explosive device on some crazy blogger's car. That's what Hardin and Madden are for," he said.

I remained silent for such a long time that

I thought he might have fallen asleep, but that didn't matter. I had a burning question on my mind. "Do you know anyone in the police department who might know something about car bombs?"

"Go to sleep, please."

I did. I slept right through the alarm, Crawford's shower and dressing, and the breakfast making that he undertook in the kitchen. I only awoke when he presented me with a bacon and egg sandwich, the smell of which roused me from my slumber. I sat up and looked at the runny egg, half-cooked bacon, and stale roll. But I also took in Crawford's pleased face — he's not much of a cook so making this sandwich must have taken a tremendous amount of effort — and decided that I needed to eat it and look like I was enjoying it heartily. He was in a much better mood than the night before.

"I would have brought you coffee but you don't have any," he said. "Do you want me to go to Beans, Beans?"

"No!" I said, a little too hastily. I didn't want anything to do with that place. At least for the time being. "The juice is fine," I said, taking a large gulp that sat in my midsection as though I had swallowed an entire orange. What the hell was wrong with me?

Maybe Crawford's insistence on my seeing a doctor was warranted. I figured I'd give it the day and then make a decision. I ate around the half-cooked parts of the bacon and avoided the egg yolk, feeding bits of the sandwich to Trixie when Crawford wasn't looking. He wears a lot of equipment to his job, and putting on all of it takes an inordinate amount of time, so his back was turned for the better part of my breakfast. When he turned back around and saw that I had finished, he was clearly pleased. He's a nice guy, that Crawford; I am glad I didn't disappoint him.

"I'll call you later," I said, getting the sense that he was heading out. "I've got interviews with the potential English majors from the freshman class today. Always a delight."

"Sounds good," he said, and leaned over the bed to give me a kiss. "Are you sure you're feeling better?"

"I'm fine," I assured him. "The weekend kind of sucked and I'm looking forward to getting back to work." I threw the comforter back and stretched. "Did I really say that? How could I be looking forward to going back to work?"

"I don't know," he said, "but try to have a good day." And he was off, leaving just the lingering odor of his clean laundry smell in his wake. No wonder I was a little dizzy.

After walking Trixie, I went through my closet, attempting to come up with an outfit that conveyed the gravitas that assigning future English majors required. I settled on a short-sleeved wrap dress and a pair of sandals, opting for comfort over seriousness. The dress was a little low-cut, but being as there was nary a safety or straight pin in sight, I pulled the material together, putting a little tape between the dress and my skin. I knew it wasn't going to hold, but I also knew that it would make me feel better, knowing that I had done something to rectify the situation. I pulled my shoulder-length hair back into a low ponytail and threw on some earrings. I was on my way out the door fifteen minutes later after checking in with the dog walker, reminding her that the party was over; I was back at work full-time.

I was planning on walking to the train that morning because the weather was beautiful, and I was definitely on my way there when I found myself veering off at the end of my street and ending up at Beans, Beans. I paused in front of the window of the store. Never in my wildest dreams did I think I would come back here after what had transpired just forty-eight hours previous, but I felt compelled and a little guilty. I had thought many bad things about Greg's coffee over the past two days and, in actuality, it wasn't that bad. Okay, it was terrible. But I didn't want the guy to fail and I wanted to show my solidarity. See? I was here and I had witnessed the whole thing! I tried to make eye contact with the other people on the street in front of the store, but imagined that I looked like a crazy person trying to strike up a conversation and ceased after the third person hurried by me. The store looked no worse for wear; a quick look inside told me that everything was as it had been right before Carter and George had started their fight ending in Carter's death. Greg was at the counter, all alone, not a customer in the store. Seeing him going about his business in silence, all by himself, made me sad. Against my better judgment, I opened the door and walked in.

His face lit up at the sight of me and, I have to say, it was not a bad way to start the day. He came out from around the counter and gave me a big bear hug, the kind that I really don't enjoy, particularly from people I don't know very well.

"Alison! Hey!" he said, hustling back around the counter. "What can I get you?"

"Nothing, Greg. Thanks," I said, quickly changing my mind when I saw his disappointed face. "A large black coffee, please."

He turned around to fill a cup of coffee for me. "You're my first customer of the day and I've been open since six." He turned back around and handed me the hot cup. "Be careful. That's hot."

I pulled a little sleeve from the stack next to the counter and slipped it on my cup before burning the pads of my fingertips. "Thanks for the warning," I said, opening the lid and taking a little tiny sip. "No business today?"

"Not yet," he said, wiping down the glass-topped counter with a wet rag even though it was spotlessly clean.

"They'll come," I assured him. "If you make the coffee, they will come," I said gravely, making him laugh.

"I hope you're right." He leaned onto the counter. "How are you doing today?"

"Me?" I asked, surprised that he even cared about my well-being.

"Yeah, you." He smiled. "You got a lot more than you bargained for on Saturday."

I raised an eyebrow. "You, too." I put my coffee on the counter.

"You're not drinking your coffee," he said.

"Oh, I will," I said. "I've haven't been feeling so great since last week. A little queasy."

Greg smiled broadly. "Something you want to tell me?"

I couldn't figure out why he was looking at me with such a broad grin on his face until he made a motion with his hand over his belly. "Pregnant? Oh, no," I said. I shook my head back and forth so vigorously I started to get dizzy. "No. Not pregnant. Sick, maybe, but not pregnant." I put my hand on my abdomen, wondering if my physique was giving the impression that I was with child. Yes, the usual paunch was still there, but it was nothing to write home about. A steady diet of Devil Dogs and vodka martinis will eventually take its toll. Was it time to start using the Ab Roller that I had bought from the Home Shopping Network one long, sleepless night a few weeks back?

"Well, okay, then," Greg said, his tone suggesting that he didn't think I was telling the truth. In order to prove him wrong, I picked up my fully caffeinated coffee and took a long drag, forgetting that it was screaming hot. My scorched tongue reminded me for the rest of the day that a simple denial would have been appropriate under the circumstances.

"Let me ask you something, Greg," I said,

attempting to articulate with a sore and numb tongue. "Did Carter come here a lot? Or was Saturday just a fluke?"

"He was here every day," he said.

"So I guess he didn't say anything nasty about you on his blog?"

Greg laughed. "Oh, sure he did. But I'm a forgiving soul, Alison. It takes a lot more energy to be negative than to be positive. And I'm all about putting positive energy into the world," he said, closing his thumbs and forefingers together on each hand. *"Namaste."*

"Namaste," I replied, and left the store thinking that I should take a page from Greg's book.

I was at school within the half hour, my tongue still numb from the scalding coffee. I entered campus, feeling that I was safer here than in my own village, and started my trek to my office. St. Thomas University sits majestically, high on a hill, overlooking the Hudson. On a day like today, the walk to my office was absolutely gorgeous, a view of the river at my left the entire time. Hoping to see some of my colleagues after the nice summer break, I decided to go in through the front door of the school rather than through the secret back door that was closer to my office but which offered a far less scenic view. But when I entered the marble hallway of the main building where most classes were held, it was pretty much desolate, letting the wind out of my sails a bit. This wasn't an auspicious beginning to the semester.

I trotted up to my third-floor office and encountered Dottie Cruz, the poorest example of a department secretary one could find on campus. She was making her way through the *Daily News,* New York's hometown paper, commenting to the guy delivering mail about the sorry state of the Mets.

"Wright's gotta stop swinging for the fences!" she said, getting a hearty nod from the mail guy. "Let's get some singles, David. Save the home runs for play-off season."

Save the home runs? Was that such great advice? How about giving us home runs whenever you wanted? Or could? I decided to pick up my mail and beat a hasty retreat to my office. "Hi, Dottie," I said, pulling out a stack of textbook catalogs and brochures for study-abroad programs that really didn't pertain to my academic subject of English. Dottie and I really don't get along; she's an inveterate gossip, and since I'm usually the one supplying the grist for the gossip mill but am tight-lipped in her presence, she doesn't consider me an ally.

Add in that I complain vociferously about her to anyone who will listen at least once a day, and I would have to say that we had become archenemies.

"The holy father is looking for you," she called after me. I realized that despite her nosy nature, she never mentioned my black eye, and for that, I was most grateful.

I turned around, unable to resist the snappy comeback. "Really? Pope Benedict is looking for me?"

She looked confused, and rightfully so; in her world, the "holy father" was one of my best friends and the school chaplain, Kevin McManus. He was not holy, nor was he a father (except in the ecclesiastical sense), so I just referred to him as "Kevin."

"You know what I mean." The mail guy had left during this scintillating exchange so she turned back to her newspaper. Seemed to me that she would have a lot of work to do for freshman orientation, but she didn't share my sense of urgency or work ethic. But she did have a beau who was a colleague of Crawford's, and she seemed deliriously happy every time he called or stopped by campus. I stared at the back of her head for a second before asking her a question.

"Hey, Dottie?"

"Yes?" she said without turning back

around. I guess we were in a fight when I had considered our latest exchange just our usual banter.

"Are you happy with Charlie?"

She turned around, her face lighting up at the sound of his name. "Charlie? He's the best. You know that."

"He seems like a nice guy."

"He's the best," she repeated.

"So if he asked you to marry him, would you?"

"Of course!" she said. "I've been alone a long time. I'd love to be married again." Her eyes narrowed. She didn't really trust me or this line of questioning. "Why do you ask?"

"Oh, no reason," I said. "You just seem very happy."

Glad that one of us was able to make a decision on our love life, I let myself into my office, leaving the door open behind me so that students could come in freely, or more important, so I could see when the rest of my colleagues on the office floor arrived.

"Well, if it isn't Chesty Morgan!"

Kevin stood in my doorway, his hands cupping his pectorals. I didn't know what he was talking about until he pointed at my chest. The Scotch tape had predictably gotten loose and both my bra and a pretty healthy portion of my breasts were hanging out of the front of my dress. No wonder the mail guy had been stricken mute at my arrival. I hastily gathered my dress back into an appropriate show of neck and cleavage and held it there with my hand. "Well, if it isn't Father Inappropriate. Welcome back from your vacation, Your Excellency." I offered him the chair in front of my desk with a wave of my hand. "And who's Chesty Morgan?"

"Just one of the most famous exotic dancers, by way of Poland, in the seventies and eighties," he said, sitting down. "Are you doing that to draw attention away from your black eye?" Kevin has known me long enough to know that I am a klutz of the highest order. He didn't seem surprised by the Technicolor band around my eye.

"And you would know about this Chesty woman how?"

"I have four brothers, remember? She had a seventy-three-inch chest. That's not something you forget hearing about." He smiled. "Especially if you have taken a vow of celibacy."

I held up a hand. "Okay! Enough!" I leaned back in my chair. "How was your vacation?" Kevin usually takes the month of

August to travel, and this year he had gone to Paris for two weeks.

"First, the eye." He leaned back in his chair. "Explain."

"You first," I said. "Tell me about the vacation."

"It was great." He reached into the pocket of his black trousers and pulled out a small package wrapped in tissue paper. "Here. This is for you."

I opened it up and found a small medal with the image of the Blessed Mother printed on it. It was blue surrounded in gold and very pretty. "Why, thanks, Kevin," I said, truly touched. I knew what these kinds of medals meant to him, and to be given one that he transported back from France was truly special.

"It's from the Church of the Miraculous Medal. It's the actual place where our order of nuns here was founded. How great is that?" he asked, beaming. From strippers to churches, that was my Kevin. After accepting my heartfelt and profuse thanks, he changed the subject. "Oh, hey, I saw that there was a weird death in your village this weekend. Something about a guy around my age dropping dead in a coffee shop?"

"Oh, Kevin, do we have a lot of catching up to do," I said.

"Make sure you put in the part where you ended up looking like Jake La Motta."

"I will." I went through the whole story, starting with the blog, going into great detail about the black eye and the death of Carter Wilmott, and ending with my conversation with Ginny Miller on the street.

"Sounds like this guy had a lot of enemies and any number of them could have wanted him dead. And it's pretty easy to get information on terrorist tactics off the Web, too, so just about any of them could have figured out how to make an explosive." Kevin knew a lot about many more things than I gave him credit for. "What was his motivation in writing the blog?"

I pondered that. "Good question. No idea, actually. I know he was a rabid liberal to the point of socialist, despite being one of the richest men in Westchester. But beyond his taking issue with most of the politicians and public officials in town, I don't know why he did what he did." But I can find out, I thought. My previous day's shame at poking around Lydia Wilmott's home and life was gone and I was now back to my old nosy self.

Kevin got up. "Gotta run. I've got a ten o'clock with Etheridge."

Mark Etheridge was the college president

and a bit of a horse's rear end, but he was our boss and we were suitably fearful of him. "What's that about?" I asked. Getting summoned to the president's office was never a good thing.

Kevin was dismissive, however. "Oh, nothing. I'm not sure but I think it's about the installment of the student Eucharistic ministers. You know how he loves to keep his hands in all things liturgical."

A student poked her head in the doorway and was immediately taken aback at the sight of Kevin in his Roman collar and Birkenstock sandals. I assumed this was my first appointment of the day and I shooed Kevin out of the office after giving him the address of the blog, which he requested before taking flight from the room. The student — a young woman who looked like she was twelve but who I knew to be almost nineteen — took a seat and I began what would be the first of ten interviews.

I watched Kevin's back as he trotted back out into the main office area and through the door to the flight of stairs that would lead up to Etheridge's office. Unlike Kevin, I wasn't so dismissive about his being summoned to see the president. My experience had led me to believe that if Etheridge wanted to see you, it couldn't be good.

I fingered the Miraculous Medal on my desk and said a quick Hail Mary.

NINE

Remind me again why I do this teaching thing?

The day was long, the students not really prepared, the answers to my questions verging from inane to so bad that they were brilliant. Most of them eyed my shiner suspiciously, looking at me as if I were not someone to be trifled with. That was a good thing; setting a good precedent for toughness never hurt. There were a few gems in this crop, those students whom I would be proud to call English majors, but I prayed that the rest of them would think about nursing or communications as viable majors when the time came to choose.

I packed up and went out the back door, careful to avoid the cracks in the risers of the steps on my way up to the parking lot where I had left my car. My mind on things other than school — namely, how *does* a seemingly healthy man drop dead if not from a blow to the head? — I missed one step and took a header toward the next step, catching myself with my hand but not before banging my shin and wrist. Oh, for God's sake, I thought, will it never end? My messenger bag went flying and, with it, all of the papers that had been inside. Fortunately, it wasn't windy, and everything stayed pretty much where it was supposed to. The unfortunate part? The wrap part of my dress, which was doing a poor job of holding everything in to begin with, was now ripped from the force of my fall and holding nothing in. I quickly gathered the front of the dress together, got up, and began to shove everything back in my bag, not even knowing if I was hurt, but knowing that I was fully humiliated.

A few freshmen had gathered on the hill next to the steps and were staring at me, a college professor with a black eye, and probably a skinned knee, her boobs hanging out in the ugliest bra they had probably ever seen. "I'm fine!" I called over and they stared at me in gape-jawed wonder, probably reconsidering what it was that they saw in this school and its curriculum in the first place. Not one of them made a move to help me, so I quickly jogged up the rest of the steps, noting a sharp pain in my wrist but able to move freely otherwise.

I cursed and muttered all the way to the car. I'm not known for my grace, but this was just ridiculous. I had been trying so hard to avoid falling down and had fallen harder than I would have anticipated. Still holding my dress together, I sped out of the parking lot, slowing down for one of the many speed bumps around campus that always hampered my time getting out of there. I looked to the left and to the spot where I usually said a silent prayer to the stone angel sitting on the wall in front of the library that had been there since before I had been a student at St. Thomas. Instead, all I saw was an empty pedestal, no angel in sight.

The angel was gone, apparently ripped right off its antique perch. This was going to be quite a class if they were already vandalizing the campus.

I continued home, ready to wash my wounds, and wipe this day right out of my mind.

Things picked up considerably upon my arrival home. The sight of Crawford, drinking a beer and sitting on my front stoop, did more to cheer me than anything could have at that moment. Trixie sat beside him, overjoyed at seeing me; her tail wagged back and forth, slapping Crawford in the face. I stopped at the end of the driveway and called out to him. "What are you doing here?"

"I took some lost time," he said. "Come on. I'll take you to dinner."

I pulled the car up the length of the driveway and parked in front of my detached garage, gathered my bag and a sweater I had left on the front seat, and hobbled over to Crawford, who had come around to the back of the house. He took in my appearance and whistled.

"That's a good look for you," he said, taking in the ripped dress and the fully exposed décolletage.

"I'm not in the mood, Crawford."

"Must have been a tough day at school," he said, taking my bag and sweater from me. "What happened to you?"

"I fell," I said, as if that weren't apparent. "Those stairs behind my office have been there since the eighteen hundreds and nobody would think to fix them. Wait until some kid with a lawyer father falls down. Then they'll get fixed." I extended my left arm for Crawford's examination. "Does my wrist look swollen to you?"

"A little," he said. He took it in his hand and examined it carefully. "Probably sprained but doesn't look broken." He had me run through a series of agility exercises that included flexing my fingers, bending my wrist, and then putting my arm around my neck, which he admitted was just so he could get a better look at my boobs through the ripped dress. He kissed the tip of my nose. "The wrist goes nicely with the black eye."

"Not. Funny." I went through the back door, noticing that the screen had been replaced. I softened immediately. "Thanks, Crawford," I said.

"Not a problem," he said. He put my bag on the table and leaned against the counter. "Now, do you feel like going out or staying in? If we go out, we'll have to go to a place that doesn't have a 'no shirt, no shoes, no service' rule."

"Out. Definitely out," I said.

"Are you feeling better?" he asked.

"I'm fine. It was just the weekend, Crawford. I was just wigged out."

"That's understandable."

"Let me get changed." I started for the hall stairs. "If I find an Ace bandage, would you wrap this thing for me?" I asked, holding out my wrist. I went upstairs and took stock of the situation while sitting on the toilet lid. The dress was a goner, the wrap part having been torn from the waistline and getting ripped in the process, but my shin was surprisingly unharmed. My elbow was a little scraped but nothing I couldn't live with. I rummaged around in the drawers of the vanity and came up with an Ace bandage because the wrist was clearly the most troublesome of all of the injuries.

I handed it to Crawford when I reentered the kitchen; I had put on a pair of jeans and a linen shirt and looked slightly more presentable. He had me sit at the table, wrapping my wrist tight and affixing the metal clip. "How's that?" he asked.

"Better," I said. My wrist was now immobile but felt better as a result. I hadn't had time to ice it so I figured this was the next best thing.

We decided to go to a restaurant right on the river that was within walking distance of my house. Crawford asked the hostess for a table in the corner so that we were far away from the cluster of diners who were seated at the tables that ringed the restaurant and had the best view of the river. We saw each other so infrequently during the week that the river view wasn't a lure but privacy was. After we sat down and each had a drink in front of us — me, my usual Ketel One martini with three olives, and him, a bottle of domestic beer — I told him about the missing angel.

"I loved that angel!" I said, stuffing an olive in my mouth. "You know it. It's the one with the broken wing tip. That angel's been through a lot but it's always there and that makes me feel better when I drive onto campus."

"Sounds like a troubled class already," he said. He pulled a piece of bread from the basket and slathered it with butter. "Did I ever tell you about my first call as a rookie at the Fiftieth?"

"I don't think so."

He smiled at the memory. "I'm on the job maybe two hours when we get a call from the Avenue Cab Company . . ."

"Ahhh, I remember it well," I said. The Avenue Cab Company — 555-5551 — was a favorite of St. Thomas students when I was there. It ferried us back and forth to Broadway where all the bars were. I spent many a night in the back of one of their cabs, smelling like beer and cigarettes. And best of all? No matter how drunk you were, you could always remember their number. Usually.

". . . that they dropped a fare off at St. Thomas but that the cabbie had asked permission from the resident assistant on duty to use the bathroom and had gone inside. When he came back out, the cab was gone. Apparently, someone — and we never found out who that was — had stolen the cab and taken it for a joy ride. We found it down by the river, running, with all of the doors locked." He took a big bite of bread. "Come to think of it, you were there then, right?"

"I guess I would have been. You're on the job almost twenty, right?"

He nodded.

"Then I was there." I took a sip of my martini.

"Do you remember hearing about that?"

I nodded. "It was all the talk for about a week or two."

He dug into the bread basket and pulled out another roll. "It wasn't you, right?" he said, his face serious.

I almost spat out my martini. "No! Why would you even ask that?"

He smiled. "I was just kidding. You? You were probably studying for a test that was two weeks away, or polishing the nuns' silver." He leaned in close. "I know you weren't a bad girl."

But I am now, I thought, but didn't say it. "You're right about that." I speared another olive. "Straight as an arrow."

He finished his bread. "It's a good thing we never found out who did it. I don't think that kid realized that they were in for a heap of trouble if they had been caught. Stealing a car is serious business."

The waitress dropped our salads in front of us. "Well, I hope it didn't give you a jaundiced eye toward all students at St. Thomas," I said.

He pushed his salad around on his plate. "Nah. It seemed like the whole lot of you were just a bunch of immature, naïve girls. That's why the cab getting stolen seemed so out of character for the type of girls we usually met from there."

"You didn't go trolling for girls on campus, now did you?"

"I was married. Remember?"

"Oh, right," I said. I was trying to forget that, actually.

"And speaking of marriage . . ." he started.

"Yes?"

"Are we going to talk about it?"

"I'm having a tough week, Crawford," I said, looking over his head at the river view beyond. Max is the only person who knows why August is the worst month for me; although I had alluded to it once with Crawford, I never did tell him just what a complete funk I go into at the thought of approaching both my mother's birthday and the anniversary of her death. Fortunately, he'd been working a lot and hadn't gotten the full force of my melancholy this month. I know — I love him and should share everything with him. I just feel like I'm a lot to handle and have a lot of baggage so I need to keep things to myself, especially when his job requires him to confront death on a daily basis.

If asked by one noted television psychologist, "How's that working out for you?", I would have to admit: not very well.

"You're always having a tough week when we start to talk about this." He exhaled, frustrated, but he let it go, just as he had the few other times it had come up. "You're either too busy, or too tired, or changing the subject." He laughed but it was a laugh devoid of humor. "I'm starting to get a complex." It was clear that he was getting tired of trying to get a true, honest answer out of me, but he had been with me long enough that he knew that if he pushed too much, my reaction was unpredictable at best. His assumption, if I had to guess, was that my first marriage had left me with some deep wounds, and he would be right. But there was much more to the story and I really didn't feel like getting into it now or ever.

The waitress came back to the table. "How's everything here?" she asked.

"Wonderful," I said. Not exactly saved by the bell, but close enough. Saved by — I squinted to read her name tag — Tameka. Thank you, dear Tameka. "Excellent, as a matter of fact. Where's your restroom?" I asked, knowing that it was right by the front door. I figured the longer I kept her engaged in conversation, the more likely it would be that Crawford would start his salad and get distracted. Tameka gave me directions to the bathroom and I headed off, assuring Crawford I wouldn't be long.

I was entering just as Lydia Wilmott was exiting. I was taken aback, not expecting to see her until the funeral, which I would eventually attend, but which had been put on hold until the coroner released the body, according to the local paper. She gave me the once-over, her eyes lingering on my wrapped wrist.

"Alison. Hello," she said.

"Hi, Lydia. How are you?" I asked, giving her an awkward hug. We weren't really friends, but we had shared an intimate experience, albeit indirectly, so I felt like a verbal greeting wasn't enough. By her stiff response to my hug, I guessed I was wrong.

"I'm doing the best I can," she said. "We have so many house guests that I decided that we should go out to dinner. Do something normal." She fiddled with the diamond heart necklace around her throat. The size of the heart, coupled with the size of the diamonds in it, made me think it cost about the same as what I made in a year.

"That sounds like a good idea," I said.

Her eyes went back to my wrist. "What happened?" she asked.

"This? Oh, I fell at school," I said, rolling my eyes at my own stupidity. "The stairs behind my office are about a thousand years old, well, not really, but it seems that way, but they're old, and they're cracked, well, some of them are, and I was walking, running actually, and I fell, and ripped my dress —"

She interrupted me, thankfully. "Are you okay?"

"I'm fine. Just sprained, I think."

She stared at the wrist and then at me for a few more seconds before speaking. "Are you here alone? You can join us, if you'd like."

"No, I'm with my boy . . . with Crawford. Remember? The guy you met at the supermarket?"

"I remember," she said tersely. "The police officer."

"Right." I put my hand on the bathroom door; we seemed to have run out of things to talk about. "Well, good to see you," I said, and headed inside, relieved to be away from Crawford and his marriage talk, Lydia Wilmott and her appraising gaze, and the wilted salad that had been served to me before I had abruptly departed the table.

But the thought of my martini, sitting there undrunk, would eventually lure me back.

Ten

Any good will I had toward Ginny Miller evaporated the next time I saw her.

This woman was turning out to be a pain in the ass.

I was taking out the garbage, ironically as it turned out, when Ginny appeared curbside in a beat-up blue Subaru Outback. So I now knew the identity of the person who had followed me from Tony's until Crawford had scared her off with his backward driving. I glared at her a little bit as she turned her car off.

I was a little cranky, I admit. I had broken my one-martini-on-weeknights rule, and you try showering with a headache and a sprained wrist. By the time Ginny pulled up, spraying gravel onto my bare legs and throwing her car in park, I had managed to drag the garbage can down to the edge of the curb with my one good hand. Any vestige of the sweet wife who loved her husband was gone, and the cranky nurse was back. She got out of the car and approached me. "Bergeron!"

"Why do you always call me by my last name?" I asked. "My name is Alison, or if you prefer, Dr. Bergeron. But this last-name stuff is getting old. You sound like an army staff sergeant and I don't think that's what you're going for." I crossed my arms over my chest. "And why were you following me?"

"I don't know what you're talking about."

"Cut the shit, Ginny. Yes you do. You were following me and Crawford that same day everything happened. Why?"

She shrugged. "I'm not sure, really." At least she was honest. "I was out of my head."

"You could have gotten us killed," I said. "Crawford's got a gun and he's not a guy who takes kindly to being tailed."

She took that in but didn't respond. She came up short when she saw my wrist. "What happened to you?"

"I fell." I tossed the garbage into the can, wishing that Crawford hadn't gone home the night before and was around to experience what I was sure was going to turn into complete unpleasantness. Ginny was dressed in scrubs, clogs on her feet. Judging from the circles under her eyes, she was returning from — rather than going to — work. "Why were you following me the other day?"

She looked surprised that I had figured out her identity. "I wanted to talk to you."

"So you followed me from Tony's? I have a phone, you know. I'm even in the book. You could have called."

"Yeah, whatever," she said distractedly. "George went to White Plains to lockup. He's being arraigned this afternoon." Her lips were set in a grim line. "I'm not sure what happens after that."

"You need a good lawyer."

She got closer to me and gave me a poke in the sternum. "No. What we need is a good witness."

"Which I'm sure your good lawyer will get when he or she needs one. Nobody has contacted me." I stepped back. "Don't poke me."

She got so close to me that I could smell the French roast on her breath. "You're really not understanding what I'm saying, are you?"

I threw my hands up. "Ginny, I get it. George is going to jail for killing Carter Wilmott and you're upset. I don't know why you think I can help you."

She backed up. "Aren't you a college professor?"

"Yes. What does that have to do with anything?"

"You're book-smart."

"Probably."

She stared at me, and again I was taken with her beautiful black eyelashes. Spectacular. "Not so street-smart."

I sighed and threw my hands up. "I guess not," I said, exasperated. "Where are we going with this?" She continued to stare at me and I tried to figure out why she was there, why her mood had changed so radically since the day before, and what she wanted from me exactly. It finally hit me. "You want me to lie."

"I didn't say that."

"Yes, you kind of did. You want me to lie and say something like Wilmott instigated the fight or that he swung first or that George was just an innocent bystander who got dragged into this." I had just given her George's defense without realizing it. "But that's not true. Wilmott's been dragging you and George through the mud on the blog for months and George had it up to here," I said, bringing my hand to my browline for emphasis. "He started that fight and you know it."

She crossed her arms and gave me a half smile. "You're not as dumb as you look."

"And you're not as tough as you'd like me to think," I said, and turned on my heel, starting up the driveway. "Did you get Greg to promise to lie? Because he saw it, too, and he's never going to do it. Oh, and what about the cops who were there? Joe and Larry? They're not going to lie, either."

She chose not to respond. "If this goes any further, they're going to call you to testify," she shouted after me. I guess she thought that was a threat that would intimidate me beyond belief. It was her trump card.

I turned around and changed course, starting down the driveway toward her. "Yeah? Well, bring it on. I'll tell them exactly what I saw just like I told the police. You think testifying against George scares me?" I pointed at the house next door. "See that house?

She looked over at the large, newish construction that sat next to my tiny Cape Cod. "Yeah? So what?"

"I found a body over there, missing its hands and feet. You probably remember the story. I also got attacked by the husband of the lady in the ground and almost lost a finger." I held up the hand with the Ace bandage and showed her the long scar running down the side of my index finger where the knife wielded by my murderous neighbor had entered. She seemed somewhat impressed by its severity, still pink and shiny after several months of healing. "You're going to have to get up pretty early in the morning to scare me, Ginny."

She decided to try a different tack. "What? Are you a knight of the fucking Round Table or something? Haven't you ever told a lie?"

She hit a nerve. "No. I have never told a lie," I said. Even that was a lie but I wasn't going to admit it; my intentions were good and that had to count for something. "No." I held my ground on the front lawn, but I could feel my toes sliding forward in my wedged sandals. I wouldn't be able to hold my ground much longer if this kept up.

"I'm trying to save my husband," she said, her voice barely a whisper. She left me with that sentiment as she sped off in her Outback, leaving me at the curb.

I went back into the house, leaned against the back door and closed my eyes. Why did buying a cup of coffee have to turn into a complete and total disaster? Why couldn't I just have made a cup of coffee at home? "Because you never have any food in the house!" I exclaimed, waking Trixie, who was lounging on the cool tile under the kitchen table. "Sorry, Trix." I took a sip of the coffee that I had made before taking out the garbage and retched at its taste. As I poured it down the sink, I thought about my next move while trying to calculate how many days it had been since my last period. Being as I couldn't do two things at the same time, I went back to thinking about my next course of action. As usual, it involved calling Crawford.

"Fiftieth Precinct. Homicide. Detective Crawford. Can I help you?"

His litany of greeting never ceased to bring a smile to my face. "Yes, I'd like to report a murder."

"Alison?"

Dang. Busted. "Yes. It's me. I just wanted to see how you react to someone reporting a murder."

"That's not funny."

"Well, it's not exactly a murder yet but I'm seriously considering killing Ginny Miller."

"Still not funny."

"I'm not kidding. That woman is proving to be a giant pain in the ass." I recounted my latest run-in with Mrs. Miller and her threats and recriminations.

"You're not going to lie, are you?"

"I. Do. Not. Lie." I enunciated very clearly so that there was no mistaking my thoughts on the subject. Deep in my heart, I knew that saying I didn't lie was, in fact, a lie.

He thought for a moment before answering; whether he was considering my declaration of complete transparency or something else, I couldn't tell. "You could probably get a restraining order against her."

Now that was an interesting turn. "Really?"

"But she's right. You'll probably have to testify at George's trial, if it gets that far. Maybe you'll get lucky and he'll plead guilty."

I looked at Trixie with exaggerated alarm. I knew that this was the case, but I hadn't thought that far in advance to the reality of what that meant. "I know."

"But you don't lie, so you'll just tell the truth, the whole truth, and nothing but the truth."

"Are you taunting me, Crawford?"

"No," he said.

I was unconvinced.

"Hey," he said, changing the subject. "When can we reschedule the meet-and-greet with my parents?"

"I don't know. Say, when I don't have a

black eye and I'm in bathing-suit shape again?"

"When will that be?"

"Twenty fifteen." That was a conservative guesstimate.

"No, seriously."

Crawford rarely has time to talk to me while he's at work, but today? All the time in the world. I tried to think of a way to get off the phone. "Listen. I've got to get to school."

"Liar."

"Can we talk about this later?" I asked.

"We could but we won't." He let out an audible exhale into the phone. "They want to meet the woman I want to marry. What's wrong with that?"

Well, when you put it that way, how could I say no? I thought. I immediately got a pain in my stomach. "I have to go." Before I had a chance to say good-bye, he had hung up. I looked at Trixie who was enthralled by the conversation, or so it seemed. "That went well," I said to her. She gave me an exasperated sigh and threw her head to the ground. "Not you, too?" I asked. "Are you all turning against me?" She looked up at me from her spot on the floor and seemed to pass some kind of judgment. I stared back at her. "I'm going to school. Don't eat any shoes."

It was hot and sticky outside and I was glad that I had chosen not to wear panty hose under my skirt, a violation akin to heresy at St. Thomas. I'm sure that the nuns who wore long habits had on thick black tights, even in summer. On their heads, they wore bonnets which tied under their chins. Me showing up for school in a knee-grazing skirt with bare legs? A scandal at best. Coupled with the fact that I was wearing a sleeveless top, chances were that I would be fired by day's end if I didn't at least put a cardigan over my shoulders.

My head was pounding from a combination of one too many martinis the night before and the oppressive heat. I should have gone to Beans, Beans for an iced coffee because I was single-handedly keeping the place in business, but I was running out of steam and couldn't face Greg and his empty store. My choices were limited as to where to get the caffeine I so desperately needed. I found myself at Tony's, knowing that he could hook me up before I headed to school.

Tony was standing behind the counter, wiping his hands on his long white apron. The jangling of the bells over the door announced my arrival. "I was worried about you!" he said when he saw me. "But you look as beautiful as ever. You have a glow about you. You must be fine." He leaned over the counter and tried to grab hold of my hand. "You are better?"

"I'm better, Tony. Thanks," I said, peering around him to see if the elusive yet angry Lucia was anywhere to be seen. "Can I get an iced coffee, please?"

He responded the same way he always did when I asked for something. "For you? Anything." He turned and started to prepare my coffee. "Milk and sugar?"

"Black," I said, and looked around the store, deciding to make good use of my time while I was waiting. "Hey, Tony? When was the last time Carter Wilmott was in?"

He stopped mid-pour and turned back around. He put a finger to his lips. "Do not say his name," he whispered. "The thought of him makes Lucia very upset."

"I'm sure it does," I said. "Did he come here often?" I thought about how despite the fact that he wrote horrible stuff about Greg and Beans, Beans, he continued to patronize the store. I didn't think Tony and Lucia were "forgiving souls" like Greg had proclaimed to be, but you never know.

"I spit on the ground he walked on," Tony said, and spat on the deli floor to illustrate. "But Lucia? Lucia would have killed him if he had entered the store."

That revelation didn't surprise me. Lucia had wanted to kill me, too, and that was only because she thought I was interested in Tony. "She was that mad, huh?"

"She hated him," he said flatly. "But Mrs. Wilmott? That was a different story. She is always welcome every time she comes here. She is a real lady."

It didn't surprise me that Tony had the hots for Lydia, too. He was after almost every woman in town, even my neighbor Jane, who had stopped coming to the deli long ago for fear of being mauled by Tony and his meaty, cold-cut-covered hands. "Mrs. Wilmott comes here?"

Tony nodded. "At least once a week. She loves Lucia's chicken cordon bleu." He smiled at the thought of Lydia. "When the cook's off, that's what she gets because she loves it so much."

I'm sure she did. Lucia was a complete lunatic but an exceptional cook. If I could stomach coming back here and getting pawed at, I would have to try the chicken cordon bleu. If I played my cards right, I could probably even pass it off as my own to Crawford. I thought about that as I pulled a few dollars from my purse and put them on the counter after Tony handed me my coffee. He looked nervously toward the back of the deli where I guessed Lucia dwelled, and when he saw that the coast was clear, he pushed the money back. "All I need is a kiss," he said. "No money."

"I'm a taken woman," I said, laughing nervously.

"Please. Just one kiss," he pleaded.

I pushed the money back across the counter. "I can't, Tony. I'd never be able to explain to my boy . . . to Crawford."

"It will be our secret," he said.

I blew Tony a kiss. "That's as close as it gets," I said, and hurried from the store, grateful to be back out on the sidewalk, even if it was close to a hundred degrees. It couldn't have been any hotter or more uncomfortable in the deli than it was outside.

I drank my coffee and mulled over my severe commitment issues as I maneuvered my car through town and toward the Saw Mill River Parkway. Could anyone blame me for not wanting to rush into marriage after what I had been through? Sure, my days of being married to a serial philanderer were long behind me, but the pain still resonated. And God knows, I hadn't been in love with Ray when I married him; I knew that I had done it out of some kind of duty to my deceased mother who had made me promise that I wouldn't die alone. Who would have thought that I'd be the only married woman in America who would indeed die alone, had I stayed with Ray? He was surrounded by a bevy of willing mistresses, yet I slogged away at school and at home, under the delusion that I was happily married to a man I thought I should love. That had been a mistake and delusion of colossal proportions.

And now I had Mr. Perfect. Sure, he had his shortcomings, not limited to his love of the Cheez Doodle or safe, German-engineered cars (which were now made in Mexico, I wanted to remind him), or his ability to stay incredibly calm under the most stressful of situations (which is extremely annoying, I guarantee you), and yet I was dragging my feet, my Ring Pop engagement ring now safely hidden in my underwear drawer so that I couldn't gaze at it every day and night when I was in my bedroom. Crawford hadn't mentioned its absence and I hadn't brought it up. I knew I had to make a decision — and fast — and I figured I would eventually acquiesce, but was acquiescence an acceptable response to a marriage proposal from a man I truly loved? Maybe I'd be more excited after I acquiesced.

I decided that I couldn't handle this on my own, so I decided to find Kevin the first chance I got and dump it all on him. He was my best friend and a priest; who would be a better dumpee?

I managed to get to school, and park without incident. The back steps would be another story so I sat in the car and went through my messenger bag to see what I could leave on the passenger seat and lighten my load for the day. I had rewrapped my wrist that morning and had done a pretty good job. It was immobile and didn't hurt as much as it had the night before. My elbow was a little scraped up and my eye was more bluish purple than black. Things were looking up. Sort of.

I had a half hour or so until I needed to meet my first freshman of the day and decided that I would run up to Kevin's residence, on the top floor of the dorm outside of which I park my car. I needed to get his opinion on my latest tale of woe. I had lived in this dorm for six weeks the previous semester and the smell of floor polish and teen spirit still lingered in my nose. I signed in with the resident director whom the dean of housing had thankfully hired to replace me and told him that I would be heading up to see Fr. McManus on the top floor. The new resident director, a young man who seemed really gung ho, sent me up and went back to reading his school manual as I waited for the hundred-year-old elevator to make its way down the shaft and to the first floor. When it arrived, I boarded it and pulled the gate closed, praying the entire time that it would take me to the sixth floor without incident.

I reached the top floor after a far longer journey than I should have had to endure and hung a right toward Kevin's one-bedroom suite with the spectacular view. I reached the doorway and noticed that his name plate — FATHER KEVIN MCMANUS — was gone. All that remained was an unvarnished rectangle that had been covered by the brass-plated sign for the last several years. I knocked on the door, even though it was slightly ajar, and waited a few seconds. No answer. I pushed the door open and called Kevin's name, hearing only silence.

As the door swung open, and the panoramic view of the campus greeted me from the floor-to-ceiling windows at the far end of the suite, it became obvious that no one would return my greeting.

The rooms were empty.

Eleven

My heart was racing by the time I reached the bottom floor of the dorm, having decided the stairs would be quicker than the ancient and quixotic elevator. I had called Kevin's cell several times while standing inside his barren residence, each call going directly to voice mail. The sound of his voice on the message made me even more frantic. When I finally reached the lobby floor, the new resident director, a young, buff, and extremely handsome African-American man, stared at me as I skidded toward the desk, obviously hoping I'd stop myself before having to use the desk as a landing pad.

"Where's Father McManus?" I asked, out of breath and feeling as though I were going to have a heart attack.

His face told me that he couldn't conjure Kevin's identity up immediately, but after a few seconds he seemed to recall the school chaplain. He laid down his reading material, the college rules and regulations handbook that all freshman received — and promptly discarded — and left it open on the desk. I noticed that he was reading the section entitled "Why Are We a Dry Campus?" with great interest. If he got the answer to that question, I sure wanted to know what it was, because right now? I needed a drink bad. I thought the head of the modern language department kept a bottle of Chambord in his desk drawer, and if he did, I was going to head down there immediately after finding Kevin.

"Have you seen him?"

"Not today."

"Did a moving van come around either last night or this morning?"

"Oh! So that's what woke me up!" he exclaimed, slapping his forehead with his hand. "I looked out the window and saw a white van, but I didn't know what it was for."

I took a deep breath; the dorm wasn't going to be very safe with a guy who slept through an entire apartment of furniture being removed on his watch. "My name is Alison Bergeron and I teach in the English department. If you see Father McManus, would you please tell him that I need to speak to him right away?"

The new RD, far younger than I was when I did the job last spring, and probably more suited to the position as well, grabbed a notepad and jotted down the information, sticking it in the mail slot next to his desk that held the residents' mail. "Sure thing." A look of surprise crossed his face. "Oh, you're Dr. Bergeron!" he said.

I wasn't sure if that was a good thing or not. Around these parts, I'm never sure.

"I replaced you as RD!" he said, his demeanor changing. He stood up and shook my hand. "Cal Johnson," he said. "Nice to meet you."

"Nice to meet you, too." I wiped my hand across my brow, now in a complete sweat after running down the stairs. "Are you sure you haven't seen Father McManus?"

"I haven't. But I'll let him know that you're looking for him if I see him." He smiled broadly. "Any secrets to doing this job well?" he asked, so sincere and earnest that it almost broke my heart. The job stunk; you were a combination babysitter slash house sitter slash den mother to a group of coeducational infants who were randy, horny, and loved to acquire booze any way they could to bring onto this "dry" campus. Oh, and don't forget the pot. They loved that, too.

"Just . . ." I started, at a loss. But I came up with something quickly if only to give this guy the idea that he had just landed the best job on the planet. "Just make sure you keep all the doors locked and have everyone sign in and out, just like the handbook says."

"I'm really psyched for this job. I was a psych major at Joliet and always loved this campus, so this is a great opportunity for me."

"Calm down, Cal, you've already got the job," I said, laughing.

He smiled. "Sorry. I am just really excited to have a job." He quickly corrected himself. "*This* job."

"Well, good luck."

He held his hand out again to shake. "Hey, do you think you'd be able to grab a cup of coffee sometime so we can talk about the job? I'd love any additional insight you might have so that I can hit the ground running."

You might think that I've lived in a cave my entire life but that isn't the case. But Cal sure looked like it was when I looked at him sadly and said, "Oh, Cal, I have a boyfriend." I probably have the least "game" of anyone I know, and that was woefully apparent as I took in Cal's pitying face as he stared at me and stammered to come up with a response. It then dawned on me that, yes, Cal just wanted to have a cup of coffee to talk about the job. He wasn't asking me on a date. I wasn't a panther, or a lemur, or a gazelle — what was it they called older women with hot, younger men anyway? — but a pathetic excuse for a middle-aged college professor. I wanted to say, "You should have seen me yesterday in my ripped dress and dingy bra. Now, that's some kind of sexy."

"Dr. Bergeron —" he started.

I held up a hand. "Forget I said that. Yes, I would love to have coffee with you. To discuss the job."

But I had scared Cal sufficiently and he backed off. "It's okay. I'm sure I'll learn as I go." He picked up the handbook and returned to reviewing the rules regarding a dry campus.

I was so embarrassed that I forgot why I had even come to the dorm. Right. Kevin. I reminded Cal that I needed to talk to Kevin and I skulked back toward the front door. If I had a tail — and given the distaste on Cal's gorgeous face, I wasn't sure I didn't — it would have been between my legs.

I went back to my office and sat dejectedly at my desk, worried about Kevin, wondering when my black eye would go away, and fiddling with my Ace bandage. The queasy feeling that I had been fighting for the past few days was back with a vengeance and I took a sip of water from the aluminum bottle on my desk and made a face; it was warm and made me feel queasier, if that was possible. Kevin was gone, his apartment was empty, and he hadn't let me know where he was going. I thought back to our conversation the day before and remembered that he was going to see Etheridge after we caught up on our summers. Did I have the nerve to go upstairs and demand an explanation from the college president? I had visited the widow of a recently deceased man not forty-eight hours before, so probably. But before I could formulate my questions for Etheridge, I heard a knock at my door, and freshman number one had arrived.

I spent the rest of the day explaining the origins of my black eye, my Ace bandage, and the course requirements for freshmen entering the college and planning on an English major at some point in their academic careers. I had almost forgotten about Kevin.

Almost.

Once the last freshman had left, the sun

starting its descent over the river, and I was safely in my car away from the prying eyes of Dottie, I pulled out my cell phone. Stored in the phone was the number of Kevin's extremely handsome and single brother, Jack, a former almost paramour, who liked me way more than I could ever explain. He also possessed the most perfect set of teeth on a human being and they were his. None of these veneers or implants. I had checked. With my tongue.

He answered after a few rings, surprised that I was calling. "Alison? Hi!"

I cut to the chase. "Jack, where's Kevin?"

"I'm fine. How are you?" he said, clearly not realizing my reason for calling.

"I'm serious. Where's your brother?"

"I'm assuming he's at school. You haven't seen him?"

I decided not to alarm Jack until I knew more. "No. I was wondering if he was back from Paris?" This lying thing was working out well for me; I would just have to keep track of all of the half-truths that I had told in the last forty-eight hours.

"You're his best friend, Alison. If you don't know, then I surely don't," he said, chuckling.

That was concerning. I made a little more chitchat with Jack, talking about the New

York Rangers — my favorite hockey team and Jack's employer — and finagling two tickets to a game in December from him. Before we hung up, Jack asked me a question.

"You're not concerned about him, are you, Alison?"

"No!" I said, a little too brightly.

Jack hesitated. "Well, okay. If you hear from him, tell him his brother wants to take him out to eat."

I hung up and dropped the phone into my lap. I stared at the dashboard of my car, watching minute dust particles swirl around in the humid air, trying to figure out where to look next for my missing priest. The phone vibrated in my lap, scaring the heck out of me but giving me a sensation that wasn't altogether unpleasant. "Hello?"

"It's me," Crawford said. "Are you still at school?" When he heard that I was, he asked, "Want to grab some dinner?"

I left school with a spring in my step; although I had suspected that he was a little peeved with me over the failure to answer the proposal question, he wanted to have dinner with me. How mad could he be? Ten minutes later, I met him at a pub close to school that had better food than its name — Poindexter's — and ambiance — early fake medieval — would imply. That's the beauty of dating a homicide detective who works in your precinct: we can be together in mere minutes if the planets align. Fortunately, he is not a picky eater since he eats at his filthy desk or in a car most of the time. I had to drive home and he was technically still on duty so we both had Diet Cokes, which we sipped in silence until we got a little caffeine rush after our long workdays. I started. We had a lot to talk about.

"George Miller was arraigned today in White Plains." I had looked at the county paper on my computer before I had left school to see what the update was.

Crawford was unimpressed. He had probably been to a thousand arraignments, and more to the point, he didn't really care about George Miller, black eye notwithstanding.

"What do you think will happen to him?"

"He'll either have his bail set or be released on his own recognizance. I'd imagine it's the latter if he doesn't have a record. What did they get him on? I'm thinking manslaughter."

"Manslaughter, it is then. You're usually pretty accurate about these things." I scanned the menu and decided on my dinner, snapping the leather-bound book shut.

"And I thought the new resident director at Siena dorm asked me out today when, in fact, he just wanted to have a cup of coffee and talk about the job."

Crawford winced.

"It gets worse."

He raised an eyebrow.

"Kevin's missing."

That got his attention. "Missing?"

I explained how I went to his room and it had been cleaned out and how his cell phone kept going to voice mail. Crawford took this all in, watching me intently as I related the details of the story.

"Where do you think he is?" he asked.

I threw my hands up. "Not a clue. But the last thing he said to me was that he was going to Etheridge's office to talk about something and he wasn't sure what it was."

Crawford drummed his fingers on the tabletop. I wasn't sure what that meant, so I was overjoyed when he said, "Let me do a little poking around."

"Thank you!" I said, and lunged across the table to kiss him, taking down my soda, his, and the bread basket with one fell swoop. The soda all went in his direction, soaking him from the solar plexus to his shoes, and several rolls ended up in his lap.

He stood. "I guess I won't be going back

to work," he said, and sauntered off toward the men's room.

TWELVE

Crawford went home after we ate our dinner, despite the fact that his pants were soaked with Diet Coke. Although he was scheduled to go back to work, he took what is mysteriously called "lost time," a term that the NYPD employs yet which I don't understand. However, I realized that term could have accurately described my marriage to my ex-husband. Maybe instead of describing myself as "previously married" I could just say that I had taken some "lost time."

Now I was nervous that the marriage issue *hadn't* come up. Crawford hadn't touched on it once and that made me think that he was done with the whole discussion, a development troubling and annoying in its own way.

I got in my car and saw that Max was calling.

"You don't take what I do seriously," she said.

"Yes I do," I said as patiently as I could. This was a conversation that we had every so often and that usually ended up with me sitting in a Crime TV conference room watching the pilot of the latest reality show that Max had conjured up.

"No you don't." Her voice was more high-pitched than usual. "Fred just told me what you call my new show."

Uh-oh. "He did?"

"Yeah. 'Dicks with Tits'? Ring a bell?" she asked. "Nice."

I needed to have a word with Crawford. I had told him that in complete confidentiality. I know he thought it was funny but he had used supremely bad judgment if he believed that telling Fred was a good idea. Didn't he know that pillow talk was not to be repeated? "I was just kidding, Max."

"I don't make fun of what you do."

How could you? Being a college professor really doesn't lend itself to comedy. But being the head of a cable television station that airs such scintillating and highbrow programs as *Juliet McKeever: Paranormal Crime Solver* and *The Ten Most Sexually Depraved Court Cases* did. I did feel bad that I had upset her. Which is how I ended up sitting in a white, unmarked production van across from a very expensive high-rise apartment building on the West Side of Manhattan, watching some Hooters waitresses case the joint. The inside of the van smelled like stale coffee and body odor, both of which I attributed to the remote-camera guy, Jerry, who was the only other person in the van besides me and Max. I had drawn the short straw, so to speak, and had to sit closest to Jerry, who kept his eyes on the monitor on which I could see three young women strutting their stuff up and down the street in front of the building.

"Shouldn't they be more undercover?" I asked, taking in the tank tops that were stretched thin across the three young ladies' ample bosoms.

"Do I tell you how to teach?" Max asked. She swiveled in her chair and checked out another monitor that was trained on the inside of the building. "Jerry! There he is," she said.

A tall, distinguished-looking man of about sixty strode from the elevators toward the doorman's desk and outside onto the street. The three Hooters waitresses — excuse me, "private investigators" — snapped to attention and got into various stances that indicated their readiness to take down this unassuming-looking man who had not a clue that he was about to be pounced on by three young women.

"I've got him, Max," Jerry said, fiddling with the knobs on his console.

I tried to yawn with my mouth closed but was unsuccessful. Max shot me a look. "Are we keeping you up?"

"No," I said. "It's just that I have a lot of work to do when I get home."

"Let's just get this scene and then I'll release you to your precious work," Max said, her gaze focused on the events playing out on the street next to the van. Jerry turned up the sound and I listened as one of the Hooters waitresses, a tall, athletically built African-American woman in a blond wig, approached the man and asked him where he was going.

"Not Hooters," he replied.

That was enough to send the Hooters waitresses into a tizzy. They accused him of cheating on his wife, threw out some details about his mistress and her location, and detailed his most recent assignation in graphic detail. I put my hands over my ears when they got to the most salacious parts. I watched as the man's face went pale under his spray tan.

The "cheater," as Max referred to him,

got a little mouthy with one of the Hooters waitresses and the one with the blond wig took umbrage. It wasn't long before she had the man pinned to the ground and was whispering something in his ear that none of us could hear. I looked at Max. "Are they supposed to do that?"

"Do what?"

"Manhandle the cheaters?"

Max looked at me, solemn. "They are to do whatever it takes to make these men realize that what they're doing is immoral and wrong."

"And get ratings?"

She gave me a look that told me she didn't appreciate my take on the situation. "Get a tight shot on Queen," she said to Jerry.

I assumed that Queen was the waitress in the blond wig. The name rang a bell but I couldn't come up with why. She pulled the man to his feet by his collar, sending him on his way down the street. That was one strong Hooters waitress.

"And cut!" Max called to no one in particular. She clapped her hands together, apparently in a good mood now that they had gotten what they had set out to shoot. It was a reality show and I was naïve enough to think that there were no scenes to be shot and that we had just happened upon this sordid scene. I now knew that I was wrong on that count. Although the target didn't know that they were going to confront him, Max's team had done "recon," as she called it, knowing his every move so that the waitresses could be in position when the moment was right. They knew he'd be leaving his apartment at exactly that time that evening, and hence they'd been able to pull off this entire, elaborate setup. It wasn't exactly staged, and it wasn't exactly scripted, but close enough. Max told Jerry to let the girls know that they were done for the evening; the girls were wearing earpieces and Jerry communicated this information to them. They took off in different directions down the street, disappearing without a word as if nothing had transpired in front of the building.

Max asked me if I'd like to get a bite to eat, but having been cooped up in a van with Jerry and having witnessed a rather lurid situation unfold, I told her the truth: I had no appetite. Plus, I had already eaten. Even though that usually didn't stop me from eating again. She seemed to have forgotten that she had been mad at me and that was a good thing. A mad Max is a scary thing indeed, but like everything else in her life, her mood changes so swiftly that if you just wait it out, she'll come back around. I got out of the van and took in a deep breath of New York City air, which smelled mountaintop fresh after my having breathed in eau de Jerry for the past two hours.

I went home to my dull, boring, beige house, so glad to see it after spending a few hours in Max's world. The dog walker had conveniently left the mail on my kitchen counter, and Trixie, although excited to see me, had just been walked, according to the note on top of the mail. I spent a few minutes giving Trixie the love and attention she so richly deserved. I looked through the mail quickly, tossing the phone, cable, and electric bills to the side to deal with later and ending up holding a letter that was addressed to me in beautiful handwriting but which had no return address or mark of a business stamped anywhere on the crisp white of the envelope. I tore it open and read the pamphlet inside:

> It may seem like you deserve what has befallen you, but you don't.
>
> Seek help before IT IS TOO LATE!
>
> We can help you get out, and more important, GET UP again.

This day was shaping up to be a doozy.

The cryptic message was followed by a 1-800 number and a note written in very elegant and left-leaning script: "we can help you" was the repeated message. I wondered if I had mistakenly received a message about erectile dysfunction, but from what I had gathered, ED doctors and pharmaceutical companies had no qualms about advertising their wares openly. I assumed it was the same for the sufferers, so none of this cloak-and-dagger stuff would suit them. I dialed the 1-800 number and expected to receive a recorded message but was disappointed. The number just rang and rang. I listened to the ringing for about twenty seconds before hanging up. I held the letter between my fingers and gingerly placed it back in the envelope, then put the envelope into a Ziploc bag. After I closed the bag, I looked at it. What did I plan to do with it? Fingerprint it in my fingerprint lab? Run it over to Crime Scene? I laughed slightly when I realized that Crawford was rubbing off on me, but I kept the letter and envelope in the bag nonetheless, thinking as I walked upstairs to change what the message might mean.

"Get up again?" I asked. Had I been on the ground and not realized it? I decided that I would hash this out with Crawford once I heard from him about any Kevin

developments. I sat on the bed and looked around. My buttinsky cleaning lady, Magda, had been here and the room and its adjacent bathroom were spotless. My underwear had also been rearranged in such a complex pattern of panties, bras, and panty hose that I was sure that Magda had spent a good deal of her time in that drawer looking for what I had no idea. I had eaten dinner. I had no schoolwork. There was nothing to do but wait until it was an acceptable time to go to bed, and checking my bedside clock — which said 8:34 — now was not that time.

Time on my hands is never a good thing. I realized when my feet started tapping the ground that I needed to change and get out of the house, if only to walk Trixie for the second time in an hour. Who knew where that would bring me?

Apparently, to the boat slip at the river, that's where.

Trixie and I often meander and we often end up by the river. It's beautiful, close to my house, and affords her all kinds of access to things she shouldn't have but instinctively is inclined to prey upon: birds and fish primarily. Despite the NO DOGS ALLOWED! signs that dotted every fifth or so piling along the docks, we haven't been caught yet, so we continue our illicit evening walks when the mood strikes us. Seeing all of the boats lined up in their individual slips and the beauty of the Palisades on the opposite side of the river at dusk convinced me that we needed to get down to the dock area more often even if that made us scofflaws. My French was good enough so that I could always pull the "je ne sais pas" defense when presented with one of their signs. Trixie was thrilled; nothing better than the smell of murky Hudson water and the idea that gulls might be around to pique her interest.

At the very least, maybe a walk along this tranquil pier would clear my head about everything and give me some insight into where Kevin might have gone. Without telling me. In the middle of the night.

The days were getting shorter, signifying the beginning of school and end of summer, always a bittersweet time for me. Trixie and I walked along the wooden dock in the twilight, my feet making no noise in my sneakers, her nails making their usual rhythmic clicking noise in time to my footfalls. I'm accustomed to carrying a flashlight on my nighttime walks with Trixie, and tonight I had it stuffed into the pocket of my jeans knowing I would need it to navigate our way home. In the dying light, I looked at the names of each boat, admiring their amenities until I settled on one almost at the end of the dock.

The Lydia.

How quaint. And how predictable. I should have guessed that Carter Wilmott's boat would be named *The Lydia.* When I happened upon it, I stopped, remembering his white foot and the tan line that started a few inches above it; until this moment, I had forgotten that he was an avid boater and kept his boat docked right here. As I took in the craft, I noticed that it was swaying more than slightly in its slip, unlike every other boat, which sat almost stock-still in the very calm Hudson on this humid end-of-August evening. The rocking gave me pause, but as usual, not enough pause to stop me from approaching it, looking out for other sailors in the area. A few boats were missing from their slips, their owners out and about on this nice evening, but being as it was a weeknight, most of the boats were safely fastened to their moorings.

I didn't know anything about boats, but it was clearly a sailboat with a big motor and an impressive-looking one at that, despite its relatively conservative size compared to the other hulking behemoths in other slips. It was well appointed with a mahogany steering wheel and some really comfortable-looking padded seats. Trixie and I decided that it wouldn't hurt anyone to step onto the boat and take a load off for a few minutes. I took a deep breath, stepping over the side of the boat, careful not to look at the water, still curious as to why the boat was swaying ever so slightly. Carter was dead. Was Lydia here? I looked down at the water again. Water always makes me nervous. After stepping gingerly onto the deck and taking a quick look around, I sat down, but not before I ran my fingers around the steering wheel, which was stained dark and very shiny and which was very smooth to the touch. Trixie made herself right at home and jumped up onto one of the padded seats and threw herself into a lounging position, head hanging off the side of the bench, tongue almost meeting the floor.

"Make yourself at home," I whispered to her. She picked her head up and gave me her doggy smile, the one that never failed to make me happy. After I had finished touching every luxurious piece of leather, expensive wood, and shiny granite that was on the boat — and then wiping everything I had touched with the edge of my shirt, realizing, too late, that putting my hands all over everything was a supreme error in judgment — I started down into the sleeping quarters, mainly out of curiosity to see how many people the boat could sleep but mostly to see how the other half lived. As I descended the stairs, I heard a sound from deep within the sleeping quarters and froze. I looked back at Trixie, and while she lifted and cocked her head, she didn't make a sound, as paralyzed with fear as I was. Or completely uninterested. It's hard to tell with her.

The door to the sleeping quarters was solid so I couldn't even peer through a porthole or a little window to see who might be inside. And I didn't want to. I started back up the stairs, backward, keeping an eye on the door and hoping to make a getaway before whoever it was made their presence known and maybe killed me. I had just reached the top step, my eye trained on the door handle, when I saw it turn slowly. I didn't waste any more time, grabbing Trixie's collar and pulling her down, her right claw leaving a giant gash in the seat. The sight of it, stuffing spilling out and creating little puffs in the air, sent me into a mini fugue state and I stood stock-still at the end of the banquette, as close to the edge of the boat as I could get without falling over. When I heard the sleeping area's door open and bang against the wall of the boat, rocking it back and forth violently, I came to.

Ginny Miller burst from the sleeping quarters and ran up the stairs, seemingly intending to run past me and into the now dark night. One mystery solved. Now if I could just figure out the other various mysteries of life, like why Magda washes white shirts with black socks, I'd be all set. I grabbed the back of Ginny's tank top and heard it rip, the force of her momentum matching the force of my grip, the whole thing coming off in my hand. She turned to me, red-faced, and bared her teeth. Trixie stood next to me and let out a low growl, which, loosely translated, said, "Back off, lady."

"What are you doing here?" I asked, genuinely curious.

Ginny had no intention of answering me. Rather, in an action that first surprised and later angered me, she took advantage of the rocking boat and pushed me over the side and into the murky Hudson, where I plunged deep into the water. Me. The nonswimmer. I was fortunate that the boat next to me was out on the river and the gap between Carter's boat and the one next to it just wide enough so that I didn't hit my head on the way down. The water was colder than I would have thought, and muddy, something that its glassy surface belied. I held my breath and kept my mouth shut, kicking violently to get to the top. I finally broke through after furious arm and leg activity and swallowed in a gulp of humid air, seeing a blur of red running pants wrapped around an ample behind and pistonlike legs charging down the dock, a golden ball of fur closing in on its prey. I had almost regained my breath and was trying to remember how to tread water when I heard a yelp. I saw Trixie in front of me, a piece of red nylon in her mouth, which she dropped on the dock. Convinced that I was engaged in some kind of fun swimming activity, she launched her body and did a belly flop into the Hudson, emerging slowly and starting a vigorous doggy paddle that made my swimming attempts look ridiculous at best.

My parents had schooled me in a lot of useful endeavors, but swimming was not one of them. I cursed both of them at this moment in French, Spanish, and Mandarin, three languages that they insisted I take as electives in high school.

Ginny was gone by the time I reached the dock; the splashing had attracted a fair amount of attention from the few boaters who were on their docked crafts and I was surrounded by concerned yachtsmen and women of various ages in no time. Two men pulled me onto the dock. One of the younger, stronger men helped me get Trixie out of the water by grabbing her back legs while I struggled to get purchase on her slippery front legs. Once on the dock, she paced excitedly, obviously thrilled that she had given chase and then had the opportunity to take a refreshing swim.

Ginny Miller was in the wind. Whatever regimen she had begun in the wake of those unflattering pictures being posted on DF Matters, it was working. That woman was fast and strong. As the crowd asked after my well-being following my precipitous dip, all I could think about was this strange woman and her relation to the Wilmott family.

I managed to extricate myself from the crowd, whose number had grown to about ten by the time I left. Thankfully, there was nobody among them who recognized me, but they all learned that I was a sad, almost B cup based on my involuntary participation in the wet T-shirt contest. I walked home along streets that were now cast into complete darkness, my flashlight held in my bandaged left hand, Trixie's leash in my right, a pathetic sight indeed in my sagging, drenched jeans. I thought about Ginny Miller, yet another resident of my quaint village, whom until two days ago I had never laid eyes on. What was she doing on Carter Wilmott's boat? And why did we keep running into each other? I knew Trixie wouldn't know the answer to those questions, so there was no point in asking. But there was nothing that I couldn't figure out while staring into the icy depths of a dry martini in a frozen glass, wrapped in my terry-cloth bathrobe.

THIRTEEN

I was convinced that I still smelled like the river when I got to school the next day, a suspicion confirmed when Mark Etheridge walked into my office shortly after I arrived and lifted his nose in the air.

"Good morning, Alison." He settled into the guest chair across from my desk and crossed his legs. "What's that I smell?" He leaned in close and my heart sank. I really *did* smell like fetid river water and that would do nothing to endear me to the already suspicious administration. "Do you wear Chanel No. 5?"

I did today. I practically had bathed in it. "Why, yes, Mark, I do."

"My grandmother's favorite scent," he said proudly. "She was a real lady."

That did nothing to buoy my spirits; Etheridge was a good ten to fifteen years older than me so that put his grandmother . . . well, never mind. Suffice it to say, I was not interested in smelling like Grand-mère Etheridge, despite his protestations of her status as a real lady. And here's the thing: Etheridge isn't very nice to me usually. So his dropping by and complimenting me on my choice of Chanel No. 5 — the scent worn by grandmothers all around the world — was suspect. In the nicest way possible, I asked him to cut to the chase.

"Hey, Mark, what brings you here?"

His fakey-fake smile faded and I was confronted with the true face of Mark: sullen, nonsmiling, and decidedly unsunny. I could only imagine the energy it had taken him to keep up the façade of dedicated and faculty-loving president that he had put forth for the thirty seconds preceding my question about his visit.

"Have you spoken to Father McManus?" he asked.

"No. And as a matter of fact —"

"Yes, he's gone."

Thank you, Captain Obvious. Now, the question was, why? Followed by, and where did he go? "Hmmm . . ." I said, stalling. "Where did he go?"

"He's taking a sabbatical. He wasn't sure if he would have time to tell you, so he asked me to communicate his leaving to you. I wanted to get to you as soon as possible. I knew you'd be worried."

"And how did you know that I knew he was gone? And more important, how did you know that I didn't already know why?" Yes, there was an easier way to ask those questions, but I've found that when trying to get the answers you want, confuse 'em with words. Works every time.

Except for this one. I hadn't taken into account that my theory was only effective when dealing with lying coeds. Someone of Mark's superior intellect could find another way to not answer the question and his was to get up and start for the door. "You can talk to Father McManus when he's ready to communicate with you and you can ask him about what he'll be doing from this point on." He stopped midway in his trek and tossed a verbal grenade in my direction. "On his sabbatical, I mean." Yes, whatever that meant. Priests don't get sabbaticals. The church elders treat them like Amish children except that the poor men of the cloth don't get their version of a rumspringa.

I got up quickly and tried to follow Mark, but my skirt got caught on the corner of my open desk drawer and by the time I extricated myself, he was gone. "But why did he leave?" I called after him, hoping for some indication of where Kevin had gone and why. I raced into the common area that the offices opened up onto and tried to catch a glimpse of him. To no one in particular, I muttered, "Who the hell does he think he is? The freaking Green Lantern?" I had never seen a disappearing act like that one.

"Alison! Your mouth. Young lady." Sister Alphonse — aka the Fonz — couldn't see very well but apparently she could hear and she knew exactly who I was just by the sound of my voice. She peered at one of the office doors, and convinced she was where she needed to be, rapped loudly with her bony, arthritic knuckles, drawing herself up to her full six feet two inches. "Louise? Are you in there? I'm ready for my blood pressure check."

"Sister, that's Coach Burton's office." I took her arm and guided her to Sister Louise's office. And I knew she didn't want to see Bill Burton, the head of the phys ed department. He wouldn't be able to tell the difference between a blood pressure cuff and a microwave. I deposited her in front of Louise's office door.

"Three Hail Mary's, dear, for that flagrant foul," she called after me. The Fonz is blind but she's got a good sense of humor. And she played a mean center for the St. Thomas girls' basketball squad back in 1942, the last time the St. Thomas Blue Jays had a winning season.

I went back into my office and hurled myself into my desk chair, rapidly checking my e-mail to see if I had any messages from Kevin. Not a one. Then I checked my local paper online, where a huge headline filled the page: " 'I'm Innocent!' DPW Chief Claims." A picture of a rather pathetic-looking George Miller, propped up by his weirdo wife, Ginny, accompanied the story.

You might be innocent, George, I thought, *but something tells me that wife of yours isn't by a long shot.*

I was eating a Lean Cuisine, rather indelicately, when Crawford called that night.

"So I guess you've seen the paper?" he asked.

"You mean George Miller protesting his innocence?" I tried to lick some sauce off my fork before it dribbled onto my T-shirt. Too late. "What did we expect him to do? I don't know how he's going to get out of this one. He's got me and Greg as witnesses. We saw him punch Wilmott in the head. I'm sure he didn't mean to kill him, but he did. Plain and simple."

Crawford was silent for a moment. "So

you're back on that? You know you're going to have to testify, right?"

I changed the subject. "I got pushed into the river last night."

Nothing I could tell him would surprise him but this definitely piqued his interest. "By whom?"

"By Ginny Miller." I explained the whole story, starting with the note instructing me to "get up again" and ending with my impromptu swim.

"You know you were trespassing?"

I guess I was. But that didn't matter. "Doesn't it make you wonder what she was doing on the boat?"

"Sure. But you were trespassing. You were on someone else's property. You can't do that."

"Neither can she," I said. "Don't forget that."

"I'm more concerned about you. I couldn't care less about Ginny Miller. If you get jammed up with Hardin and Madden again, though, it's not going to be good." He paused. "And I won't be able to help you because they're not that fond of me, either. Guilt by association."

"I. Know." I forked a little more lemongrass chicken, some of which was burning hot and some of which was ice-cold, into my mouth. Damn that cheap microwave. "And I know the definition of 'trespassing.' "

An audible sigh let me know that we were heading into an area where the wrong word would start a fight. Crawford and I don't generally argue but the proposal had become the elephant in the room, and I suspected that any movement in that direction, conversationally, would bring one on. I didn't have to wait long to find out if he was going to bring it up. "So are you ever going to give me an answer?"

I played dumb, something I do quite well after years of practice. "About what?"

"Don't play dumb, Alison."

"Did I mention that I got pushed in the river yesterday?" His silence on the other end of the phone was troubling. I kept chattering so that I wouldn't have to listen to dead air. "I really don't want to have this conversation on the phone . . . I've had a lot going on and we really haven't had time —"

"We've had all the time in the world. You don't want to have this conversation, ever. That tells me a lot."

I sputtered a little bit, trying to figure out a way to disagree with him, but when I thought about it, he was right. I didn't want to talk about it. "There's a lot to discuss, Crawford. For one, where would we live?"

"I don't care."

"I think you do. Do you really want to move to the suburbs after you've lived in the city all of your life?"

"We could move by St. Thomas. It's half suburb, half city. We'd both be happy."

Wow, he'd really thought this through. That was a mighty fine solution but I was loath to agree. "Well, maybe you would, but my life is here. I have friends . . ."

"Who?"

"Well, Jane, for one. And . . ." I couldn't come up with another one who lived in the area. "Greg?"

Again, the pregnant pause.

"Really, do we have to talk about this right now?" I asked, bending over at the waist to restore my equilibrium. I had felt fine all day; all of the sudden, the taste of the Lean Cuisine clogged my throat and I stood up and flung the half-full container into the sink. "I don't feel very well."

"You never feel well when we start talking about this," he said softly. His next sentence hit me like a punch to the solar plexus. "Maybe we should take a break."

"From talking about this?" I asked hopefully.

"No. From everything," he said. His voice was barely a whisper. "I'm not Ray, Alison."

"I know you're not!" I said, feeling the tears spring to my eyes. "I just need time. There hasn't been enough time."

"There's been plenty of time," he said. I heard the usual commotion of the Fiftieth Precinct detective squad in the background. "I have to go."

And then he was gone. And I was alone in my kitchen with my beautiful dog and a half-empty container of lemongrass chicken.

It was hours before I moved from the kitchen table and into the hallway where I found a single sheet of paper that had been slipped under the front door. It was written in the same handwriting as the note that I had received the night before. This time, the message was a little more insistent and a little less cryptic.

GET OUT BEFORE IT'S TOO LATE.

Funny thing was, I think I just had.

FOURTEEN

The next morning, I considered my options. I couldn't call Max because I have found her to be absolutely no help in these situations; her attention-deficit disorder always gets in the way of her giving any sound advice. And Kevin? Well, he was my go-to guy on matters of the heart but he was missing. Jane, my across-the-street neighbor, is a good friend, divorced like me, but in a very stable and loving relationship with her partner, Kathy. I decided that she was my best bet.

I wrote her an e-mail from school asking her if she was available for an early dinner that evening. She wrote me back a few minutes later to accept, suggesting a little bistro that was walking distance from our houses. That set, I decided to turn my attention to other matters, mainly, the disappearance of Kevin. I sent him an e-mail to his St. Thomas account, something I hadn't thought of doing the day before. It was returned to me immediately, marked as "undeliverable."

Curious.

I dialed his cell phone again, expecting to be confronted with his full voice-mail box, and was surprised when he answered. So surprised, in fact, that I began to choke on the muffin I had bought in the cafeteria, a piece of which I had just shoved in my mouth.

"Alison?"

I started coughing, spewing muffin crumbs all over my desk and my computer monitor. I finally managed to swallow the crumbs, washing them down with the remainder of my cup of coffee. "Kevin?"

"Alison?"

"Where the hell are you?" I asked, rather indelicately, given that I was speaking to a man of the cloth.

"I'd rather not say."

"And why did you leave?"

"Again, I'd rather not tell you."

"Okay," I said, seeing that I wasn't going to get anywhere. "Are you all right?"

He sighed. "I guess."

"Does your family know where you are?"

"They know I'm fine and that's all they

need to know right now. You spoke to Jack, right?"

"Briefly." I didn't understand all this cloak-and-dagger stuff but he obviously didn't want to talk about it so I wasn't going there. I had already picked the scab off the wedding conversation wound with Crawford and I wasn't going to take any chances that I had blundered into something distasteful again. "Just tell me that you'll be back?"

"I don't know if I will. I can't say any more." He sounded bereft. "Listen, I have to go. I'll call you soon. I promise." And then he was gone. The men in my life were hanging up on me with regularity. Time to find some new guy friends.

I continued my presemester work with the candidates for Freshman Comp, along with reviewing some papers for the senior seminar course that I'd be teaching this and the following semester. Students had been asked to choose an author to study in depth and I was relieved to see F. Scott Fitzgerald and Kurt Vonnegut among the choices of the ten students who were taking the course this semester. I wasn't so happy to see a few contemporary authors whose books were blockbuster sellers but whom I considered a little cut-rate, and I made a mental note to talk to the students on the list whose authors didn't pass muster. I'm all for the "Jesus and Mary Magdalene had a baby" thing but St. Thomas isn't, so it looked like Dan Brown would be off the list. I looked out my window and toward the cemetery that rested on the hill beyond the access road behind the building and contemplated the various goings-on in my life.

I was being harassed to change something in my life by a nameless, faceless letter writer who thought I either suffered from erectile dysfunction or some other peccadillo that was getting in the way of my emotional health.

A woman named Ginny Miller had become a major thorn in my side.

One of my best friends had gone missing and was being extremely coy about where he was and why.

And oh, yeah, the topper? My boyfriend, the one who adored me and wanted to spend the rest of his life with me, thought we should spend some time apart.

I considered all of this as I stared out the window at the various tombstones that dotted the hillside behind my office. And I felt sick to my stomach most of the time. When I added all of it up, I became pretty depressed.

I walked into the main office area and approached Dottie's desk. She was engrossed in the *Daily News*'s Jumble and was trying to unlock the word that was comprised of the letters *v-i-e-s-o-l*.

"Olives," I said. Because if it's one thing I know, it's how to spell "olives."

She looked up at me, not aware that I had been standing there figuring out her Jumble. "Thanks," she said, and folded the paper up, sticking it into a half-open drawer. She eyed me suspiciously. "Can I help you?"

I picked up our conversation from a few days prior as if there had been no interruption. "So if Charlie asked you to marry him, you are absolutely, positively sure that you would say yes? How can you be so sure?"

Dottie has been wronged by more than one man and her attennae went up. "Why? What do you know?"

"I don't know anything," I assured her. "I just want to know how you can be so sure that you want to spend the rest of your life with him. Doesn't he annoy you or get on your nerves? And haven't you lived alone for a long time?"

"Honey," she said, waving a hand dismissively, "I've lived alone so long that anything that man could do to annoy me or get on my nerves would be a welcome change of pace."

I chewed on that for a minute. "Yeah, but what if you do get married and then you decide that you made a mistake? That it wasn't the right decision?"

"Aren't you divorced?"

"Well, I was before he ended up dead. I'm not entirely sure what that makes me."

There was no question in her mind. "That makes you divorced."

I nodded. "I guess you're right." She didn't respond. "So what are you saying?"

"If you made a mistake, you divorce his ass. But if you love him, nothing he does will annoy you enough to make you think you made a mistake."

I went back into my office no closer to a decision. But I did know that things had taken a very weird turn if I was using Dottie as my barometer for good decision making.

I left my office around five with the intention of driving straight to the restaurant where I was to meet Jane, an ice-cold martini in my immediate future. I arrived at Chez Madeleine with twenty minutes to spare and took a seat at the small, granite-topped bar. Two tables in the restaurant were filled with early birds, but the bar was empty, much to my relief. I didn't feel like making small talk with anyone, let alone the bartender, a young guy who really took his role as liquor-serving therapist seriously.

"You look like a lady who could use a drink," he said with a sad smile, placing a napkin in front of me. "Let me guess. Chardonnay? Something oaky with a hint of blackberries?"

"Ketel One martini, three olives. Up."

He gave me a winning smile. "That was my second guess." Before turning to mix my drink, he looked up at the television placed over the bar, tuned to our local Westchester news station. They were doing a story on Carter Wilmott. "Hey, did you hear about that poor guy who dropped dead in Beans, Beans?"

"No," I said, playing dumb for the second time in as many days. "I've been out of town. What happened?" I always love to hear other people's take on a story in which I've been involved. It's a weird combination of rubbernecking and gossipmongering, but interesting nonetheless.

He leaned in conspiratorially. "Got into a fight with the head of the DPW and was killed."

"Really?"

"Really." He pulled a martini glass off a rack above him and filled it with ice. "Apparently, the DPW guy really knocked the stuffing out of poor Wilmott. Killed him."

"Wow," I said. "How awful. Were there any witnesses?"

"Well, apparently, there was the guy who owns Beans, Beans. You know. The big hippie guy?" he asked, shaking the cocktail shaker within an inch of its stainless steel life. "And some college professor who lives in town but nobody seems to know anything about except that her ex-husband was murdered last year."

I shrugged. "Can't imagine who that might be."

He looked up at the ceiling, trying to remember something. "Bertelsman? Bergerson?" He put the cocktail shaker down and leaned his hands on the counter. "Oh, it will come to me." My mouth was watering, waiting for my drink. Open the damn shaker! I wanted to scream at him. "Anyway, nobody's seen her since it happened."

"Sounds like she doesn't want to be seen."

He finally poured my drink into the martini glass and placed it in front of me. Despite being extremely chatty, he clearly knew what he was doing in the drink department. The first sip went down very easily and helped take the edge off just slightly. The bartender watched me with interest, holding out his hand after I had put the drink back on the napkin. "My name is Jamie."

I took his hand. "Maxine." If ever there was a time to channel Max, now was it.

"Hi, Maxine," he said warmly, resting his elbows on the bar. "So, having a bad day, Maxine?"

"The worst."

"Does it have something to do with the black eye?" he asked. "Or is it man trouble?"

"You could say that." As a matter of fact, you could. I saw a guy get dead, my priest has gone missing, and my boyfriend thinks I'm a commitmentphobe. If that wasn't man trouble, I didn't know what was.

"Well, Maxine, I might be able to help in that department."

I took in the bartender's young, handsome face, glossy black hair, and long eyelashes and decided that there might not be anything wrong with being single again. But then when I noticed just how much he resembled a younger and more filled-out Crawford and realized that he probably was just above the legal age, I hovered between devastated and horrified. I realized that I couldn't carry on this charade of being a hip chinchilla or whatever they called women my age who dated younger men. I looked nervously toward the door of the restaurant, hoping against hope that Jane would be early and would rescue me from this most uncomfortable situation.

"Well?" he asked, giving me a dazzling smile.

"Well, I don't need as much help as you might think," I said, laughing nervously. "As a matter of fact," I said, spotting Jane ambling toward the front door, "I'm not sure my girlfriend would approve."

He looked at me quizzically.

"Would you have my drink brought to my table?" I asked, getting up from my bar stool. I wrapped Jane in a big hug and took her hand. "You're early!" I said.

Jane was shocked by my public display of affection and gently extricated herself from my grasp. "I am. I got out of work a little early tonight."

"I'll explain everything when we sit down," I whispered in her ear as we followed the hostess to our table, tucked into the front corner of the restaurant and thankfully out of view of the bartender. We sat down and she ordered the oaky chardonnay with the hint of blackberries after my martini had been delivered to the table.

She studied her menu quickly and snapped it shut. "Try the scallops if you like seafood." She unfolded her napkin and put it on her lap. "So what's going on?"

"Well, I'm your significant other if the bartender asks, and Crawford and I have broken up." I had to spit the whole thing out; if I had spent more time thinking about how to phrase it, I might have broken down and become the mess that I had been the entire night before.

She didn't know where to start. "You? Me? Crawford?" She shook her head, her hair coming loose from the elastic band holding her blond hair in a low ponytail. "Start over."

I started with the Ring Pop, because that was the most logical place to start, and ended with Crawford hanging up on me. "Then, the bartender started hitting on me," I said, holding up a hand when I saw the incredulous look on her face. "I know. Hard to believe, but true. So I told him you were my partner just to save face."

"His or yours?"

I shrugged. "No clue. His, I guess."

Jane swallowed the rest of her chardonnay in one gulp and motioned for another one. "Well, that's quite a story. And that's not even taking into consideration your run-in with Carter and that guy from the DPW."

I touched my black eye instinctively.

"Tough couple of days."

"That's putting it mildly."

"So what do you want to do about Crawford?"

"Marry him, I guess."

She smiled. "Doesn't sound too convincing."

I put my head on the table, careful to avoid the bread basket. "I'm just not sure."

Jane put her hand over mine. "Listen, I had the great, good-looking husband, the nice house in Larchmont, the two great kids, and the dog and the picket fence, and it just wasn't right."

"Yeah, but you're gay."

"True," she said, laughing, "but when something doesn't feel right, you need to listen to your instincts."

"But what if your instincts have been proven to be consistently wrong?"

"I know a thing or two about that, too, believe it or not," she said.

I bet she did, what with the twists and turns her romantic life had taken over the years. We focused on our new drinks and the salads we had ordered that had arrived while we were talking. After a few minutes of disconsolately munching field greens, I brought up another topic if only to get my mind off Crawford and the fact that I might never see him again, let alone be with him again. "Tell me about Lydia Wilmott."

Jane looked surprised. "Why?"

"I don't know. Just curious. We met the other day but that was under very tragic circumstances, obviously. What was she like when Carter was alive?"

Jane chewed on that for a few minutes. "She was happy. She adored Carter. And they seemed to have a wonderful marriage."

"But . . ." The specter of a caveat hung heavy in the air.

"But all I heard was her side of things. She always went on and on about how they were soul mates and perfectly suited to each other but I don't think they spent that much time together. And she stays very busy with her volunteer activities so I always wondered if that replaced what she was missing from her seemingly perfect marriage."

I had replaced what was missing from my seemingly perfect marriage with doughnuts. Volunteer activities? That was a route I had never considered. "Did you like Carter?"

"Hardly ever saw him," she said. "But we did socialize a few times and he was just a very negative person with a lot of opinions. He spent a lot of time on that blog and his boat and didn't do much else. That's what leads me to believe that things weren't perfect between the two of them."

"Are they ever?" I asked. "Perfect?"

"Of course not. I don't know what it is, but I don't think Lydia was completely happy. That's all I'll say."

Made sense if you subscribed to the "methinks you doth protest too much" school of reasoning. If I thought about her blog postings, it made sense. Lydia was a woman trying to convince herself that everything was okay in Wilmottville when in fact she had a distant and removed husband who thought about nothing but his incendiary blog and his boat.

"He's being buried tomorrow," she added. "There's a memorial service at the Unitarian church."

I thought about that. I wondered if I could go and not feel like a rubbernecker.

Or if taking a sick day this early in the semester, before it had even started really, would give me a figurative black eye with administration.

It didn't matter. I was going.

Fifteen

I had to break my "no lying" rule and call in sick to school, even though I was as healthy as a horse with just a little nagging nausea. A petite horse. I laid it on thick with Sister Mary's assistant, Jolene, and brought it home with a gagging noise that made her hang up quickly after promising to tell Mary that I was under the weather.

Being as I hadn't attended too many celebrity funerals, and Carter Wilmott was a bit of a celebrity around these parts, I never took into account the fact that every major local news outlet would also be in attendance. As I strode up to the church, feeling fine in my sleeveless black shift and high-heeled pumps, I got a knot in my stomach, knowing that pictures of this event would be splashed across every Westchester paper, not to mention a few New York City papers, whose reporters often wrote about the goings-on in sleepy towns in the area, especially if such goings-on were as sordid and juicy as the Carter Wilmott death/murder.

I got inside without being photographed, or so I thought, and slid into a back pew, trying to remain as inconspicuous as possible, black wide-rimmed sunglasses covering my black eye and, hopefully, my identity. I didn't look out of place among the many well-heeled mourners who were all in chic black clothing and dark sunglasses. This is a village that really dresses for its funerals. I wondered how many of them were wearing girdle-topped panty hose like I was and in danger of losing consciousness from having their diaphragms cut in half. Lydia strolled in through a side door wearing her usual uniform of crisp white shirt, big, chunky, expensive-looking necklace, and dark sunglasses. The only thing different about her outfit was that instead of her usual size-two designer jeans, she wore a beautifully cut black pencil skirt that showed off her amazing figure and long legs. If her late husband was distracted and distant from *that,* he had been a complete idiot in life. She sat in the front pew with several other family members, her two young-adult children, and her frumpy and rather odd sister, Elaine, who thankfully had shed her sweatpants for the day and wore a black sack dress.

I was raised in a devout Catholic household so a Unitarian service, to me, was pretty simple and scaled back in its pomp and circumstance. A few Cat Stevens songs, followed by some generic prayers and a couple of speeches that made Carter sound like a cross between Nelson Mandela and Mother Teresa. I also noticed that there were hardly any tears shed; must have been some kind of lapsed-Protestant way of dealing with things. Even we Catholics were allowed to cry a little bit if the spirit moved us. But during this service, there was complete silence, nary a sniffle, and no evidence of moist eyes or cheeks.

After forty-five minutes or so, just long enough for me to determine that, yes, I would have to cut myself out of my girdle-topped panty hose, the ceremony abruptly ended, with Lydia standing in her pew and receiving the condolences of the assembled. I saw my neighbor, Jane, envelop Lydia in a tight embrace. I looked around but didn't see Jane's partner, Kathy, which I thought was odd; if a friend of mine had died — or even if it was the husband of a friend of mine — Crawford would be there. I thought about offering my sympathies, but figured that I already had, and didn't want to make a spectacle of myself as I had a few days earlier when I visited the Wilmott estate. Instead, I moved out of the back pew as quietly as I had when I had entered and headed out onto the sidewalk, where I had the good fortune to run into Detective Madden, clad in one of her ubiquitous navy pantsuits.

She nodded at me, not unkindly. "Professor Bergeron."

"Detective Madden." I looked down at the pavement and caught sight of a very nice pair of navy pumps peeking out from under Detective Madden's sensibly cut pants. Now that was a surprise. I figured her for a dowdy pair of loafers, but even though they were blue, you could tell that her shoes had set her back a few hundred dollars. "Nice shoes," I said.

"Thank you," she said, a little surprised that anyone had noticed. Did she not know who she was dealing with here? I may not look like it but I can tell the difference between Payless and Via Spiga. "What are you doing here?"

"Oh, just paying my respects," I said, trying to sound casual and nonchalant.

"Go to a lot of funerals?"

"Not if I can help it."

She pursed her thin lips together in contemplation.

"Listen. Can I be completely frank with you?" I asked.

I took her silence to be tacit acceptance.

"I saw the guy die. I felt it was only right to be here." I stuck my little clutch purse high up under my arm in the hopes of soaking up a bit of the moisture that was present there. Why did I always feel like this lady was interrogating me? Maybe because she was?

She looked at me for a few minutes. "I guess that makes sense." She looked around. "But Greg from the coffee shop isn't here. George Miller isn't here, either."

"Well, he killed the guy so why would he?"

"Is that what you believe?"

I thought about Ginny Miller and her threats and her begging me to lie. "I don't know. I'm not a medical professional. I just thought that was what everyone else was thinking."

"Maybe. Is that what you think happened?" God, she was good at being cryptic. She reminded me of a therapist I once had who had promised to patch up my and Ray's relationship and make our marriage as good as new. I left our tenth session with no husband, a bruised ego, and no self-esteem after enduring her vague musings and open-ended questions. Detective Madden might consider a new career.

"Again," I said for emphasis, "I'm not sure. Isn't that why you arrested George Miller?"

"Could be."

That was enough of that. Sufficiently aggravated, I stomped off toward the parking lot and made my way toward my car. Before I got there, an overly coiffed blonde wearing lots of pancake makeup with breasts like giant cantaloupes got in my path and shoved a microphone in my face.

"You were there, right?" she asked, moving backward as I kept moving forward. "LeeAnne McDermott, News47 Westchester."

Oh, yes. "The One to Watch!" Especially if you wanted inaccurate weather reports, extended rantings about traffic, and nearly naked news from toothsome anchorwomen not unlike this one shoving the microphone down my throat.

"I was where?" I kept an eye on the camera guy who was walking backward as well and in danger of stepping into a giant pothole. "Watch out!" I said, distracting both of them enough to run to my car, jump in the front seat, and lock the door. This would look fabulous hours later on their six o'clock broadcast when all of the nuns, Sister Mary included, were having their aperitif and realizing that the woman whose car window was being banged on was mine. I smiled as broadly as I could as the whole scenario played out, faked a cough for good measure in case I did end up on the news, and peeled out of the parking space, doing my best not to run over the camera guy now wedged in the pothole.

I screeched out of the parking lot, any attempt at being inconspicuous now ruined by the Dallas Cowboys cheerleader masquerading as a news reporter and her inept camera guy. I sped up and came to a traffic light that turned red faster than I was expecting and I slammed on the brakes so as not to run the light. I sat a little straighter in my seat while waiting for the light to change and tried to bring my breathing back to normal. From the driver's side window of the car I glanced at the cars lined up along Main Street next to the shops and restaurants. One car caught my eye and I looked closer.

Oh, hello, Ginny Miller.

Ginny stared back at me from the safety of her Subaru Outback and gave me a half smile that was basically indistinguishable from the snarl she usually wore. The only giveaway was that her lips turned up slightly at the corners. I gave her a little smile back and kept my eyes on the light, wondering why she was parked on the street across from the Unitarian church. What did she care if Carter Wilmott was being buried? The fact that he was being buried at all was because her husband couldn't keep his ham-hock hands to himself. Surely she wouldn't want to be seen within ten blocks of the place, but there she was, hiding in plain sight, and watching everyone come out of the church.

Rather than using common sense and going back home to hide from news cameras and overzealous reporters, I chose the nontraditional route. That included pulling an illegal U-turn in the center of town, in full view of Detective Madden, and following Ginny Miller to her final destination.

Which happened to be the Stop & Shop, a fortunate choice because I was out of milk.

I followed Ginny into the store with her completely unaware that I was tailing her. We meandered through the aisles, her picking up an item here or there and throwing it into her shopping cart, me keeping a safe distance while riffling through my bag for coupons. I was here, wasn't I? Might as well get some shopping done. I stuffed a package of English muffins under my arm and continued toward the spice and "international foods" aisle, which was only international because of its selection of Goya bean products.

I rounded the aisle thinking that fajitas might make a tasty dinner, singing along to the Muzak version of Metallica's "Enter Sandman," and ran right into Ginny, who was lurking around the corner from where I had been. I slammed into her solid torso — had we been playing basketball, I clearly would have been charged with an offensive foul — and dropped my English muffins.

"Want to tell me why you're following me?" she hissed while smiling at an elderly female shopper who was angling her cart past us, running over my toes in the process.

"Want to tell me why you were spying on Carter Wilmott's funeral?" I asked, stooping down to retrieve my breakfast muffins and rub my sore toes.

"None of your business," she said.

"It just seems weird," I said. What was even weirder was that she was clad, once again, in her gym wear. I realized I had never seen this woman in any material other than spandex except for that one time she was in scrubs. Wasn't she a nurse? Wouldn't common sense dictate that she would be in scrubs more than occasionally?

"Why? You were there. That's pretty weird when you think about it."

I chewed on that. I knew that it was, obviously. But I would never admit that to Ginny Miller.

Ginny moved her cart a bit. "Are we done here?"

"I wish we were, Ginny, but I'd also like to know what you were doing on Carter's boat." I handed the same elderly lady who had run over my toes a can of black beans from a high shelf. She didn't say "thank you" which I thought was extremely rude.

"Once again," Ginny said, pointing at me, "same question for you."

"I was looking for something."

"Yeah? Well, me too." She started down the aisle, passing the elderly lady now reaching up for a can of garbanzo beans and perilously close to bringing down the GOYA? OH BOYA sign. I hurried after Ginny, grabbing the beans and throwing them in the lady's cart. I had a hard time keeping up with the yoga-pant-clad Ginny, who made haste down the aisle and into the main area of the store by the checkout lines. I skidded to a stop at the end of the aisle and called to Ginny. The old lady, now exhibiting remarkable agility, plowed into my rear end with her cart. I burst forward from the aisle into the middle of the store. "And you owe me an apology for pushing me into the river!"

The din of the grocery store evaporated into thin air and I realized that we now had about sixty pairs of eyes on us, from the elderly shoppers who had come in the minivan from the over-fifty-five complex down the road, to the cashiers, to the mothers with little children in line and making less of a ruckus than I was. Ginny turned to glare at me and gave me a warning scowl. I heard someone on one of the checkout lines whisper, "That's Ginny Miller."

Sadly, when someone whispered, "And who's the other one?", not one person knew the answer. Welcome to my world.

Ginny flushed deep red and disappeared into the frozen food section. Confident that I had caused enough trouble for the day, and convinced that I needed to get her alone to find out just exactly what she was up to and what she was looking for on the boat, I headed out of the store, leaving my English muffins behind a copy of *The National Enquirer.*

If I kept this up, I might find myself as the lead story in a future issue.

SIXTEEN

I ran into the house and went immediately to the phone. I had dialed the area code and first few digits of Crawford's phone number before I realized that I couldn't call him anymore, at least not for a little while. Seemed like we needed a cooling-off period or maybe a heating-up period? Any way you sliced it, we were on a break and I needed to respect that. I put the phone back on the handle and stared at it for a few minutes, wondering how I had gotten myself into this mess. My boyfriend and I had broken up and now I was fighting with townspeople in the local grocery store. What was next? Causing a commotion at the hair salon?

I decided that I would call Max since I couldn't get the good Lord's advice from Kevin, His mouthpiece. She picked up on the first ring. "Well, well, well. If it isn't Ms. Commitmentphobe." Although he only speaks in a series of grunts and clicks, Fred had obviously taken the time to give Max a blow-by-blow of my argument with Crawford.

"Max, this is not the time."

"Oh, this most certainly is the time. What is wrong with you?"

"How much time do you have?"

"I'm serious."

"So am I." I leaned against the kitchen counter and picked absently at a banana in a bowl of fruit that had seen better days. "Listen, I want this to work as much as you do. I just don't know if I'm ready to make that kind of commitment. Or maybe I am. I don't know." I forgot that I was talking to someone who had married her husband after weeks of courtship, broken up with him months into the marriage, and had taken him back — all in the same calendar year. I asked a question I should never pose her, under any circumstances. "What should I do?"

"The first thing you should do is set that house of yours on fire for the insurance money so I never have to look at that hideous Crate and Barrel coffee table again. Or your selection of horrific St. Thomas T-shirts. Then, I think you should crawl on your hands and knees to Crawford and beg him to take you back."

"Great solution, Max."

"Seriously. Marry the guy. You love him. He loves you. What else do you need?" She gasped audibly into the phone. "This is about your mother!"

"It is not."

"It is. It's August. You go crazy in August. That doesn't account for the rest of the summer, but this is always when you go crazy."

She was right, something I'm always surprised to acknowledge when it happens, say once every five years.

"If it's not one thing, it's your mother."

"What?" I said.

"Never mind. Listen, marry the guy or let him go. This is getting really annoying."

I was still mulling over this advice as I changed into one of my "horrific" St. Thomas T-shirts and a pair of jeans. At the thought of marriage, my stomach lurched and I found myself hugging the toilet bowl in the bathroom, unable even to commit to throwing up. I finished dressing and lay on my bed, not sure how any of this was going to turn out but knowing that whatever did happen was going to be my fault alone. And wondering why I felt as if I were going to throw up all of the time.

I wanted to touch base with Jane but

didn't know when she'd be back from the funeral and the afterparty, which is the only way I can think of the gathering that takes place after the ceremony. I waited a few hours before checking in with her to see how things had gone after I had left and had contributed to *l'affaire* Stop & Shop. I'm sure the bus ride back to Leisure Village had been exciting, with everyone giving their version of what they had seen transpire in the store between me and Ginny Miller.

I put Trixie on her leash and walked outside, noting that Jane's car was in the driveway. I knocked on her front door and let Trixie sniff around the boxwood hedges while I waited for her to answer. "Hi!" she said, surprised to see me. She opened the door wide to let us in.

"I hope I'm not getting you at a bad time."

She was still dressed in the outfit she had worn to church: black pants, a black sleeveless top, and kitten-heel pumps. Her blond hair was pulled back into its usual low ponytail and her makeup was expertly applied. As is often the case when I'm with Jane, I felt like a slob, and my jeans, St. Thomas T-shirt, and flip-flops did nothing to counter that feeling.

"No," she said. "It's a good time. Come on in."

We walked back toward the kitchen, and settled in at the breakfast bar. Jane grabbed two Diet Cokes from the refrigerator and two glasses from the cabinet. "Soda?"

I guessed it was too early to ask for a martini, so I accepted the soda. Trixie flung herself into a sunny patch by the back sliding doors and let out a long sigh. Things hadn't turned out the way she had expected when I had put her leash on. For me, either, I wanted to remind her.

Jane handed me a cold glass of Diet Coke. "Your eye looks better," she said.

"Thanks," I said. "It was kind of scaring people, so I was hoping that it would start improving."

"And the wrist?" she asked, pointing at my Ace bandage.

I flexed it back and forth. "I fell down, or maybe it was up, the stairs at school and sprained it. It's better, too, though."

"You're like a walking accident," she said, smiling.

"I guess I am." We moved on to the memorial service. "Lydia seems to be holding up well," I said.

"She's doing better than I would be under the same circumstances."

I waited a few seconds before asking the question that I had come to ask. "Do you know Ginny Miller?"

Jane blanched. "Why do you ask?"

Interesting reaction. "Well, I've run into her a few times over the past few days, so I was wondering if you knew her at all."

Jane looked away and toyed with a corner of the newspaper on the counter.

Oh, good. There's a story to tell, I thought.

She looked up, her blue eyes steely. "Let's just say that Lydia does not have any fond feelings for that woman, nor do I."

I waited a few more seconds for the rest of the story to come out, my mind reviewing the horrible pictures of Ginny Miller taking out the garbage in sweatpants and posted on Carter's blog. "What did she do?"

Jane laughed but it was not a happy sound. "I don't know why I'm trying to protect him. He's gone. And Lydia can move on."

"What is it, Jane?"

"She slept with him."

I gagged on the sip of soda that I had drunk. "Ginny Miller? And Carter Wilmott?" The thought of it was too bizarre to consider. I grabbed a napkin from the holder on the counter and blotted the front of my T-shirt.

"I know. Right?" Jane said. "Hard to believe."

"When?" I thought of the unflattering pictures on the Web site; I didn't know when they had been posted but I remembered thinking that they hadn't been in the too-distant past.

"George Miller went to Iraq for an eighteen-month tour about three years ago." Jane looked up at the ceiling, trying to piece together the time line. "Yes. Three years ago. So that's when it was."

"Wait. George Miller was in Afghanistan?"

"Yes. He was working for some contractor before he became head of the DPW. Something with munitions." Her distaste for the Millers was obvious. "You didn't know?"

"How would I know?" I asked. "I lived across the street from you for five years before making contact. I have no idea what goes on in this village and wish that I had never heard of the Millers or the Wilmotts." I grimaced. "Yikes."

I thought back to my first conversation with Ginny and when I had asked her if George had ever been to war. She had said no, which technically was true. But he had been in Afghanistan, a war-torn country, and was obviously familiar with explosives. She was asking me to lie while at the same time lying to me. That was even more curious to me than the fact that Ginny had slept with Carter. And that was an extremely odd pairing. The spandex-wearing gym rat and the hoity-toity yellow blog journalist. Takes all kinds.

It seemed to me that George Miller had been planning to kill Carter all along. He certainly had the means; he had explosives experience presumably if he worked for a munitions company who outfitted American soldiers and their Iraqi counterparts. He certainly had motive. His wife had slept with Wilmott. And he had opportunity. One needn't look any farther than Beans, Beans and what had probably been a chance encounter. The fight was just a sideshow diversion that ended tragically before Carter would have blown up in a bomb-rigged car.

I downed the rest of my soda and grabbed Trixie's leash. "I've got to go, Jane. Thanks for the soda."

We left Jane's and took a side trip to the next block, Trixie's favorite watering hole, so to speak. Rather than return home immediately after Trixie's business was done and her mind on chasing squirrels, I decided to take advantage of this day off and meander around the neighborhood and spend some time outdoors. God knows, once school really got under way, I would be inside a lot.

I thought about Kevin, still puzzled about what had made him leave without warning. I could only guess that he had gotten on the wrong side of Etheridge once again and that had led to his departure. Kevin and I are always on the wrong side of Etheridge; it was starting to seem as if pissing off the president of the college was our collective goal in life, when in actuality we were pretty hapless. We weren't determined to make him hate us; circumstances sometimes conspired against us. I got a little worried even going there in my mind. Was I next? Would my next unintended gaffe be his reason for letting me go?

Even though the day was gorgeous and I should have been in good spirits, a lot of things weighed heavily on my mind. I thought things couldn't get any worse. I was wrong.

For when I arrived home, there was another note tacked to my front door, this one more urgent than the last.

YOU WILL DIE IF YOU KEEP THIS UP.

If I kept what up? Harrassing unsuspecting shoppers in the grocery store? Asking questions about Ginny Miller and Carter Wilmott? Who knew? For some reason, and with everything else going on in my life, getting these notes amounted to a giant annoyance and nothing else. The Catholic-school, Palmer-method handwriting probably contributed to that. If someone had truly wanted to scare me, wouldn't they have cut out individual letters from magazines, like the serial killers on television did? People who wanted to scare other people into submission didn't do so with lavender-scented note cards. I suspected that was a general rule in the art of written intimidation.

My guess was that they were coming from Ginny Miller and I really wasn't afraid of her. I don't know how far she would go to protect her husband but I didn't think whatever she chose to do would involve me. After all, I was just a nuisance. With a black eye and a taped-up wrist. I couldn't help her because of my strict "no lying" policy, and I couldn't hurt her any more than I had. Unless she found out that I knew what everyone else seemed to know and not care about: that she had had an affair with Carter Wilmott, an interesting little tidbit that I hadn't seen turn up in any of the newspaper reporting on the case. Maybe only those closest to all of the players knew about it and nobody else. Because surely that would give George Miller ample cause and motive to beat the heck out of Carter Wilmott.

I was taking that information to my grave along with a few other items.

I called the number on the note again and listened to the phone ring and ring again. What kind of organization and/or psychopathic killer puts a phone number on its intimidating notes only to let the phone ring? I fingered the note, taking a deep whiff of the lavender, which had the opposite effect of the note's intent: it made me relax. I didn't know who sent the note or what they were referring to. The only thing I did know for sure was that if I spent any more time away from Crawford, I certainly would die. I stuffed the note into my jeans pocket, deposited Trixie in the house with an admonishment against eating anything that wasn't actually a food product, and got into my car.

If you're trying to win your boyfriend-slash-fiancé back, it is probably a good idea to look a little bit better than I currently did. But what the hell? He already loved me, warts and all, despite the fact that he was a bit perturbed with me at the moment. I knew it was a long shot that he would even be in the precinct but I figured it was worth taking a drive.

I rehearsed what I was going to say to him once I got to the precinct. I didn't think that blurting out "I love you!" in the middle of the detectives' squad room was the right course of action, but it was approaching dinnertime and I was hoping that we could sneak away for a drink or even something to eat so I could explain to him why I was the way I was. I went over all of my concerns in my head ranging from "how will your daughters feel about this?" to "my closet isn't big enough for your giant clothes," realizing how inane all of these objections sounded. I didn't want to go to the lying, cheating husband well again — Crawford was right, he wasn't Ray — but I had to get it all out.

And then, answer his question once and for all.

The precinct was its usual beehive of activity or den of iniquity, depending on how you looked at it. I had found a parking spot that seemed like three miles from the building, so by the time I jogged through the front doors, I was sweating, disheveled, and more than a little ripe. Any of the makeup that I had put on earlier in the day had melted off. It wasn't exactly the way I wanted to begin my "Please Forgive Me" tour but it would have to do. I walked up to the front desk and spoke to the sergeant on duty.

I tried to catch my breath. "Um, hi," I said, realizing, too late, that I was more out of breath than I originally thought. "Is Detective Crawford here?"

The desk sergeant, one Sergeant Tierney, a florid fellow reaching retirement age, stared down at me. "Um, hi," he repeated, obviously getting a kick out of my attempt at a greeting. He looked sideways at another police officer who was pretending, unsuccessfully, to be engaged in typing a form on a computer.

I took in a stale gulp of police station air. "Let me start over." I smiled. "Is Detective Crawford available?"

"Are you here to report a homicide?" he asked.

If you call murdering a relationship a "homicide," well, then, yes. "Uh, no."

Sergeant Tierney looked at me expectantly. "Then who should I tell him is looking for him?" he asked, taking in my sweaty St. Thomas T-shirt and wrinkled jeans. "The flip-flops are a nice touch," he said.

I ignored that. I already knew that I looked a mess. "Tell him it's Alison Bergeron." I smoothed down the front of my T-shirt. "Is he even here?"

"Well, we'll just see," he said. He snickered a bit with his cohort at the computer but I wasn't in on the joke. He picked up a phone and turned his back as if he were privy to the Pentagon's secrets. After a few seconds, he turned back around. "You're in luck! He's here," he said, and waved his arm toward the flight of stairs that I knew would take me up to the detectives' squad room. "Right this way."

I left the main area and trotted up the stairs wondering if the job made you crazy or Sergeant Tierney was just somewhere on the manic spectrum. I stepped behind the flimsy partition that separated the hallway from the squad room and looked toward Crawford's desk, trying to judge his mood from twenty feet.

When he saw me, he smiled. That was a good sign.

And he held up a sheet of paper with both hands and proclaimed, "I know where Kevin is."

Seventeen

We were in Crawford's "personal vehicle," otherwise known as his Volkswagen Passat. He had logged out of work with the lovely and talented Sergeant Tierney and we were headed down the Henry Hudson Parkway at an alarming speed, me hanging on to the door handle for dear life.

"So what's Sergeant Tierney's issue?" I asked after we took a hairpin turn on the parkway.

"He's a tool." Crawford is a man of few words but the ones he uses are usually right on the mark.

"I'll say."

"Did he give you a hard time?" he asked.

"I wouldn't say that. I would just characterize him as exceptionally sarcastic."

Crawford gave a little harrumph. "Well, charm isn't really a prerequisite for a desk sergeant but he's just a —"

"Tool?" I offered helpfully.

"A tool." Crawford slowed down to pay the toll at the E-Z Pass machine and waited for the mechanical arm to rise. It didn't. The cars behind us, stacked up during rush hour, began honking noisily. Crawford reached into his pants pocket, pulled out his badge, and held it aloft outside the car window in full view of most of the honkers. And a great silence befell the earth.

A uniformed cop rushed over and swiped something through the machine and the arm rose. "Sorry, Detective."

I eyed Crawford as he sped through the lane. "Wow, that's impressive. Where can I get one of those?"

"One of what?"

"One of *those,*" I said. "A gold shield. They're like the keys to the city."

"Well, I can't get you one, but I can get you access to one," he said. "You know, close enough, if you get my drift."

I took a deep breath. "That's why I came to see you."

He remained silent. His expression told me that he already knew that.

"Listen, Crawford —"

" 'Listen, Crawford' doesn't exactly sound like a promising start to this conversation. Or any conversation, for that matter."

He had a point.

We merged onto the West Side Highway. Once we passed the huge Fairway grocery store and its glaring neon sign advertising FRESH-KILLED POULTRY, he spoke again. "Let's focus on one thing at a time."

"One thing at a time?"

"Yes," he said. "Let's find Kevin first." He took one hand off the wheel and put it over mine. "Let's get through this month," he said, his perception about my emotional state astounding me. I looked out the window. "Let's find Kevin first," he repeated.

"Thanks, Crawford," I whispered, watching the scenery speed by, a blur of blue river and green trees.

He chuckled. "If we can't find him, who's going to marry us?"

Under normal circumstances, a line like that would bring on gastrointestinal distress, but the twinkle in Crawford's eye, accompanied by his hand squeezing mine, made me think that the eventual conversation we would have to have might turn out better than I hoped. He knew. He had probably known all along. It was obvious to me that he knew the problem was not with him or my feelings for him, but with me and my complicated past, my emotional baggage, and a host of other things that he probably knew he'd have to put up with if — sorry, *when* — this marriage took place.

I knew I was lucky. The question was, why? The guy was a gem, but even guys like Crawford are likely to run out of patience. I decided to focus on his current good humor as well as the task at hand.

I pulled out the piece of paper that Crawford had handed me. Kevin had gotten two parking tickets — a day apart — in a trendy West Village neighborhood, leading Crawford to believe that our prodigal priest was staying somewhere in the vicinity of the poorly parked car. I had driven with Kevin long enough to know that *(a)* he's a crappy driver and *(b)* an even crappier parker. He can't parallel-park to save his life so once he got his car into a spot, he was probably going to leave it there. He can turn water into wine and bread into body, but get into a spot with his Honda Fit that would normally fit a Hummer? Not on your life.

And the West Village? Another curious clue in the story. Kevin only goes two places: the Food Emporium by St. Thomas and his mother's house in the Throgs Neck section of the Bronx. There was nowhere else, in his world. So to think that we had to track him down in lower Manhattan was completely unbelievable to me. Crawford slid into a parking spot behind Kevin's Fit that was semilegal and put his police credentials in the window. He turned to me and told me that we would just have to wait.

My growling stomach told me that this was not going to be easy, and given our environs — a bustling West Village street filled with bistros and trattorias — I mentioned to Crawford that it might be using our time more wisely if we got a snack while waiting. Or an appetizer. Or dinner.

He didn't need much convincing. We were happily ensconced at a table at the Riviera Café and Sports Bar in seconds, across the street from his and Kevin's parked cars. An extra five to the hostess got a seat at one of the tables that sat along a bank of almost floor-to-ceiling windows, affording us a perfect view of Kevin's car and the apartment buildings near it. We decided that Crawford would sit facing the window and I would have my back to it, because as we all know, I'm easily distracted. But even better than our seats was that just two minutes after we had sat down I had a giant Ketel One martini in front of me with my requisite three olives. I decided that the Riviera Café was my new favorite restaurant. Things were back to the way I liked them, the Damoclean sword of the proposal not swinging over my head and threatening to impale me at every turn. I stuck my hand into my jeans pocket and pulled out the lavender-scented note card. "What do you make of this?" I asked.

Crawford read the note, his eyes growing wide. "When did you get this?"

"Today." I popped an olive in my mouth. "It's the third one of these that I've gotten. The first one encouraged me to 'get up' or 'get it up' or something like that. The second one was shorter but equally cryptic." I looked around for the waitress. "We need bread," I said to myself. I was starving.

"You've gotten three?"

"Yes," I said, distracted. I couldn't remember if our waitress was the actress-model who looked like Tyra Banks or the one who looked like Halle Berry. I finally grabbed a busboy and asked him for a basket of bread. "And butter!" I called after him.

"This is disturbing," he said.

"It is," I agreed, my mind on a completely different topic. "You'd think that they'd give you bread and butter automatically."

"No, not the bread situation. The notes." He flipped the note over. "Did you try this number?"

I looked at him as if to say, "what do you think?" "Nobody answers."

"That's weird." He sat back in his seat.

"This is concerning."

I looked at Crawford and was momentarily stunned by just how adorable he really was. Especially when he was concerned about me. What in God's name was wrong with me that I couldn't commit to this guy? "You think?" I knew it was, but I was trying to downplay my reaction. I've been through a lot during my time with Crawford and I was loath to think of our relationship spiralling into one where I continually played the damsel in distress. This situation, I thought, called for practiced nonchalance.

"Uh, yes." He downed a bit of the glass of merlot that he had ordered. "When did the first one come?"

I thought back. "A few days ago?"

"You're not sure?"

"So much has happened, Crawford. I can't remember a lot since Carter's death. It's been a blur."

"What about the second one?" he asked. When I shrugged, he asked, "Did you tell Detective Madden about this?"

Thankfully, the busboy came back with a big basket of bread but only two pats of butter. I grabbed his arm. "We're going to need more butter."

Crawford waited before asking me again.

"Did you tell Detective Madden about this?"

"No. I never want to see her again, let alone talk to her. I don't think she needs to get involved." I put forth my lavender-scented note card/good penmanship theory.

"I don't agree. And I want to see the other notes." Crawford looked around the restaurant before returning his gaze to the car across the street. "What else has happened since I entered my self-imposed exile from you?"

That was an interesting way to put it. "Not much." I dug through the bread basket for a roll. "I went to Carter Wilmott's memorial service. Ginny Miller was there."

Crawford raised an eyebrow.

"She was actually in her car across the street, but she was looking for something. Or someone. I followed her to the Stop and Shop."

Crawford didn't take his eye off the window but his exasperation with me and my handling of the situation was palpable. "You didn't."

"I did."

"I hope you didn't try to buy cold cuts."

"I didn't. But I made quite a scene, if I do say so myself. And I prevented an old lady from knocking an entire display of Goya garbanzo beans to the ground." I slathered some butter on my bread and shoved it in my mouth. "Good bread."

Crawford stood up abruptly, knocking my drink into my lap. Now there was a first. I'm usually the one knocking things over. He ran from the restaurant and out onto the street, his long legs a blur as he ran across the street, against the light and toward Kevin, who stood on the other side by his sensible and energy-efficient Honda Fit.

In mufti, Kevin looked like a normal, everyday denizen of Greenwich Village. Even up close, nobody would have had any idea that he was a man of the cloth. In his baggy jeans, hipster T-shirt with a slightly ironic saying on it, and Puma sneakers, he could have passed for a bike messenger, barista, or young dot-com executive. But I knew the truth. And I also knew that if Kevin was under deep cover, as he appeared to be, something was seriously wrong. I exited the restaurant, promising the hostess that we would return, but probably with an extra diner in tow, and headed across the street.

EIGHTEEN

"How did you find me?"

I rolled my eyes. "It wasn't hard, Kevin," I said, as if I had had anything to do with it.

Crawford graciously acknowledged my noninvolvement by not making an issue of it. "What's going on, Father?"

We were back at our table at the Riviera, me starting my second martini, Crawford having switched to coffee, and Kevin with an untouched chardonnay in front of him. I had finished the basket of bread and was waiting for my entrée. I raised an eyebrow at Kevin, who remained silent. "Well?"

Kevin took a deep breath, seemingly marshaling his courage. "I've been accused of 'inappropriate behavior' toward a student."

I was more comfortable with the "priest on the lam" charade that I had conjured up; in that fantasy, Kevin had gotten tired of the Catholic Church and pastoring to a bunch of uninterested college students and was living the life he had intended to live with a wife and twin sons. "Inappropriate behavior?" That was startling and discomfiting, to say the least.

Crawford was able to remain impassive, a gift we did not share upon hearing unsettling news. "Tell me what happened."

And Kevin did. A sophomore whom Kevin would not name had been seeing him for counseling for several months for a problem he would also not name. Kevin had helped the student as best he could, but he could sense that the situation this student was in was worsening and that this person was in serious trouble. He wanted to alert the kid's parents, the school, or anyone else who might be able to help further, but this suggestion sent the student into a rage that Kevin never anticipated.

"And the next thing I knew, I was in Etheridge's office being put on notice and told that I had to vacate the premises immediately while the situation was under investigation." He rolled up the end of the tablecloth and worried it between his fingers. "Remember, Alison? That was the day I saw you in your office."

I did remember. What we thought was an innocuous meeting turned out to be much more. “They can’t do this to you, Kevin.”

He smiled at my naïveté. “They can, Alison. And they did.”

Crawford jotted a few notes into the notebook he kept in his jacket pocket at all times. “What can we do to help, Father?”

“Well, you can start by calling me Kevin.”

“Okay. Kevin.”

“I don’t think there’s anything you can do to help. I’m playing a waiting game right now and Etheridge holds the key to if and when I can return.” He looked at me beseechingly. “I didn’t do anything wrong, Alison.” He looked at Crawford, his eyes sunken beneath giant dark circles, then back at me. “You believe me, right?”

“Of course I do,” I said. I did. Kevin was a lot of things — terrible homilist, lover of all things Broadway, and shitty driver — but he was true blue. And he took his vows very seriously. I had once seen a fellow professor make a pseudopass at Kevin, but he had shut her down in the kindest and most delicate way possible. It was clear that he wasn’t interested and she got the message — loud and clear.

Crawford stretched his long legs to the side and reviewed his notes. “What else can you tell us?”

“Nothing,” Kevin said. “Well, I should say

nothing without compromising this person's privacy and my vows. What someone tells me in confidence remains in my confidence. You know I can't reveal anything else, Bobby."

Crawford nodded. He did know.

Our food arrived but I was the only one who dug in. Kevin pushed his French fries around on his plate, and Crawford only picked at his meat loaf. I came up for air and asked Kevin who he was staying with. He was vague. "A friend."

"Anybody I know?" Realistically, I knew that Kevin must have other friends — I had actually met a few — but I liked to think that I was his only true friend.

"Somebody from the seminary."

"And he lives down here?" I asked. "How come you can't get a gig like that?"

Kevin smiled. "Long story."

Without pouring on too much of the guilt, I asked Kevin why he didn't let me know that he was leaving.

"Not enough time," he said. "I'm sorry." He took off his glasses and rubbed his hands over his eyes, exhausted.

Crawford gave me a tight smile that indicated that I was not to go any further with this line of questioning. I concentrated on my chicken and waited, hoping Kevin would take the conversation in a new direction. He didn't. We sat silently, eating our dinners and trying desperately to pretend that we were just three friends out for a leisurely and enjoyable dinner. Although I ate, I felt as if I had a large pit in my stomach when I finished, and I declined the server's offer of coffee or dessert.

Kevin looked at me suspiciously. "Are you all right?" He knew that I ended almost every meal with dessert so not having it was definitely a bad sign.

"I just don't feel like it," I said, the enormity of the situation coming down on me. I resisted the urge to cry; Kevin looked so dejected and I knew that this charge of impropriety was weighing heavily on him. His wan pallor telegraphed that he was dying inside. I leaned over and wrapped my arms around him. He leaned back in and a little sob escaped his throat. I held on to him a long time, until I was sure he had stopped crying and then held him at arm's length. "You let me know what I can do to help." I pushed his shaggy blond hair off his forehead. "And remember, Etheridge is a tool."

Crawford signaled for the check. "You like that word, huh?"

"It seems like an appropriate designation

for him. My other nicknames have never done him justice."

We parted on Seventh Avenue South, Crawford promising Kevin that he would make the parking tickets go away if Kevin agreed to find a legal spot for the Fit in the next few hours. As we drove back to the Bronx, I asked Crawford if he had any thoughts on Kevin's situation.

"It sounds pretty serious," he said in his usual understated way.

"Yes, but do you think they can really let him go?" I asked, in no mood for understatement. I wanted Crawford's emotional intensity in response to the situation to match my own and that just wasn't going to happen, no matter how hard I pushed.

"If he's guilty."

"Well, he's not guilty and you know that!" I said, a little louder than I intended. Crawford flinched slightly. I dropped my voice to a whisper. "He's not guilty."

"Right," he said, pulling off at the exit for the precinct. "He's not guilty."

But he didn't sound convinced and I was too tired to pursue the subject. I told him where my car was and he pulled up alongside it. He sighed. "You have a parking ticket, too."

I got out and plucked it from under the

windshield. Crawford opened his window and I dropped it in his lap. "Take care of this for me?"

He gave me a little salute. "You got it."

I leaned in and gave him a long, lingering kiss on the mouth in full view of a pair of uniformed cops who were starting their shift and walking their beat. They gave Crawford a sidelong glance, one of them uttering a muffled, "You go, Detective." Blushing, Crawford pulled back and told me to drive safely. I watched as he drove off down the street, waiting until he was out of sight before starting for home.

I checked my phone for messages when I got in the car and saw that I had a message from Max. *I need 2 talk 2 u soon* was all it said in typical cryptic, yet dramatic, Max fashion. I flipped my phone closed and threw it onto the passenger seat, making a mental note to carve out a piece of time during the evening to call her and find out what was so urgent.

My mood on the ride home fluctuated between overwhelming sadness and intense hatred toward Etheridge. How could he take the word of a student over that of Kevin, a trusted and loyal employee? It didn't make sense to me. But once I regained my emotional equilibrium, it occurred to me that

Kevin was in a "guilty until proven innocent" situation and nothing he could say at this point would change that fact. I pulled into my driveway feeling an urge to throttle Etheridge — a feeling I was well acquainted with — along with an urge to shout Kevin's innocence from the rooftops, one that I suppressed.

I went around back and noticed, once again, that the screen was ripped. Max. I didn't see a car, but that didn't mean anything. For all I knew, she had taken the train and walked here from the station. She had left me the urgent message and had obviously come here to talk to me; not finding a way in, she used her usual mode of entry. In the darkness, I could make out a lawn chair parked under the window. It was pitch-dark now and I regretted not having put on the back light so that I could find my way into the house. I hadn't anticipated being gone as long as I had and never guessed that it would be almost nine o'clock by the time I arrived home. As my anger flared in the form of a deep flush to my cheeks, I unlocked the back door, throwing it open and entering the kitchen in a full rage.

"Max!" I called. Upstairs, I heard Trixie's muffled barks, coming from somewhere directly overhead, meaning that she was in the guest room. She rips the screen *and* she locks up my dog, I thought. I fumbled for the kitchen light preparing to lambaste Max as soon as I located her. But my next words were drowned out as a piece of tape was slapped across my mouth and a hood was thrown over my head. After that, I was flung over the shoulder of a very large man, I guessed by the cloying smell of musky after-shave and the size of his broad shoulders, who carried me out into the dark night.

NINETEEN

The basement was dark and musty, but with the hood off my head, I could tell it was also filled with priceless antiques, the kind you don't regularly see at the places I shop. Although my hands and feet had been bound while I was in the vehicle that had taken me here, they no longer were. I had looked around for a pit, not unlike the one in which Buffalo Bill from *The Silence of the Lambs* had kept his victims, imploring them to put the "lotion on its skin" so that he could keep his ultimate skin jacket soft. I was relieved to not find one. What I found was a giant slop sink with two empty cans of Benjamin Moore paint in it, a small bathroom with a toilet (thank God) and a full roll of toilet paper in it, and a full-sized Jenn Air refrigerator fully stocked with soda, juice, and by golly, chardonnay. I was sitting in an original Chippendale chair, having exhausted myself looking for a way out, drinking a glass of dry, oaky chardonnay from a crystal goblet that I had found in what appeared to be an original Louis XIV china cabinet. I didn't know where I was or who had brought me here, but I did know that I was extremely pleased that I had left a deep scratch in the top of the mahogany dresser on which I had leaped, trying to find a window to break.

It hadn't taken that long to transport me to this place, just a few minutes. So I knew that I was probably still in the village proper, and if I had to guess, I was sure that Ginny Miller had something to do with this. Heck, maybe I was even in Ginny Miller's basement. But as I took in all of the antiques and paintings — was that an original Georgia O'Keeffe over there by the Stickley end table? — I wondered how Ginny Miller had acquired such taste and class. She was an oncology nurse and her husband a civil servant. They probably did well but not well enough to have a treasure trove of rare, and very old, furniture. And my general consensus is that people who wear spandex generally don't have a ton of antiques in their basements. It wasn't a proven theory, okay, but it was a guess that seemed to hold true.

When it came right down to it, this dark, musty, and cobweb-filled basement was almost nicer than my living room. It certainly didn't belong to Ginny Miller, driver of a beat-up Subaru and hider of recyclables.

I put my head between my knees trying to figure out my next move. I suddenly had an upside-down yet full view of a collection of antique fencing sabers behind me. I jumped from the chair, pushing it aside, and grabbed a long and pointy foil.

I had been kind of a shy and moody teen, so in an effort to connect me with other shy moody teens, my mother had enrolled me in fencing classes in Elmsford, not far from where I grew up. Every Tuesday, from four in the afternoon until six, I would advance, rapelle, lunge, and do a bunch of other things long forgotten in a white jumpsuit and face mask. I was a fair to middling fencer and did not make one friend. But I did fall in love with Gilles, my very French and very married fencing teacher who always called me Abigail and was not attracted to me in the least, and I never competed in any fencing competitions. Generally, fencing class had been a giant waste of time. But I did learn how to manipulate a foil and that had made my mother somewhat happy. I gripped the foil in my hands and lunged forward. Yes. This would do the trick. I still had my old moves even if it felt as if I'd dislodged a vertebra in the process.

Movement overhead, along with the sound of muted and muffled voices, put me on high alert. I stood at the bottom of the stairs, hiding behind the giant mahogany dresser, and waited while I heard someone unlock the door and start down the stairs. As the sound of the footfalls got closer, I lunged out from behind the dresser and posed with my foil. Instead of shouting "En garde!" out came "Lydia!" and I was surprised and then not surprised that my captor was Carter's widow.

Lydia grabbed her chest, almost losing her breath at the shock of seeing me jump out from behind the dresser with her antique foil. "Oh, Alison. Put that thing down," she said. "You scared the life out of me."

I don't know why, but I was inclined to do what she said. I rested the foil against the dresser and crossed my arms over my chest. "So this is an interesting twist. What the hell am I doing here?"

"Would you like dinner?" Lydia asked. "Chef has made coq au vin. I know it's a bit early in the season but I had a yen."

I *was* kind of hungry. The Riviera's chicken piccata was a distant memory.

"No," I said definitively. My growling stomach was a dead giveaway. "Kind of."

"Why don't you come upstairs?" Lydia asked, as if my coming here had been my idea alone.

"I think I'll stay here," I said, realizing how ridiculous it sounded.

Lydia regarded me with something akin to pity, but not quite. "Suit yourself," she said, starting up the stairs.

"Wait!" I called and followed her up the stairs. When I got to the top, I was back in the kitchen with the spectacular view of the Hudson that I had been in only days before while offering my condolences for Carter's death. Elaine was seated at the granite counter, drinking the same chardonnay that I had found in the refrigerator below. She was in head-to-toe cotton, her purple sweat suit accentuating the big roll of fat around her waist. I had a hard time buying these two women as sisters; they were polar opposites. Also at the counter was a giant man who reeked of the same cologne as the man who had brought me here.

Lydia made introductions all around. "You remember Elaine," she said, holding a hand out. Elaine gave me a sullen nod. "And this is Clark, Elaine's husband."

I held my hand out to Clark as if meeting

him under these circumstances were the most natural thing in the world. Clark, you need to lay off the cologne, brother, was what I wanted to say, but I shook his hand politely. I surreptitiously brought the hand up to my nose. Yep. It smelled like cologne. That was some pretty potent stuff and, most certainly, not a lady killer. Clark was a hulking mass, not unlike Max's Neanderthal husband, but while Fred was bald, Clark sported a slicked-back black ponytail that hung below his massive shoulders.

Lydia reached into a cabinet and brought out an expensive-looking wineglass. My guess was Baccarat. These were some fancy people, these Wilmotts. "Do you want some chardonnay? It's Conundrum. One of their special vintages and one of our favorites."

"Thank you," I said graciously, until I realized I no longer had to be gracious. We could pretend all we wanted that I was a guest who had come to sample the special vintage from the Conundrum vineyard, but I was essentially a hostage. I had been brought here with a burlap sack over my head. I shook my head to clear the cobwebs. "No! No chardonnay. What I want are some answers." I stared at Lydia in her usual white shirt and pricey designer jeans. "What am I doing here?"

"Have some wine," she said, pouring me a healthy glass of this special vintage.

I took a sip. I had to admit: it was excellent, far better than anything I had ever purchased. But even that didn't alleviate the stress I had felt being kidnapped and brought here under duress. I banged the glass onto the counter and demanded some answers. Elaine jumped a little bit.

Lydia looked at me sadly. "We're just trying to help you."

"Help me? With what?"

Elaine recited some kind of gobbledygook about denial being the first stage of something or other.

"Alison," Lydia said gently. "We all know what's going on."

"Well, then could you let me know?" I punctuated my outburst with a long slug of wine. Clark eyed me but didn't say a word.

Lydia gave me that pitying smile again. "The eye. The wrist." She looked down at the counter. "The abusive cop boyfriend."

The eye, the wrist, the abusive cop boyfriend? What in God's name was she talking about? Who in God's name was she talking about?

Elaine took over. "Alison, we're part of an organization called WIMP." When I looked at her blankly, she explained. "Women in

Major Peril. Well, it's actually Women and Children in Major Peril but we didn't want to add any letters."

Lydia jumped in. "You see, Alison, Elaine and I know what it's like to live in fear. Our father was a police officer, too, like your boyfriend, and he was very violent. We grew up in a small town in upstate New York, not unlike this one, and everyone thought that he was a wonderful man. But we knew what he was: a drinker and an abuser. We decided that if we got out of our house alive, we would devote our lives to helping other women and children in similar situations. That's why we started WIMP."

I stepped back from the counter, still holding my wineglass. "You're kidding, right?"

Clark spoke for the first time, his voice a jarring and uncharacteristic high tenor. "I wish we were."

It all came together: Lydia's obvious dislike of Crawford, a man she didn't even know; the lavender-scented note cards imploring me to get it up or pick myself up or something to that effect; and Jane's reference to Lydia's all-encompassing volunteer activities. Lydia and her bizarre cohorts — Clark and Elaine — were part of some militant, underground organization that tried to help battered women. By battering them, it seemed. Because if slapping duct tape over someone's mouth, putting a hood over their heads, and carrying them from their homes qualified as anything, it was *battery.*

Lydia attempted to explain what she considered all of the good works that they undertook after they had kidnapped and battered their clients. "We give women places to stay, money to get started, and a chance at a new life. We do very good work, Alison. We are very well intentioned."

"You kidnapped me," I said.

"Sometimes we have to resort to desperate measures to make sure that the women we seek to protect accept our help."

"You are all completely insane," I said, and placed my wineglass back on the counter, but not before sucking down every last drop of the lovely and delicate white wine. "And what kind of legitimate organization could you be if your phone number doesn't even work?"

Elaine shot Clark a dirty look. "I told you that you need to fix that."

Clark cowered slightly at the wrathful gaze of Elaine and promised that he would get on it right away.

"You'd better," she said.

Lydia grabbed my arm. "Alison, please. Just hear us out."

"You hear *me* out," I said. "I'm not an abused woman, nor was I ever. True, I married a lying, cheating piece of pond scum, but he never abused me. And Crawford would never lay a hand on me." The idea that they would even consider Crawford a batterer made me sick; talk about jumping to conclusions based on nothing. I pointed to my black eye, slowly fading into a light green and purple miasma of color. "This is from your husband."

Lydia gasped.

"Yes. Carter and George Miller flung the door open during their stupid fight and it knocked me silly. That's how I ended up with a black eye." I held up my bandaged wrist. "And this? I fell at school, something I do about once every two months." I straightened up to my full height and smoothed down my T-shirt, trying to regain some sense of composure. "I'm sorry I had to tell you that, Lydia, particularly on the day when you buried your husband, but it's the truth." I prepared to leave. "And let me just add that 'WIMP' is a spectacularly bad acronym for a battered women's rescue group. And lay off the cologne, Clark," I added. This day felt like it had been a thousand hours long. I took one last look at the gorgeous Hudson view — I thought it was a pretty safe bet to assume that I would never be invited back here — and strode from the house onto the dark street.

TWENTY

"Ever hear of a group called WIMP?"

Crawford hesitated. "Uh, no."

"Women in Major Peril."

"Still, no."

I was sitting on the edge of my bed, attempting to fasten the strap on my pumps while talking on the phone. It wasn't going well and I gave up. I had to leave for school in ten minutes but I wanted to give Crawford an update on what had happened after we parted. Yes, it was Saturday but since classes began in a few days, it was "all hands on deck." Etheridge had designated this entire weekend for extra orientation and expected everyone to be in their offices to attend to any students who might have questions or concerns before school officially started.

Crawford's first reaction to my story? "That's what happens when you lie about being sick to your boss," an "I told you so" that I didn't appreciate one bit.

"WIMP is an underground battered women's rescue operation and, apparently, Lydia, her creepy, sweatpants-wearing sister, Elaine, and some castrato named Clark are deeply involved with them."

Crawford was in his car on his way to work. "I must have misunderstood you. Did you call someone a 'castrato'?"

"I did."

"I'm impressed."

"Don't be. They think you're a batterer."

"What?"

"You know, the black eye, the taped-up wrist."

He interrupted me. "I hope you disabused them of that notion."

"Of course I did."

"So you're not hurt, and they're not too sinister, and all's well that ends well?"

"I guess."

"Do you want to press charges?" he asked.

I thought for a moment and decided that I didn't.

"Okay. Take the screen off the back window and bring it to the hardware store. And keep that back window locked, all right?"

"Got it." I managed to thread my shoe strap through the buckle and fasten it. I worked on the other one. "Hey, Crawford?"

"Yes?" he said in his comic, deeply serious voice.

"See you soon?"

"You bet."

I wasn't sure why he had come around, and so quickly, but I decided not to push it and ask for an explanation. It seemed that we were falling back into our old pattern and I was happy about that. The question was: how long would he be happy?

I thought back to our conversation about WIMP. We've had a lot of these types of conversations, and the fact that he still cares enough to hear the details, as ridiculous as most of them are, was a testament to his gentle nature. The idea that Lydia and company could consider him a wife beater was absolutely preposterous but I decided that there was no reason to try to convince them that they were way off the mark. But I would tell Jane that her friend Lydia was a certified nutcase.

I stood up in front of the full-length mirror on my closet door and assessed my appearance: black eye fading? Check. Wrist almost fully mobile? Check. Stockings unsnagged and without runs? Check. Things were looking up. I put on a pair of diamond stud earrings — the remaining material vestige of my marriage — and headed downstairs to let Trixie know that I was on my way out.

She still wasn't talking to me after last night's debacle. See, I didn't think I'd be gone for as long as I was, but then again, I hadn't counted on being mistaken for a battered woman and being kidnapped. By the time I arrived home, she was beyond manic, pacing back and forth in the guest bedroom where Clark had stowed her after he had broken in and lured her away with a giant bone. I don't know how she interpreted that to be my fault, but she was cool and distant when I came down to the kitchen and refused to look at me before I left.

"Suit yourself," I said, leaving money on the counter for the dog walker.

It was another hot and humid day and I prayed that the weather would break before the semester actually began and I had to start teaching. My office was air-conditioned but most of the classrooms where I taught were not. And to top it all off, most of the windows in the nearly one-hundred-and-fifty-year-old building didn't open so it made for some interesting teaching experiences. Fortunately, today would be spent in my office, my presence at school a mere formality. Classes hadn't started and I didn't have any more prospective English majors to interview. I was going to get myself organized for the new semester and make sure I could hit the ground running. Or so I thought.

Dottie was waiting for me with a look on her face that radiated glee. She was happy to report, before I had even fully set foot into the office area, that Dr. Etheridge was looking for me and that I was to see him immediately upon arriving at school. I wanted to smack the smug look off her face but good sense prevailed and I only thanked her for the message and exited the space by her desk as quickly and as gracefully as I could. No reason for her to know that even hearing Etheridge's name made me break out in a cold and clammy sweat.

Fran Voigt, Etheridge's gal Friday, was typing at her computer when I arrived on the fourth floor, her back to me. Fran is one of those people with eyes in the back of her head. Without turning around, she said, "Hi, Alison. They're waiting for you."

They? Who was "they"? I didn't have to wait long because I opened the heavy wooden doors leading to Etheridge's office and was confronted by the president himself, and a short, baby-faced man in a Roman collar and with a thick shock of perfectly coiffed black hair, artfully arranged into a semipompadour. This wasn't going to be good. I stopped short. "Good morning," I said.

Etheridge waved me into one of the guest chairs in front of his desk. "Alison, good morning." He gestured to the priest standing beside the other guest chair. "Let me introduce you to Father Dwyer."

I shook hands with Dwyer, noticing instantly that he had hands as smooth as a baby's bottom. This was a guy not accustomed to hard labor, that was certain. "Nice to meet you, Father," I said, still not sure what the purpose of this meeting was or who this chubby little mystery priest was.

"Likewise, Alison. I've heard a lot about you," he said.

Once again, that couldn't be good.

We sat down in the guest chairs and Etheridge began his spiel. "Alison, I've invited you here to meet Father Dwyer because he will be replacing Father McManus as chaplain of the university."

"You did? He will?" was all I could get out.

"I told Father Dwyer about your special relationship with Father McManus —"

"We're friends!" I protested, turning to Dwyer. "We're friends," I said more calmly. "We're just good friends," I threw in for good measure in a whispered tone.

Dwyer nodded at me in probably the same way that he would nod at a patient in a mental hospital who had told him he had just seen the Holy Trinity.

Etheridge stood, indicating the end of the meeting. "I hope you'll do everything in your power to make Father Dwyer feel at home."

"Of course I will." Was he really that concerned that I wouldn't? Etheridge really did think I was kind of a sociopathic lunatic if he thought I wouldn't be nice to the new priest. I had a modicum of class. And I was afraid of going to hell.

Father Dwyer smiled serenely. "I'll be making a few changes to the liturgy in the coming weeks and the faculty will be apprised of what those might be."

I felt the hair go up on the back of my neck. "Changes?"

Dwyer clasped his hands in front of him. "Small things. Little changes."

"Like what?" I asked, my smile insincere and frozen on my face.

Dwyer bared his teeth in a facsimile of a smile. "Well, for one, we'll be having a daily rosary."

Okay . . . that didn't sound terrible. I like the Blessed Virgin as well as the next lapsed

Catholic. She's a mother, something I hoped to be someday before all of my eggs dried up. And the rosary is always a good excuse if you're putting something off, e.g., I'll grade these papers after I say the rosary.

"We'll also be offering a Latin mass once a week. For our more tradition-minded students," he said.

I couldn't think of one student I had who would attend a Latin mass but didn't think now was the right time to offer up that little nugget of information. I looked at Dwyer who seemed like he wanted to add something else, but couldn't.

He hemmed and hawed for a few seconds, almost prompting me to prod him to "spit it out." I wisely kept my mouth shut. "We'll be changing the demographic of the altar-serving population."

I tried to diagram that sentence in my head but was having a hard time. I managed a "Huh?" instead.

"We'll be doing away with female altar servers."

That one was hard to stomach. I looked at Etheridge. "Does Sister Mary know about this?" Mary might be a pain in the ass when it came to being my boss, but she was a feminist of the first order. And the altar-serving program was hers alone; she coordinated the whole thing and used it as a way to reevangelize students, and in particular, female students, who may have become lapsed in their faith. She wasn't a convent pusher by any stretch of the imagination and I had lived through many convent pushers during my time here at St. Thomas. She just felt strongly that it was a way of involving young women in their faith and in the liturgy. Her program had other aspects but this was a main component. She was a smart cookie and had created a successful model for other Catholic schools in the area.

Etheridge waved his hand toward the door, trying to usher me out, but I wasn't having any part of it. "Everyone will know soon. We'll be issuing a release on our new regulations." He tried to smile but was unsuccessful, something I noticed only happened around me. "So we're done here."

I stood. "We're really not." I turned to Dwyer. "How can you do that? That can't be . . . legal," I spat out, for lack of a better word.

"Alison," Etheridge said, from behind me. "We're done."

I looked into Dwyer's beady eyes and decided that there was nothing there that was remotely Christian and turned on my heel to exit. Fran raised her eyes slightly above her monitor and gave me a look that said “I know.”

Before I reached the doors to the hallway, I heard her mutter, “If only my son hadn’t decided on that masters, I’d be outta here already.” St. Thomas grants the students of all employees free tuition for undergraduate and graduate work, so I understood Fran’s conflict.

I stepped out into the hallway, undecided about which way I wanted to turn. If I went right, I could hit Mary’s office and let it all out. But if I went left, I could head straight back to my office, pick up my briefcase and keys, and leave the premises before I did any damage.

I went with option B.

Twenty-One

I typed "WIMP" into my search engine and waited for the list to load.

I hadn't had the time, or the inclination, to read up on my captors prior to this moment, so in shock was I that I had been kidnapped and stuffed in a basement with a wine cellar to rival the best that many New York City restaurants had to offer. But now, back from school — AWOL, so to speak — and still steaming about Father Dwyer and his program of liturgical female alienation at St. Thomas, I decided to turn my attention to finding out just what Lydia Wilmott, creepy Elaine, and no-balls Clark had up their sleeves. And why.

I was sitting outside under the shade of my patio umbrella, my computer on my lap. I thought WIMP was so subversive that it didn't even occur to me to type in www.wimp.org but that was their Web site address, believe it or not. That was easy, I thought. The WIMP site's serene and lavender-screened home page belied the group's ugly tactics. Music began playing as a beautiful hyacinth filled the page, lulling me into a dream state for a second. There were several headers that you could click on, including one that said "Who We Are," which I scrolled over to. Who are you? is exactly what I wanted to know. But the page was disappointingly devoid of any concrete information.

> Who we are is a group of concerned citizens, some of us victims of emotional, physical, and sexual abuse ourselves. Others of us are reformed abusers . . .

. . . and now I knew who Clark was and which category he fell into . . .

> . . . who have chosen to live our lives on a path of repentance to atone for the things we've done. Still others are just concerned bystanders, hoping that nobody abuses anyone. EVER. AGAIN.
>
> . . . Pick yourself up. Get up again. Let WIMP help.

Nowhere on the site was there mention of Lydia, Elaine, or Clark, not that I really expected they would publish their names. It was all very generic and very soothing and very reassuring. Nowhere did it mention that if they even suspected you were a victim, they would bind your hands and feet, put duct tape over your mouth and a hood over your head. It all seemed very . . . voluntary. "*If* you wanted help . . ." and "*If* you had had enough . . ." They didn't list a location at which to seek help, which didn't surprise me. What were they going to write? "To donate, visit Lydia's basement"?

In order to get help, interested parties could send an e-mail to the site and would receive contact from a WIMP volunteer. I wondered if that meant the same treatment I had received.

I closed the computer. The whole thing was extremely shady and I wondered how many women actually availed themselves of WIMP's services, which included boarding at a local safe house (once again, Lydia's basement?), counseling services, and loans to relocate and "start anew." I put my computer under my arm and started off for Jane's house, deciding that I needed more information.

Jane and her partner, Kathy, were both home, enjoying a glass of wine by the pool in their backyard. Jane offered me a chair and a glass of wine. I accepted both gladly.

"I'm glad you came over," Jane said in her usual gracious way.

"Thanks for letting me drop in," I said, clinking glasses with both of them before taking a drink.

"We decided not to do anything this weekend," Kathy said. According to Jane, Kathy was a master of home improvement and spent every weekend doing some kind of major renovation. "God knows, we need it. I taught summer school this year. Ugh." Kathy taught physics at a high school in a neighboring town.

"Amen," I said. Jane asked me again why I was home so early. I gave her the *Reader's Digest* version.

Kathy shook her head. "And *that* is why I haven't been to church in years."

Jane laughed. "No, the reason you haven't been to church in years is that you don't get up before noon on Sundays."

Kathy shrugged. "Touché."

Jane pushed a plate of cheese and crackers my way. "I'm glad you came to visit." She looked at my laptop, sitting on the glass-topped table. "But why did you bring your computer?"

I cut to the chase. "What do you know about WIMP?"

Both Jane and Kathy did double takes.

"WIMP?" they both said simultaneously. Neither of them seemed to have any idea about the organization, or they were extremely good liars.

So it was more underground than I thought. If Jane, a good friend of Lydia's, didn't know about the organization, Lydia must have kept it very hush-hush. I opened my laptop and went back to the WIMP page. Jane's blue eyes scanned the screen, reading some of the same things I had read just minutes before, her eyes growing wide as I recounted my tale from the night before. "What is this?"

"This is one of the 'volunteer activities' that Lydia Wilmott is involved in," I said, using finger quotes.

Kathy sat back in her chair and looked at Jane. "I told you she was a whack job."

Jane shot Kathy a look. "I've known her a long time. Her intentions are good."

"So that's why she goes around kidnapping women in distress?" Kathy said. "Give me a break."

Jane closed the computer. "Lydia had a very sad upbringing. She has a lot of issues that she's still working out."

"Doesn't give her the right to kidnap Alison," Kathy said, her mouth full of cheese and cracker. I didn't know Kathy well and my first impression had been tainted by the embarrassing discovery that Jane was gay and I didn't know it. Kathy was taller than I was, and slightly imperious, amber-colored eyes peering out from behind tortoiseshell glasses. She signaled that she was not to be messed with by the way she carried herself. She was no-nonsense and sharp as a tack; at least I was sure about that. "And who doesn't have issues?" Kathy added.

I waited for Jane to continue, helping myself to some camembert and Triscuits, a combo that went delightfully with the wine they had served. I really needed to get out more. Apparently there was a whole big wide world out there that went beyond St. Thomas University and martinis. Too bad that being kidnapped was one of the reasons I was finding this out.

Jane seemed conflicted. "I don't know. I think she means well. And she's a good friend."

Kathy coughed into her hand. "Fruitcake." Obviously, this was a conversation that they had had more than once.

"But back to WIMP," I said. "Did Lydia ever mention it at all?"

Jane gazed out at the pool. "A little. But I didn't know it was called that and I didn't know how they went about doing the work they did. I got the impression that what they did was very good ultimately. And Lydia funded everything with her own money. She was very passionate about helping the women. I'm not sure why." Jane looked at Kathy. "But this does make sense. She always said that Carter didn't appreciate how much time she spent volunteering. I just assumed that meant working on the silent auction for our church and the other things she did to help women. I didn't realize that she was so deeply involved. I just figured she was overextended like the rest of us."

I mulled this over and decided that all of this information begged the question. "Did Carter abuse Lydia, Jane?"

Jane shot a look at Kathy before answering. "I don't think so."

"Not physically, anyway," Kathy added. "You knew him, right?" she asked me.

I shook my head. Even if you watch someone die, I don't think that qualifies as "knowing" them. Call me crazy.

"Well, he was an asshole, plain and simple. But she loved him. Did you ever read some of those 'Ask Lydia' posts that she wrote?" she asked. When I said that I had, she continued. "So you know what I mean. You could see how she adored the guy even though he didn't give her the time of day. And then, the cheating . . ."

I thought back to Jane's revelation that Carter had had an affair with Ginny Miller, something I was still trying to wrap my brain around before going into complete "system failure." Lots going on and not a lot of ways to process it. "More than Ginny Miller?"

"Way more," Kathy said, to the dismay of Jane, who reached out and put a hand on her leg to silence her. Kathy, on a roll, suddenly shut down. I think she realized that she had gone too far. She held her hands up in surrender. "I'm done." She pushed her chair back and said good-bye to me before going into the house.

"I'm sorry, Jane," I said. "I didn't mean to start an argument between you and Kathy."

Jane brushed it off. "It's nothing that we haven't discussed in the past. Kathy doesn't like Lydia. She thinks the whole Wilmott scene is dysfunctional, and I can't say I blame her. And she loves Tony's so anyone who disparages him or his food is a creep, in her book." She laughed softly and I got the impression she was only half joking.

"I kind of feel the same way," I said. I stood, picking up my computer. "Thanks for the wine and the information." I stopped midway between the edge of the pool and the gate to the driveway. I turned back around, something occurring to me. "He didn't . . . ?" I started, but Jane had already gone into the house.

I started down the driveway. The Wilmotts were certainly a complicated bunch. But just what was it about them that made Kathy see red at the mention of their names?

Twenty-Two

George Miller was out on bail.

At least that was the information I got from the latest story in the local paper. So I assumed Ginny was in a better place, mentally, or so I hoped, and that would make her leave me alone. Although things had been quiet on that front ever since the Stop & Shop incident, I never knew when the two of us might run into each other again and have an unpleasant encounter.

I was back at the house and in bed with Trixie, she and I having reached détente. She was lying at the bottom of my bed, nuzzling my feet with her wet snout while I spent some more time reading Carter Wilmott's blog, something I hadn't done since the night he had died. The home page looked exactly as it had when I first logged on; nothing had changed. I wondered if someone would take over the site or if it would eventually be taken down. Since Carter was no longer at the helm, it was hard to say what would happen. I scrolled through and looked for any mention of WIMP but there was none.

Carter included pictures of himself, particularly if he was reviewing a restaurant. In his restaurant review posts, he was always shown in front of the establishment, holding up a notebook and a pen as if to indicate that he was going to be reviewing the place. I wondered who took the picture and if it was Lydia. I also wondered what kind of service he got at these places, most of them knowing in advance that he would review them unfavorably, because, after all, that's what he did every time. It didn't take a genius to know that when Carter Wilmott was eating at your restaurant, you were going down.

I went back to his very first review and it happened to be the same local waterfront restaurant where Crawford and I had dined a few nights before. When Carter had reviewed it, it had been a popular chain restaurant that specialized in seafood and spectacular views. Carter had given the place one star, and only because they prepared an "excellent dry martini." My kind of restaurant. In the picture that ran beside the post was a robust and hale-looking Carter, not the winded, pale, and thin man that I had encountered. I remembered having the same reaction when I had looked at the blog the night after he had died. I clicked through the various restaurant review posts, starting with the oldest and going all the way to the newest. Indeed, the man had lost a ton of weight. And it didn't suit him. He looked far healthier in the earlier posts, despite the small roll of fat resting on top of the waistband of his belted jeans. A few extra pounds actually looked pretty good on him; his face was far too pale and droopy in later photos.

I wondered which version of Carter Ginny Miller had gotten: slightly chubby but kind of cute Carter or thin and bedraggled Carter? Because even as he dropped the weight and seemingly would have more options in the clothing department, he continued to wear his old clothes, cinching his pants at the waist until the last posted photo — dated two weeks earlier — had them buckling in the back (there was one side shot where this was noticeable) and bunched up in the front. Not a great look on anyone, particularly a middle-aged man.

I read through a couple of the reviews and decided that Carter Wilmott would have been well advised to invest in a thesaurus.

Because there were just so many ways to say "disgusting," "awful," and "dirty" without running out of words. Which he had.

I revisited the few slings and arrows he had aimed at Greg and Beans, Beans, a place he confessed he frequented daily. He implored Greg to get better coffee beans and to not burn his brew. Carter struck me as a guy who loved to pick a fight, even if it wasn't a fight worth picking. I scrolled down and read the comments that accompanied the post. Coffee Lover, in particular, was quite visceral in his or her reaction to Carter's ramblings. I settled on the most interesting and threatening of the commenter's responses to the post:

> Coffee Lover: *You're a moron, Wilmott. If it wasn't for Greg and his willingness to try a new business in this one-horse town, Main Street would be desolate.*

Not true. Main Street was a thriving strip of commerce with boutiques and cafés dotting both sides of the street.

> Coffee Lover: You'd better shut up. If you know what's good for you. And you don't.

Okay, not the best grammar, but the intent was clear: Coffee Lover wanted Carter to shut up and shut up quick. This guy had more enemies than I could count, but from the number of listings on the blog, he kept right on posting and right on pissing everyone off. What kind of personality disorder did Carter Wilmott actually have?

I read through some of Lydia's posts, as well, and while none overtly pointed to anonymous posters' problems with violent partners, Lydia did seem to go there more often than not. I wondered how the poor woman who had written asking how to get her husband to stop leaving his dirty underwear on the floor had reacted to Lydia's suggestion to "stop taking his abuse and leave immediately." That was a little over the top, if you ask me. My initial reaction would have been to torch all of his underwear in full view of the neighbors, but that's just me.

I puzzled over the little details that I had gleaned from the blog as I shut my computer and put it on my nightstand. I looked down at Trixie, whose eyes were peering out from under golden eyebrows. "Cocktails?" I asked, and she jumped off the bed and raced downstairs. I heard her hit the hardwood floor of the hallway and skid all the way into the kitchen. She knows that when I say "cocktails," what I really mean is a walk followed by a martini. Everybody wins.

We set out for our journey, a gorgeous end of day in which much had transpired. I didn't know how I was going to navigate the new liturgical rule that was being instituted at St. Thomas; I was a heathen at best, a heretic at worst. That was going to make things difficult, particularly if Father Dwyer and his flying monkeys made all of the faculty attend every holy day of obligation mass or become daily communicants or — gasp — become Eucharistic ministers. If that was the case, Etheridge better get some more insurance, because me in charge of the Holy Eucharist? That for sure meant that the building would cleave in two from the force of the bolt of lightning that would surely strike.

Trixie and I wandered up and down my street until a black cloud that had been hanging low overhead decided to burst open and drench us with big, fat raindrops that soaked us within seconds. Trixie didn't need any encouragement; she dragged me down the street, my arm straight out in front of me, the leash between us. We were home in less than a minute, but drenched nonetheless. I went in through the back door, which I hadn't bothered locking, flustered and anxious to get inside. Trixie and I did a simultaneous shake-off not noticing that we had company.

Max came out of the attached powder room and screamed, not expecting to see us. A young black woman at the kitchen table used her hands to shield herself from the droplets of water flying off my wet dog and me. Trixie yelped at the sight of Max and scurried off to hide under the dining room table, her "safe place." And I nearly collapsed from the sheer terror that accompanies seeing someone in your house when you're sure it's unoccupied. I had been so focused on getting home — not to mention nearly blinded by the wall of water that had fallen on me — that I hadn't even noticed Max's car outside.

Max, of course, found my screaming to be a serious affront to her delicate auditory function. "Shut up!"

I sat at the table and put my hand over my heart. "Good God, Max. Have you ever heard of calling first?" I looked over at the young lady across from me and held out my hand. I recognized her as the woman who had taken down the seemingly staid businessman in front of the apartment building a few nights earlier. "Alison Bergeron. This is my house."

"Queen Martinez." She looked at Max.

"Friend of Max, I guess?"

"She's a Hooters waitress," Max said, as if that explained everything.

"The Hooters tank top was a dead give-away," I said, taking in Queen's interesting ensemble: the aforementioned Hooters tank top; a long-sleeved sweatshirt with a hood; Daisy Duke shorts that rode up so high in the sitting position that I could only imagine what they looked like when she stood up; and red platform shoes with a cork bottom. "You waitress in those?" I asked, pointing at the shoes. I didn't remember her wearing them the night of the confrontation with the cheating husband but there had been so much more to focus on that I hadn't really noticed her shoes.

"They're surprisingly comfortable," she said, bending one ankle to admire the shoe's construction.

"Max, a word please?" I asked, dragging Max by the collar into the hallway. Once we were out of earshot, and I observed Queen playing with the dog, I tore into Max. "What is going on?"

She pulled her collar back and adjusted it. "Sheesh. You didn't have to get so rough."

"Yes I did. What is happening here?" I could only imagine given my history with my best friend. "And why have you brought

RuPaul to my house?" I looked over again and watched while Queen adjusted her very long, and very full, blond wig, which had come loose while she played tug-of-war with Trixie. She was on her knees, and half of her butt cheeks were hanging out. I needed to get this girl some pants.

Max took a deep breath, signifying that there was a long story to be told. "Well, here's the thing. Queen has run into a little trouble and needs a place to stay."

I pulled Max close so that there would be no misunderstanding what I was about to say. "She. Cannot. Stay. Here."

And then Max did something I had rarely seen her do: she started to cry. Loudly. And wetly. Queen rushed from her place under the dining room table and put her arms around my terribly misguided friend. Trixie, who we have established loathes Max, also came running. The dog herded us together, me, the tall, unkempt college professor; Max, the tiny, well-dressed cable television executive; and Queen . . . well, she defied description. We stood in a tight group, the dog circling us to keep us together. I looked down at Max and then up at Queen, who up close was stunning once you weren't distracted by the hair, the tank top/sweatshirt combo, and the short shorts.

"What's your story?" I asked.

Before she could answer, the doorbell rang. As if this day couldn't get any weirder — or truly, any worse — there stood Ginny Miller.

She looked at me sheepishly, while tugging at the seat of her spandex exercise pants. There was no greeting, nor a preamble. She just stated her business. "Hey. I need your help."

TWENTY-THREE

I don't think I could have put together a more disparate group of people, but here I was in my dining room surrounded by Max, Queen, and Ginny. While I had thought that Ginny was off my back for good with George being out on bail, it seemed that she was even more determined to make his troubles go away, and to do so, she had to come completely clean to me. That meant confessing the scintillating details of her torrid affair with Carter Wilmott to me and my new partners in crime, one in hot pants, another in a very expensive business suit, and one in a fake jeweled collar. We listened in rapt attention to Ginny's story of encountering Carter Wilmott at a town hall meeting and his insistent wooing of this slightly overweight and kind of dowdy-looking and very married nurse.

"Why did you break up?" I asked.

"Guilt."

Max snorted. "That's a good reason."

I kicked her under the table.

"And I love George."

"Yeah, but not enough to not sleep with Blogenstein," Max added. Her excessive use of double negatives left even her mildly confused and she shook her head to regain her equilibrium. Another kick under the table was intended to silence her but she kept going. "It's something I don't understand. How could you do that to your husband and another woman? Don't you believe in the sisterhood?"

I put my hand on Max's shoulder; the threat of physical harm wasn't stopping her so I thought I'd try the gentle approach. "Max, we're not here to judge. Let's listen to what Ginny needs."

Queen nodded vigorously, her blond ringlets bouncing up and down. I still didn't know why she was here but figured we'd get to that later.

Ginny rested her head on her arms that were crossed on the dining room table. After a few seconds, she picked her head up and addressed us. "Listen, I know it was wrong, but I was flattered." She waved a hand to indicate herself. "Look at me. I'm a frumpy, middle-aged woman who's married to a frumpy, middle-aged man. I've had three children and look like it. The fact that someone like Carter Wilmott was even interested in me in the least was . . . well, flattering."

You'd think that I would have been more judgmental, given my history with cheating spouses, but all I felt for her was sorrow. She was a mess. Probably an extremely competent nurse based on some of the chutzpah and clinical knowledge of the healing powers of pineapple she had previously displayed with me, but an emotional wreck nonetheless.

"Carter Wilmott was a troll," Max said. The kicks didn't work nor did the hands on the shoulder so I just shot her a death gaze that said "shut your freaking piehole." "I'm just saying," she added quietly.

"What do you need from me, Ginny?" I asked finally. Cut to the chase, sister.

"I don't think Carter died from the blow to the head," she said.

Now I was getting impatient. "We know," I said. "We've been through this, Ginny."

"No," she said. "Wait."

Queen sighed. Even she was getting tired of this nonsense and she had only been here less than half an hour.

"I think Carter was poisoned."

"At Greg's?" That statement left me

incredulous. His coffee was bad but it couldn't kill you. Could it? I started to worry.

"No, not at Greg's," she said. She looked at me intently. "At home. By Lydia."

Queen leaned over to Max and whispered, "Who's Lydia?" Max just shushed her loudly, so intent on hearing the resolution to this tawdry story. In reality, she had no idea who Lydia was, either.

"Ginny, you're crazy," I said before I had time to think of an appropriate response. "Even if you're right about him being poisoned, he still died from your husband's pummeling."

"Maybe," she said.

"No, not maybe. Definitely," I said. "I was there. I heard what the ME had to say. It's all there in black-and-white. Hit to the head? Die." I stood up. "Who wants coffee?"

Ginny stood, as well. "No. You're wrong. I'm telling you, he was being poisoned. Slowly."

I started for the kitchen but turned back around. "Ginny, I don't know which one of you I like better: angry, hostile Ginny or completely deluded Ginny. Right now, it's a tie." I went into the kitchen and pulled the filter basket out of the coffee maker. "It's not like you have proof or anything."

"Here! Catch!" Ginny called, and I turned just as a huge chunk of rock was thrown at my head. I put a hand up and caught it.

I looked at the big hunk of rock in my hand.

"Now do you believe me?" she asked.

"I would if I knew what this was," I said.

"It's arsenic." Max's and Queen's jaws dropped. "I found it on Carter's boat the night that we were both there."

"Arsenic?"

"Yeah, arsenic." She stood. "If you shave a little bit of that rock into someone's food or drink every day, it will slowly kill them. All you need is a cheese grater and a rock like this. It's basically undetectable."

I wish I had known that when I had been married. God, why do I learn about all of the cool stuff so late?

Queen stood as well. "This might not be the best place for me to stay," she said, looking at Max regretfully. She tottered into the kitchen and stood next to me at the counter. "I'll find somewhere else."

"You stay right here," I said to Queen, and then turned to Ginny. "Continue."

"It's odorless and tasteless and can kill you slowly, over time. Did you read Carter's blog?" she asked.

I didn't want to admit that I had, but I did. No sense lying about it now.

"Did you notice how he had changed in the photos?"

"As a matter of fact —"

"Well, there you go."

I started the coffee. Seemed like it was going to be a long night. "Well, if you're right, how come the ME didn't mention this?"

Ginny spoke to me as if she were talking to a dumb student. "Because they don't automatically test for poison in autopsies."

"They don't?" Max and Queen asked at the same time. I could practically see the wheels turning in both of their heads.

Ginny shook her head. "Nope. And they wanted this cleared quickly, so they went with the blunt force trauma cause of death. But Carter had called me a few weeks back and told me that he hadn't been feeling well. He wondered what some of the signs and symptoms of various cancers were. I begged him to come in and get scanned, and he did." She paused dramatically. "No cancer."

"Well, what did they find?" I asked.

"Nothing. And since it wasn't cancer, he blamed it on stress and didn't go for any more tests." Tears welled up in those long-lashed eyes of hers. "I should have made him go further. Maybe I could have saved him." She sat back down and sobbed into her hands. "Now that I think about it, he showed all of the signs of arsenic poisoning, but I was just so concerned that it was cancer. I didn't think it could be something more sinister."

"How could Lydia have come up with this plan?" I asked.

"Are you dense?" Ginny asked. When I didn't respond, she kept going. "First of all, you can find all kinds of stuff like this on the Internet. Ever heard of it? And secondly, her sister is a nurse. She knows a thing or two about toxicology."

"It's probably in your best interest not to insult the person you're trying to get to help you, don't you think, Ginny?" But even as I was taking umbrage at Ginny's insult, I was thinking back to Elaine's insistence that Carter had been "healthy as a horse" when I had gone to the Wilmotts' on the day Carter died. Was she protesting too much and giving me a clue?

"I'm sorry," she said.

I leaned against the counter and watched coffee drip into the pot. She sure seemed concerned about this man, the same one who had published extremely unflattering photos of her on his blog. I didn't know whether to believe this tale or not; she certainly relayed the details with a lot of conviction. But I had been there and I saw what happened and it was no accident that right after her husband landed a blow to Carter's head, he was dead. But there was one other little matter and that concerned the explosive device in the engine. I asked Ginny who had put that there and asked if perhaps it had been George.

"I don't know but I know that it wasn't George."

"How can you be so sure? He couldn't have been too happy about you having an affair."

She shrugged. "He doesn't know."

Now it was the three of us — Max, Queen, and me — who exclaimed in unison. "He doesn't?"

"Not that I know of."

Speaking from experience, I said, "He knows." And I bet that's why this whole thing started, I thought. And even if it wasn't, that didn't mean George Miller didn't want Carter, the little weasel who took him to task day after day on his blog, dead.

"Whatever," she said, defeated. "It doesn't change the fact that he's dead, my husband's going to jail, and our lives have been ruined."

I took some mugs out of the cabinet. "So what do you want from me, Ginny? Seems like you've got the whole thing figured out."

"I do, but I don't have proof. Besides a big arsenic rock, that is. I tried to talk to Detective Madden about it, but as far as she's concerned, the arrest has been made. It's an open-and-shut case. She doesn't really care how Carter died, she just cares that she's closed a homicide." She stood and walked into the kitchen. She picked up the arsenic rock that I had hastily placed on the counter as far from me as I could. "I know you've got a reputation for being a bit of a busybody —" I took offense at that characterization and started to protest. She held up a hand to silence me. "But you find things out. And I know you know Lydia."

Not in the way you'd think, I wanted to tell her, but I wisely kept my mouth shut.

"And your boyfriend is a cop. He can find things out, too."

"Leave him out of this. He's not going to help you, Ginny. He doesn't know you from a hole in the wall." I poured coffee into each mug and handed them to each of my guests — and I use that term loosely — now all clustered in the kitchen. I took a sip, burned my lip, and cursed a blue streak in my head. This day just keeps getting better and better, I thought.

Queen spoke up. "I'm a private investigator."

"Yeah! She's a private investigator!" Max agreed.

Ginny looked Queen up and down, a mild expression of disdain crossing her face. "Of course you are, honey."

Queen shook her head. "No, really. I am."

Max launched into her pitch about the show. I decided to keep to myself my name for it lest I incur the wrath of Max again and find myself stuck in a fetid-smelling van. Ginny looked at me. "They're kidding, right?"

"I wish they were," I said.

Ginny looked back at Queen. "How much do you charge?"

Queen seemed never to have considered this question and didn't want to get the answer wrong. "One thousand dollars a day plus expenses."

Ginny sighed. "I can't afford you."

"Okay, fifty dollars a day. No expenses."

Max clapped her hands together as if she had just brokered a deal between Israel and Palestine. "It's settled!"

I clanged my mug down on the counter to

get their attention, coffee sloshing out onto the floor, my jeans, and Ginny, who was standing closest to me. "No it's not. Queen, thank you for your generous offer of support, but Ginny needs to figure this out on her own. And Max, we still have some unfinished business, so if you'd both excuse us for a second . . ." I waved a hand toward the back door and motioned to Ginny that it was time to go.

"Help me," Ginny said one last time, her hand on the doorknob. "My husband is a good man. He just let his temper get the best of him. He's not a killer, either on purpose or accidentally. He'll never make it in jail," she added.

I felt for her but I really didn't know what I could do and told her so. "Go before the rain starts again," I said gently.

"I've made a lot of mistakes," she said. "More than anyone should ever make. And I have no excuses. I would just like to make some of this up to George. He's a good man," she repeated, and I was inclined to believe her. And then she played her hand completely. "You know, I knew your mother."

My heart leaped into my mouth.

"She was a patient on my floor, wasn't she?" she asked.

"I don't know. Was she?" I said. This was a conversation I certainly didn't want to have.

"I thought your name sounded familiar. And then I remembered. A beautiful lady, inside and out." She looked up at the sky, as I did many a night, thinking that I could feel her presence from above. "We took good care of her, Alison. I'm sorry there wasn't a better outcome." When I didn't respond, she stepped out into the backyard, just outside of the door. "I'm sorry I bothered you," she said before pulling the door closed behind her.

Max waited until she saw Ginny pass by the kitchen window before offering her interpretation of events. She wisely skipped over the last part of the story because even Max, the least self-aware and perceptive person I have ever met, could tell that one push and the whole house of cards that were my emotions would come tumbling down. "Well, he might be a 'good man' but that dude is going to jail. Then, Mrs. Miller can carry on all she wants with whomever she wants."

"That's a real change of tune," I said, my voice sounding thick from the tears backed up in my throat.

"Girl's gotta do what a girl's gotta do,"

Max said.

I stared into my coffee cup. Girl had a point.

Twenty-Four

I awoke the next morning and entered the kitchen to find a fresh-faced, athletic-looking African-American woman who couldn't have been more than twenty sitting at my table. Her straight black hair was pulled back in a ponytail and the only way I recognized her as Queen Martinez was from the St. Thomas sweatpants that she was wearing and that I had given her the night before. She had started coffee and had made some toast.

"Hello?" I said, still not entirely sure that this adorable young woman was the same one that I had permitted to spend the night — and perhaps many more — in my house the previous evening. She looked more like she was ready for a track meet than a shift at Hooters. Even the big breasts seemed to have evaporated overnight, but having had some experience with push-up bras (and not good experience), I knew that these things could be manipulated very easily.

"Oh, hi," she said. "I made some coffee. I hope that's okay with you."

"Okay? It's fantastic," I said, and poured myself a cup. "How did you sleep?"

"Fine," she said, nibbling on a piece of toast. Despite the fact that we had just met the night before and she was now staying in my house, she seemed pretty much at ease and at home.

"I only have the two bedrooms and need to use the spare for an office so I put a futon in there. I'm sorry it's not more comfortable."

She waved her hand dismissively. "It's fine. Really. I can't thank you enough for putting me up."

"I have to go to school today. Do you have to go to . . . uh, work?" I asked. What did you call what a Hooters waitress cum private investigator cum reality show participant did?

She stood and came over to the sink to wash out her coffee cup. "I have an assignment to finish for school, then a shift at the restaurant, and then I have to meet with Max and the other private investigators for an update on our latest case."

Wow, pretty busy. It made my day seem positively tame by comparison and I would probably have to run the Sister Mary, Father Dwyer, President Etheridge gauntlet at some point. "School?"

"Yep," she said, putting her coffee cup, now dry, back into the cabinet. "Getting a degree in criminal justice from John Jay."

So there was more to this young chicken wing server than met the eye. Good to know. "There are fresh towels in the upstairs hall closet. Make yourself at home," I said to this woman whom I had met less than twelve hours earlier. I knew more about my gynecologist, whom I only saw once every year or so, than I did about this woman who was now sharing my house. Max had given me no information beyond "she needs a place to stay," and I wisely did not press. With Max, it's better that way; the less you know, the better. "So, okay, well, bye," I said, not sure how one behaves around one's new roommate.

I arrived at school a little more than a half hour later and attempted to lie low, something that a nearly six-foot-tall woman with a miasma of messy hair can hardly pull off. I slunk into my office after exchanging a few benign words with Dottie about the weather — wisely avoiding any talk about her relationship with Charlie or any additional relationship advice — and settled in behind my desk. From my messenger bag, I took out the business card that I had been carrying around for the last few days and put it on my desk, smoothing down the edges. After a few minutes of manipulating the card between my fingers, I finally got up the courage to dial the number that was printed on the front.

John McVeigh, Mac the Medical Examiner, answered on the second ring, something I wasn't counting on. "ME's office. McVeigh speaking."

"Um, hi, Medical Examiner McVeigh." Was he a doctor? Or just a mister? I wasn't sure, so I went with his full title. "This is Alison Bergeron. We met the other day —"

"Of course! Alison! How are you?" he asked, full of good cheer.

"Well, I'm fine, thank you," I said, surprised that he had asked. He asked me why I was calling, and up until this moment, I had thought I would go straight to begging for the exhumation of Carter Wilmott's body, but on second thought, I went with a different tack. It hadn't occurred to me until just now that my implying that Carter had not died of what the ME said he had died of would be a wee bit uncomfortable for both of us. "I think I have some information that might be germane to the Wilmott case and I wanted to share it with you." The silence on the other end of the phone was deafening; obviously ME McVeigh was no dummy and could see where this was headed. "Hello?"

"Blunt force trauma to the head," he said dully.

"I know," I quickly amended. "That's what you said. That's probably what you even put on the certificate of death!" I said, much more cheerily than the circumstances would have required. "I actually just have a question. Regarding death. And stuff."

"And stuff?"

"Well, maybe not 'stuff,' per se, but other things." Nothing like sounding like a complete moron to solidify your credibility. "Can we have a cup of coffee?"

"I'd much prefer a scotch," he said.

"Okay! Then scotch it is. What does your schedule look like?"

"It looks like a spiral-bound notebook filled with monthly calendars."

I was stunned into silence until I realized he was joking. Not exactly gallows humor, but not exactly humor, either. "Oh, right. How is tonight? Say seven? I can meet you anywhere you'd like."

He asked me to meet him at an Irish pub in White Plains not far from his office and conveniently located across from a funeral home, an appropriate landmark when one was meeting the medical examiner for a drink. Until then, I had a few things to figure out, the first being what I was going to do now that I had a Hooters waitress as a roommate.

I called Crawford and gave him the update, leaving out the part where I was going on a first date with the ME and most of the stuff about Ginny Miller and her thoughts on poison. Crawford knew me well enough that that was just enough information to get me snooping around, and let's just say that he doesn't like that aspect of my personality.

"Wait," he said. "You're living with a Hooters waitress?" I heard him relay this information to Fred; they were in the car, riding to a homicide. "And she's a friend of Max?"

"You heard me, brother. Hooters waitress. In my house."

"Do you know anything about this person?"

"Only that she needs a place to stay."

"Oh, good. I feel so much better."

"She's a nice kid. She's getting a degree in criminal justice from John Jay."

"Sounds like a regular Mother Teresa."

Fred mumbled something in the background that I couldn't understand but it didn't matter; if Fred had been standing right next to me, chances are I wouldn't have been able to understand him, either. "I've gotta go. Call me later, okay?"

I hated deceiving Crawford but I hated him being mad at me more. I had tossed and turned all night wondering why I was helping Ginny Miller, a woman who up until last night had been my archenemy. But now I saw her for what she was: a lonely, kind of depressed middle-aged woman who had succumbed to the charms of a seemingly sophisticated — if you believed money gave you class, that is, which I didn't — and wealthy man. I didn't know a lot about the relationship but I had gleaned that much. And she seemed hell-bent on making amends and saving her marriage. I had to respect that. Albeit begrudgingly, given the way she had treated me.

And there was the added bonus of her having attended to my terminally ill mother in her last days. I had spent every day and night at the hospital for two weeks but was hard-pressed to remember any nurses or doctors whom I had met during that time, so overcome was I with grief and exhaustion. My mind wasn't my mind then; I was younger than I should have been while attending to a sick parent and it was all I could do to maintain my sanity in the midst of a horrific tragedy. My father had already died several years earlier. But I do remember that the people who had taken care of my mother had kept her comfortable, out of pain, and clean. They were angels who flitted in and did their work silently and without too much disturbance.

If Ginny Miller had been one of those angels, I was certainly in her debt.

The whole poisoning angle was an interesting twist. Although I had seen the guy die, who knew if he had died in the manner to which we all ascribed? What if he had been slowly poisoned? And by whom? It was a question that should be answered. Because if George Miller was innocent, then he shouldn't have to go to jail. That much was very clear to me and my inbred sense of social and moral justice.

It's a high horse but someone has to ride it.

The day went quickly, and when I had interviewed my last student, I hightailed it out of there. I was in White Plains, a city in Westchester where the ME's office was located and which also was the location of my rendezvous with ME McVeigh, in about twenty minutes. I found the bar easily and parked across the street in front of the funeral home.

Mac was at the bar, nursing an amber-colored liquid in a short glass that I assumed was his beloved scotch. He stood when I entered, and not knowing whether to give me a hug or shake my hand, he settled for a pat on the shoulder. "Hello, Ms. Bergeron."

"It's Alison." I slid onto the stool next to him and ordered a club soda.

"Not a drinker?" he asked.

"Not a drinker and a driver," I explained.

He nodded solemnly. "Good rule." He motioned to the bartender for another drink. "I can walk from here," he explained. Once it had been placed in front of him and he took a sip, he turned his full attention to me. "Now, remind me. Why are we here?" His blue eyes were sharp, but kind.

I spread my hands out on the bar and waited a few beats, trying to get the facts — or what I perceived to be the facts — straight in my head. "What would you say if I told you that I had information that led me to believe that Carter Wilmott died from poisoning rather than blunt force trauma?"

Mac studied his drink. "I thought you were a college professor."

"I am."

"So what makes you think that you know how to determine cause of death?"

"I don't." He waited for me to continue. "It's just that someone I know who was close to Carter seems to think that his symptoms prior to his death may link to poisoning. And this person would know."

"How?"

"They're a nurse."

"*She's* a nurse."

I was caught off guard and stammered a bit. How had he known that? Fifty-fifty guess?

Mac clinked his glass against mine. "Good luck, Ms. Bergeron. But stay away from Ginny Miller. She doesn't know what she's talking about." He swished his drink around in his glass. "The only reason I wanted to meet you in person was to implore you to stay away from her. I had a feeling she was behind this. She had already contacted someone in my office to express her concerns. But her delusions are dangerous."

So Ginny had already gotten to him; I wish she had mentioned that before I had invited him out under somewhat false pretenses. It didn't surprise me that she could get in touch with the ME; being a nurse, she probably had a lot of contacts on his staff. "What if she does know something?" I asked. "She said that you don't test for poisoning."

Mac sighed and looked up at the ceiling, as he was wont to do. "I'm telling you, if I had a dime for everyone that came and told me how somebody really died . . ."

He was exasperated but I could see that he was wavering, ever so slightly. "You don't test for poisoning, do you?"

He shook his head. "No." He shook his head again. "Blunt force trauma," he repeated, almost as if trying to convince himself.

I reached over and grabbed his arm. "I know that it will be a huge embarrassment if you have to revise your cause of death, but do you really want an innocent man to go to jail?"

He looked like he was going to signal for another drink but thought better of it. "Your eye looks better," he said, smiling.

"Don't change the subject," I said.

He sucked down the last of his second scotch. "Let me think about this."

I reached over and gave him a hug. "You're the best, Mac."

"You don't know that for a fact and I'm not promising anything." He stood and buttoned his blazer. He smoothed down the few strands of gray hair that covered his mostly bald pate. “I have to go. Reezie’s making pot roast. I’d ask you to join us but you’ve given me quite a headache and I think it would be best if we parted here while I still like you.”

“Thank you. But I have plans,” I lied.

“You teach at St. Thomas, right?” he asked before he left. He threw a ten and a twenty on the bar, a generous tipper, to say the least.

I nodded.

“My friend’s daughter went there. She’s around your age, maybe a little older. Lovely girl. Smart as a whip. Couldn’t do math to save her life.” He mentioned her name but I didn’t know her and by his description she could have been anyone; St. Thomas isn’t known for its math program. “I’ll be in touch, Alison.”

I watched him go, hands in his pockets, whistling as he walked down the street and out of sight. I believed he would be in touch. But I wasn’t so sure I would like what he had to say.

Twenty-Five

My first tip-off that things weren't going to be normal when I entered my house were the Crime TV production trucks parked at the curb. I drove up the driveway to the garage and parked the car, my hands gripping the steering wheel and my heart racing. I decided that if Max was inside the house, I was going to wring her neck. Then, I was going to mix myself a nice dry vodka martini.

First things first.

I went in through the back door; the house was a beehive of activity, and packed to the gills with strangers. I took in the three Crime TV crew members sitting at my kitchen table, devouring a pepperoni pizza. One, a young hipster-looking guy with long hair, threw a piece to Trixie, who happily jumped in the air to catch it in her mouth.

"Hey, chief," I said, grabbing the dog by the collar and pulling her away from the pizza. "I'll call you at midnight when she's throwing up pepperoni."

"Who are you?" hipster kid asked, shoving another slice of pizza into his mouth.

"Just the owner of the house," I said. I put the dog in the powder room in the hallway and walked into the living room where a bevy of Hooters waitresses had convened. I tripped over a large cable that transversed the area between the kitchen and the front door. There were lights, cameras, and microphones littered everywhere, and a technician on the stairs leading up to my second floor recording my every move. I slapped the camera out of his hand as if I were Sean Penn coming out of the Ivy in Hollywood. Max was in the living room holding court, instructing them on the next case, it seemed, while they sat in rapt attention. I was momentarily blinded by the preponderance of enormous breasts but managed not to appear gobsmacked. Or so I thought.

"We'll do a stakeout in front of the cheater's house," Max said. "Oh, hi, Alison!" she said, noticing me in the archway leading into the living room. "Everyone, this is Alison Bergeron, my best friend in the whole world and maybe the smartest person I know."

Flattery will get you nowhere. "Hi, everyone. Now get out."

Max was mid-sentence, giving the waitress/private investigators their next assignment, when she realized that hell hath no fury like a sexually frustrated college professor. She looked over at me. "Excuse me?"

"Out."

"We're having a meeting," she explained in her usual clueless fashion.

"I can see that," I said, using my supercilious polite tone. "But this is my house and I need to eat. And drink. And do some work. And generally live the life that I work so hard to have."

Max snorted. "We'll only be five more minutes." She seemed genuinely put out.

"No, you'll be gone now." I took in the doe-eyed stares of the Hooters gals, Queen among them. I pointed at her. "You can stay."

Max strode toward me, Tinker Bell in five-hundred-dollar shoes. "A word, please?"

We stood in the hallway, the camera guy training his lens on us. I turned my back on him, blocking his view. "What the hell is this?" I hissed.

"This is our preproduction meeting," Max said, as if it were the most apparent thing in the entire world. "We decided to have it here instead at the office because Queen has a lot of homework and a test to study for."

"Don't you think you should have asked me first?"

Max considered this and then made a decision. "No."

"No?"

"Queen lives here so it's kind of like her house and I didn't think you'd mind."

The cameraman was inches from my face and I gently pushed him away. "You were wrong. I'm going to take the dog for a walk. You have ten minutes to get everyone out of here. Got it?"

Max's look was a cross between sad and angry but she nodded her head dutifully. "Fine. We'll be gone in fifteen minutes."

"Ten." I turned and opened the powder room door, liberating a very grateful Trixie.

"I don't know if —"

"Ten!" I called back over my shoulder as I hooked Trixie's leash onto her collar and went out the back door into the blissful calm of my backyard. Good God, I thought, as I crossed the lawn and walked down the driveway, Trixie setting the pace. As a result, I was being dragged more than walking of my own accord. Nevertheless, I was relieved to be out of the house and on a quiet street in a suburban neighborhood and away from the prying eyes, and pendulous breasts, of a bunch of Hooters waitresses. Sorry. Make that "private investigators."

Although I tried not to, I replayed the events of the last several days in my mind, spending way too much time on thoughts of my mother and her untimely death at the age of forty-eight. Heck, I wasn't that far off from that myself. I had managed, for all of these years, to keep those emotions pressed down deep in my subconscious, thinking of her often but only focusing on the good times, when she was a raven-haired beauty with not a care in the world save her awkward, studious daughter and her place in the world. Goddamn Ginny Miller, I thought. As painful as it was to witness Carter Wilmott's death, it was way harder to sift through the emotional wreckage that was years of repressed grief over the loss of a woman whom I had treasured.

I didn't really owe Ginny anything but she had played her trump card and I had fallen for it. How could I not help the woman who had helped my mother pass from this world into the next? And how could I not help a man, George Miller, who was guilty of only a really bad temper but not manslaughter if Ginny's theory was proved? I had once been suspected of something I hadn't done and it was a very painful time. The helplessness that I felt then came rushing back to me now and gave me some insight into the hell in which George Miller resided.

I kept walking, thinking that if I gave myself enough time, I could just walk away from this whole mess completely.

But I know myself better than that. I couldn't. And I'm sure that's what Ginny was banking on. I'm nothing if not completely transparent.

My heart was heavy as I started back to the house, Trixie having been successful in her mission to mark her territory throughout the entire neighborhood. My feet hurt; I hadn't changed out of my high heels upon entering the house and I now had a little more sympathy for women who served hot wings and beer in platform shoes while running investigations. These women were to be lauded. I looked for signs of the Crime TV crew, but there were none. The trucks were gone, as was Max's bright red Mini Cooper. All that was left at the curb was a brown Honda Fit, parked at an angle, its front wheels resting on my lawn.

I ran up the driveway, the dog dragging me once again, and burst through the back door. Kevin was sitting at the kitchen table with Queen, the two of them deep in conversation. He looked at me with sad eyes.

"Is there any room at the inn?"

TWENTY-SIX

Technically, there was no room at the inn, but that didn't stop me from letting Kevin sleep on the couch. His family didn't really know what was going on with him so staying with one of them was out of the question for the foreseeable future, and he had overstayed his welcome with his "friend" from the seminary, a person about whom I needed more information. I went to bed, one Hooters waitress in the guest room on the futon, and one almost-defrocked priest in the living room on the couch.

Any more wayward souls coming into my life and I was moving into Crawford's, his "personal space" issues be damned. Yes, that's what a tampon in the medicine cabinet will get you: admonitions about personal space.

I left the house extra early the next morning, wanting to avoid giant breasts and "innocent until proven guilty" priests. I knew that Crawford had pulled a double shift and called him on the off chance that he might meet me for a coffee before he went home. I could tell, even over the phone, that he was dead tired but he agreed anyway, suggesting a Dunkin' Donuts midway between campus and his precinct. I was on my third Boston cream doughnut and second cup of coffee when he walked in.

"What's so important that it couldn't wait until the weekend?" he asked, settling his lanky frame into a small Dunkin' Donuts chair.

"Well, good morning to you, too!" I said. I realized, as I finished the remainder of my coffee, that I should have stopped at one cup; my heart was racing and I felt like I needed to run a marathon. What did they put in this stuff? Rocket fuel?

"No, seriously," he said. "I'm exhausted. What's going on?"

I filled him in on my new house guest while I had his attention.

"You're running out of room," he said in his usual cut-to-the-chase way.

"It's like a home for wayward waitresses and priests."

"They can't stay."

"And I can't throw them out," I said.

His look told me that he thought I could.

Rather than continue with this train of thought, I decided to go with the real reason I had asked him here.

"What do you know about poison?"

He pointed at my cup. "Only that that qualifies."

"I'm not kidding. Do you know anything about arsenic?"

"No. That's what we've got Crime Scene for."

"Are they chemists?"

"Some of them are." He looked around the store and decided he couldn't resist, I guess. He got up and ordered a large black coffee and a bagel with cream cheese. He carried both back to the table and started eating. "Where is this going?"

I told him about the Ginny Miller scenario, and my meeting with McVeigh. "I need to know about arsenic. How it is administered, how long it takes to act, how it kills you. Know anybody I can talk to?"

He put his head in his hands. "Why do you care?" he asked from underneath his palms.

I could feel the tears welling up before I even formulated an answer. "She took care of my mother, Crawford."

He took his hands off his face. "So what? That's her job. She's a nurse."

He was uncharacteristically short, not giving me the answer I was looking for. The minute he saw my face, he knew he had spoken too soon. He started to recant, but I closed my eyes and shook my head, attempting to silence him. "No. Don't say anything."

"I know a guy who knows a guy . . . anyway, I can help you with the arsenic thing."

"Forget it." Passive-aggressiveness is my stock-in-trade.

"Really. Just let me get six hours of shut-eye and I'll make a few calls." He passed a hand over his eyes. "I'm wiped out."

"Thanks, Crawford." This wasn't exactly how I had wanted our early-morning meeting to go; my decision to call him had been ill-advised at best. I gathered up my stuff, all crammed under my seat. "I've gotta go."

He grabbed my hand. "Do you think she may be using you? You know, for your connections and everything?"

"Oh, I know she's using me," I said, standing. "It's just that I remember . . ." I started and then revised what I was going to say. "I just remember what it was like to be suspected of something I didn't do." I decided a joke would make this encounter end better than it had started. "And George Miller is one heck of a DPW head. I wouldn't want to lose him."

Crawford smiled wearily. "Let me walk you out," he said, getting a bag for his bagel as we passed the crowded counter. Once outside, he put his arms around me. "It won't do me any good to ask you not to get involved, right?"

I shook my head. "Right."

He gave me a long hug and kissed me solidly on the lips. "Okay. Can I come over and meet the Hooters waitress tonight?"

"She's more than a Hooters waitress. Her name is Queen and she's a criminal justice major at John Jay."

"And a Hooters waitress . . ."

"And a Hooters waitress."

"So, can I?"

"Sure. As long as you know that you'll have to sleep with me, with my priest on the couch below us."

He looked up at the sky and sighed. "You don't make it easy." Crawford's got a healthy respect — bordering on the obsessive — for church authority.

"And that's why you love me," I said. He walked me to my car and made sure I was buckled in before walking away.

I didn't hear from Crawford for the rest of the day and I expected that he had slept longer than he had originally anticipated. He's a guy who needs his sleep and he doesn't get that much. He can go for long stretches without food and often does, but miss a night's sleep? The man turns into a beast. I didn't bother him and figured he would call me when he got up, got the information I needed, and was in a position to talk.

I wasn't looking forward to going home. My home was my haven. Just me, Trixie, and sometimes Crawford. Now I had Queen and Kevin and they were taking up a lot of space. Talk about your personal space being violated. Did I have to start cooking dinner every night? Do their laundry? What role, exactly, was I going to be playing in their lives besides providing a roof over their heads? I thought a house meeting might be in order to clarify our different roles.

But to my surprise, nobody was home. No Queen, no Kevin, and no Trixie. A note on the kitchen table written in Kevin's chicken scratch informed me that the trio had gone for a run down by the river and would return in about an hour with a pizza.

Maybe this roommate thing wouldn't be so bad after all.

I poured myself a glass of wine, kicked off my pumps, and settled in to watch television, relishing the quiet. I flicked through the channels, settling on the local news station, News47 Westchester, knowing that the weather report would be coming up. I don't know why but I'm obsessed with the following day's weather. Generally, News47 Westchester's meteorologist is wrong, and I'm usually not dressed appropriately as a result, but I always check. Someday, he'll get it right and I won't be wearing suede boots when the next monsoon hits.

With the exception of DPW chiefs who kill local bloggers, not too much goes on in the county. You have your usual drug busts, DUIs, and shady politicians, but as counties around New York go, it's generally a pretty safe place to live. That's why when something exciting happens, all hell breaks loose.

And hell was busting out all over.

I sat up when the "Breaking News" banner blasted onto the screen. Although overused as a notice, sometimes it represented really good, juicy, happening news. And today's interruption didn't disappoint. For when the banner rolled off the screen in a haze of red and purple, the News47 Westchester station colors, there was a woman, standing on the ledge of the highest part of the Tappan Zee Bridge, her hand gripping one of the iron beams that held the bridge together and aloft. I leaned in closer. Traffic was stopped in both directions and everyone from the bridge crew to the state police was gathered on both the north- and southbound lanes. The woman stayed on the ledge, her balance surprisingly good, as the wind whipped around her on her lofty perch.

The commentator was giving us viewers a blow-by-blow account of what had happened up until this moment. The woman had been driving in the northbound lane until she had suddenly pulled her car over in the right lane, causing a twelve-car accident, and climbed to the railing of the bridge where she had stood for the past hour, apparently contemplating her next move. Her next move seemed obvious to me: she was going to jump as soon as she got the courage. As usual with stories like this, I wondered what had her so distraught that she felt this was her only way out. I had been in many dark emotional places in my life but ending it all had never occurred to me.

The commentator was just about to throw the report back to the studio when the woman did just what I expected she would: she threw her arms out wide and executed a perfect swan dive, a beautiful sight if only the ending hadn't been preordained tragic. I grabbed my chest, horrified, and let out a strangled sound because as I watched this surreal and heartbreaking event unfold, I realized that I knew the woman.

And I knew why she had jumped.

Twenty-Seven

I was still staring at the television set when Queen, Kevin, and Trixie returned. I don't know why I was so upset; I hadn't known Ginny Miller well, but the shock of seeing her plunge to her death from the Tappan Zee Bridge was one of the more terrible things I had seen in my lifetime. News47 Westchester was going to have a lot of angry viewers; their viewership, for the most part, didn't tune in to see women fly off the railing of the bridge and into the choppy Hudson River. They tuned in to see crappy meteorologists give incorrect weather reports.

I had left the television on so I knew that although the state police had sent a police boat to the scene when Ginny was discovered on the bridge to hopefully fish her from the drink if she did jump, it had been an unnecessary measure. Because Ginny, she with all of her bad luck, had missed the river completely and jumped directly onto an old piling sticking out of the water, essentially breaking every bone in her body upon impact. She was dead instantly. Or so said the trembling News47 Westchester commentator, a young Hispanic woman who looked like she was suddenly considering a career change.

Trixie rushed over and licked my face. She was used to seeing me upset, but not like this. I'm usually hopping mad, not sobbing into a polyester-covered pillow. Queen and Kevin were alarmed, but after watching television for a few minutes, they ascertained what had happened. Kevin didn't know many of the details about the Carter Wilmott murder and Queen didn't know any. After gathering my wits about me and calming down, I filled them in.

Queen, not Kevin, made the sign of the cross at the news of Ginny's passing. Kevin let out an "oh, shit" that surprised Queen, but not me. Trixie gave a little woof in horror.

I stood up. "Why did she do it?"

Queen crossed her arms across her chest, ready to make her pronouncement. "Well, as a private investigator, in my professional opinion, I would have to say that that woman poisoned Carter Wilmott to death and jumped to her own death out of feelings of intense guilt."

Kevin took his glasses off and wiped the lenses between his T-shirt. "No shit, Sherlock," he said, striking a much more familiar, not to mention off-color, tone with Queen than I would have thought the last twenty-four hours of togetherness would have warranted. But I didn't have time to deal with that now. I needed to call Crawford.

He sounded groggy when he picked up. I skipped the greeting. "Ginny Miller just threw herself off the Tappan Zee Bridge."

"Huh?"

"You heard me. She's dead. She committed suicide. On television. I saw the whole thing."

"What channel?" he asked, now fully awake.

"News47 Westchester. You don't get that station. But I'm sure it will be on all of the local news stations shortly."

"Well, that solves that."

"Solves what?"

"The issue of the poisoning. She probably poisoned Wilmott and jumped because she felt guilty."

He's so smart he could be a Hooters waitress. "Or because she had had an affair with Carter. And maybe George found out. Or maybe because George is going to jail for a crime he didn't really commit."

"My head hurts."

"Mine does, too," I said. I looked at Queen and Kevin, who I noticed were now chowing down on a pizza at my dining room table, and were also helping themselves to a lovely cabernet that they had found in the wine rack that I had been saving for a special occasion. Heck, I guessed that now was as good a time as any and walked over to pour myself a glass before my freeloading roommates chugged the whole bottle themselves. I told Crawford to go back to bed or to at least stay in a reclining position and sat down at the dining room table. I was still in my work clothes and felt overdressed for this little gathering but proceeded to eat anyway.

Kevin and Queen eyed me as I sipped my wine and nibbled at my first slice of pizza, waiting for some outburst that wasn't going to come. I tried to put the pieces together in my head but kept coming back to the same conclusion that everyone had beat me to. Ginny had poisoned Carter and had tried to pin it on Lydia. Ginny was the nurse and the one who had the pharmacology background. If anyone had known how to kill someone by poisoning, it was Ginny, not Lydia, who had no discernible skills as far as I could tell besides being able to look gorgeous despite the situation. Had Ginny realized that nobody would believe her? When all was said and done, she felt guilty for killing Carter but only because it would have compromised George's freedom. She had loved her husband enough to not allow him to go to jail for a crime he didn't commit, but not enough to have remained faithful. She had found herself in quite a conundrum, it would seem. She had no way out, except for one.

I tried not to think of her hitting the piling and breaking into a million pieces internally. She was a pain in the ass, but a human being nonetheless, and one who had cared enough to see that my mother had had the most comfortable death she could have, under the circumstances. I didn't know how to feel. I left my pizza on my plate and excused myself from the table, the feelings of nausea returning.

Once in my room and under the covers, I thought about George Miller. Had he found out about Ginny's affair with Carter and had that been the origin of the fight at Beans, Beans? Ginny's death left more questions than answers and, like Crawford, my head hurt.

It was early in the evening, but I had been rendered useless by the hum of the window air conditioner combined with my exhaustion from being back at school after a summer break and from the events of the past week. I drifted off to sleep in my soft bed, thinking before I went into a full doze that I hoped I could stay asleep until the following morning.

It was only a few hours later that I felt the familiar shape of Crawford lying next to me, the warmth from his body bringing me comfort after a restless few hours of sleep. I burrowed into him and wrapped my arms around him, wondering if I was dreaming, but not really caring. It felt real enough.

I passed the night in a dreamless sleep, not waking until the telephone rang at the ungodly hour of six in the morning. Crawford was next to me and closer to the phone; he mumbled a greeting into the receiver before passing it over to me.

"I wanted you to hear this before anyone else." I recognized the gravelly voice of my friend Mac, the medical examiner. An apology for the early hour would have been nice, but obviously was not forthcoming.

"What's that?"

"You were right. Or should I say, 'she was

right.' " I heard him take a loud sip of something and mutter, "Jeez, burned my tongue."

I waited a beat before asking him again why he had called.

"Oh, Ginny Miller. She was right. Wilmott was poisoned." I could picture him looking at the ceiling, deep in thought. "Cause of death? Poisoning. By arsenic. A rather old method but a quite effective one."

I sat up straighter. Crawford, a champion sleeper, had already fallen into a coma and was missing the entire conversation, or at least my side of it. "Really?"

"Really."

"You know Ginny is dead, right?"

Mac chuckled. "Of course I do, Alison. She's already here. She arrived just after eight o'clock last night," he said, so casually that it seemed like she had kept a dinner reservation as opposed to a date with the autopsy table. "Okay, now I'm in a heap of trouble, so let me get back to work. Gotta figure out how I'm going to spin this one so I don't lose my job. Reezie doesn't have expensive tastes but she does like to eat."

"Thanks, Mac." I don't know why he had heeded my plea to look at Carter's tissue samples after ignoring Ginny, but I was glad that he did. George Miller was now a widower but at least he wasn't a guest of the state, as well.

"No problem," he said, adding before he bid me adieu, "I don't know why, but I like you. But I have to be honest, you are a giant pain in the ass."

"Thank you, I guess?"

"You're welcome."

I looked over at Crawford. This was an interesting but not unexpected turn of events. I leaned into his warm body again and fell back to sleep wondering if I would at least get a thank-you card from George Miller for all of my trouble.

Twenty-Eight

I didn't get a thank-you note for my trouble. What I did get was a citation from the police department for having cars parked in front of my house overnight and having obstructed the DPW's pickup on garbage day.

No good deed goes unpunished.

Kevin had done his usual ridiculously bad job of parallel-parking, and Crawford forgetting, I guess, that he wasn't responding to a homicide, had parked the wrong way on the wrong side of the street, facing east when he should have been facing west. Neither of them should have been parked on the street overnight but didn't use the sense God had given them to remember to pull into the driveway. When I reminded the two of them at breakfast that morning that they had broken a long-standing village parking rule, they both proclaimed their ignorance of village ordinance. I responded by throwing the citation, which had been found attached to my full garbage cans, between Kevin's bowl of oatmeal and Crawford's toast.

"You two can decide if you want to split this fifty-fifty or some other way." I grabbed a coffee mug from the cabinet and poured myself a cup. "I don't care. But I'm not paying it." I took a sip of coffee and noticed that we were a roommate short. "Where's Queen?"

Kevin shrugged. "Not sure. I think she's doing PI stuff. It's too early for Hooters to be open."

Crawford leaned into Kevin. "You've met her?"

"Of course. She's a lovely girl."

Dry spell or not, Crawford's insistence on meeting Queen was wearing thin. I told him to stick a sock in it.

"You're kind of mean," Kevin said, as if this thought had dawned on him for the first time.

"She is, right?" Crawford asked, shoving a piece of toast into his mouth and washing it down with coffee.

"Listen, you two. I've seen two people die in the space of a week and I'm not in the mood to listen to your opinions of me." I looked at Kevin. "Without me, I might remind you, you're homeless." I turned to Crawford but couldn't think of anything to say. Because without me, he would probably have a very calm and serene life.

Crawford got up to pour himself a cup of coffee, stopping on the way to kiss the top of my head. He stood at the coffee-maker and turned to look out the kitchen window. "Hey," he said, addressing Kevin. "Can you still do weddings?"

I gave him a look that telegraphed my reluctance to talk about the topic in front of Kevin, if at all.

"What?" he asked. "Just an innocent question. Hypothetical, really."

"We'll talk about this later," I said as pleasantly as I could. I thought the big, fake smile on my face should have given him some indication of the tone, but apparently, it didn't. He went sullen.

"Just wanted to know."

Kevin watched the two of us discuss whether or not it was appropriate to talk about the topic of our possibly impending nuptials in front of him, his head whipping back and forth depending on who was speaking. Kevin knew about the marriage talk; he had been with us when Crawford had popped the question in his straightforward way. When all was said and done, though, Crawford and I still needed to "close the deal" officially, and Kevin hadn't let us know if he could perform a Catholic wedding ceremony. My guess was no.

I had thought that since Crawford now knew the source of my reluctance, the conversation would have been toned down until at least after Labor Day. But homicide detectives ask the same question over and over and over again until they get the answer they want. Crawford, apparently, thought the same tactic would work in this situation.

"Hey, what's this?" he asked, picking up the arsenic rock that I had assumed Ginny had taken with her the other night but which was sitting on my kitchen counter. He picked it up and examined it.

"Put that down!" I exclaimed. "It's poison."

He dropped it on the counter and stepped back.

"That's the arsenic," I said. "I didn't realize it was still here. I should bring that over to Detective Madden."

Neither of the men debated me on that point, so it was just a mere forty minutes later that I was sitting in the same room where I had been the week before, toying with the rock — now in a plastic bag — and awaiting her entrance. She walked in a few minutes later, notebook in hand, and regarded me warily.

"You have some information for me?" She was crabbier than usual. It hadn't occurred to me until this very moment that she, like Mac the Knife, would be none too happy with the idea that the man she had arrested was not guilty of the crime and that she might look a wee bit vulnerable to her colleagues as a result.

I pushed the arsenic rock forward. She raised an eyebrow at me. "It's arsenic," I explained.

She picked up the bag. "Great. Thanks."

"It's probably the rock that Ginny Miller used to poison Carter Wilmott."

"Probably." Her expression was stony.

"Are you mad that it wasn't George Miller?"

She leaned on the table, her knuckles supporting her weight. "Listen. I'm happy when justice is served. I did not want an innocent man to go to jail, who may or may not be innocent of everything," she said, reminding me that we still had the issue of the explosive device on the engine to contend with. "But this," she said, pushing the plastic bag toward me, "is going to cause a whole lot of trouble for the department and the ME's office. Is that what you intended?"

I sputtered a little, caught off guard by

her outburst. "Well, no. But yes." I took a deep breath and composed myself. "I hope you're not insinuating that I should have kept this a secret."

"I'm not insinuating that at all."

"And are you completely sure that Ginny Miller was the one who was poisoning Carter Wilmott?"

Her look told me that that was a question I shouldn't have asked, but I wanted to know how they knew. It was my assumption that Ginny's suicide implied her guilt, but who knew? Carter's death had opened a Pandora's box of suspects from George to any one of the people he had maligned on the blog, including Tony and Lucia, not to mention Coffee Lover, who seemed really incensed that Wilmott didn't like Beans, Beans. Madden didn't want to answer but she did anyway. "Yes, I'm sure." She stood up straight and picked up the bag. "Good day, Ms. Bergeron." She walked toward the door and put her hand on the knob. "Make that 'good-bye,' Ms. Bergeron."

Sometimes I know when to take a hint and today was one of those times. I hightailed it out of there and made my way to school, sorry that I had any kind of civic or moral compass at all. "Leave the detecting to the detectives," I muttered to myself as I pulled into my reserved parking spot in the lot behind my building. It was something that I had been told over and over again, yet it had failed to sink into my brain as a reasonable course of action.

Dottie was reading a bodice ripper when I walked in. "Is that Fabio on the cover?" I asked.

She turned the book over and looked at the cover. "Maybe."

"I always thought he was kind of handsome," I said. As usual, my friendly attitude toward her made her suspicious and she kept her eyes on me as I collected the mail from my mailbox and shuffled through it while still standing at her desk. "So, how's Charlie?" I asked.

She slammed the book down on her desk and gave me a hard look. "Okay, so what is this about? Why are you being so nice to me? And why do you keep asking me about Charlie?"

It wasn't the first time I had misread a situation nor would it be the last. What I thought passed for innocent small talk had apparently raised Dottie's hackles. "It's nothing. I'm just curious about your relationship and how you keep it fresh after all these months of dating."

"Fresh?" She snickered. "What? Are you

watching Dr. Phil now?"

"What do you mean?"

"You don't talk like that. What gives?"

I leaned toward her desk and whispered. "Listen. It's like this. Crawford wants to get married and I'm not sure."

She leaned back and crossed her arms, happy to be in the role of relationship therapist. "Well, you were married to that cheating, lying asshole. I could see where you would have some issues."

Lady, I own the market on issues, I wanted to say, but I didn't. I was struck dumb by her perceptiveness. "Right! Issues!"

"After what you've been through, it would be hard to trust anyone."

"You're right again!"

"I understand what you're going through." Satisfied that she had correctly assessed the situation, she picked up her book.

"Wait!" I said. "What should I do?"

She gave me the same look I give my most challenged students. "You should marry him. What are you? A moron?"

Though shocked that she had decided to impugn my character while giving me advice, I decided that she was right, as was Crawford. He wasn't Ray and I wasn't making a mistake, and getting married again was a blessing, not the blind cliff jump that

I was making it out to be. I knew Crawford whereas I hadn't really known Ray. Dottie was right. I was a moron.

It all came down to one thing: I missed my mother. I had already gone through one wedding without her and the thought of going through another one gave me a palpable pain in my heart. Her advice the first time had been off the mark and borderline devastating. By telling me to marry a man I was ambivalent about at best, I know that she was just trying to protect me from a life of loneliness without my parents and without any siblings on whom to rely. It took me a few seconds to imagine what she would think of Crawford and decided that she would probably have been as much in love with him as I was. When I thought about it that way, it all made sense.

Mentally, at least, I had "closed the deal." When school was over for the day, I needed to make it official.

I started for my office, my head in a completely different place than it had been for the last several weeks. Although the pain of my mother's loss was still there, I felt lighter in spirit. My head did seem like it was in the clouds, which could be the only explanation I had for nearly colliding with Father Dwyer, also on his way to my office.

Any feelings of bonhomie that I had based on finally making up my mind were quickly squelched by the sight of our new chubby chaplain. He was dressed in full blacks — jacket, pants, clergy shirt, and black shoes. I rarely saw Kevin dressed like this so it was jarring to see Dwyer in full regalia.

"Hello, Father. Are you on your way to see me?" I asked. I opened the office door and motioned for him to go in before me.

"Age before beauty," he said, chuckling while waiting for me to precede him.

Okay, what does that mean? "Ladies first" might have been more appropriate under the circumstances, but from the little I knew about this guy, I wasn't surprised that he found himself more attractive than he found me. He settled into one of my guest chairs and took in the titles of some of the books on the shelves in my office.

"Lots of Joyce," he remarked.

"I'm a Joyce scholar," I said, resisting the urge to add "you idiot." But I was feeling generous and figured that the hundreds of volumes related to the Irish author were not a dead giveaway.

Dwyer surveyed my office, his eyes landing on a bumper sticker that was taped to the side of my filing cabinet: "If God was a woman, the world would have been created in two days and everything would have matched." The expression on his face told me that he didn't think it was funny. I decided not to tell him that it had been given to me by his predecessor, Kevin. He brought his eyes back to me, looking at me as if I had a huge piece of spinach in my teeth.

Just to be sure, I ran my tongue across my teeth. All good there. "What can I do for you, Father?"

"Nothing, really. I just wanted to meet with you and get to know you a little bit. I'm meeting with all the faculty members individually to see what role, if any, they can play in the liturgical events here at St. Thomas."

I held my hands up. "Whoa, there. Count me out. I'm not that good a Catholic to be involved in 'liturgical events,' " I said, giving him the old air quotes. I wasn't even sure what a liturgical event was. Did he mean Mass? If so, why didn't he just say that? Oh, right. He was a tool. I was meeting a lot of them lately.

He didn't look surprised. "That's another reason for my visit." I didn't respond. I already knew that I'd be in trouble for *(a)* not going to church and *(b)* admitting it in front of the overzealous school chaplain.

With Kevin, it was a “don’t ask, don’t tell” policy. With Dwyer, obviously, it was going to be much different. “It would be in the best interest of our students if they could witness, firsthand, the reevangelization of our faculty.”

Since many of the faculty members were already nuns, I could only surmise that he was talking about me. And Dorothy Koppell, biology teacher and my next-door office neighbor and a devoted practitioner of Wicca. Oh, and of course, Rabbi Schneckstein, who was a part-time faculty member in the religious studies department. But he wasn’t going to get Koppell and Schneckstein, so I was a reasonable target. I held his gaze. “What exactly are you asking me to do, Father?”

He was clear. “Go to Mass regularly. Attend Holy Day of Obligation Masses on campus when school is in session. Volunteer with our campus God Squad.”

I held up a hand and ticked a finger off for each request. Going to Mass regularly was a choice I had yet to make and I wasn’t going to have him dictate how often I would go. Same for Holy Days of Obligation. As for volunteering with the God Squad, spending thirty or so hours a week with teens and young adults was about all I could handle realistically. They were also an extremely conservative organization given to protesting things on campus that I supported wholeheartedly, like the Gay-Lesbian-Transgender Alliance. It seemed obvious: having me volunteer with the God Squad wouldn't be a good fit; was I the only person who thought so? I gave him a stern stare. "No. No. And no." Fortunately, his response was muted by the ringing of my office phone. I looked down and saw that it was a call from Westchester County based on the area code that flashed on my caller ID. I picked up the phone and asked the caller to hang on without bothering to find out who it was. I put my hand over the receiver and asked Father Dwyer if we were done.

"No, we're not done," he said.

"Actually, we are," I said, and opened the office door. "If you'll excuse me? I have to take this call."

Yes, I was going to burn in hell. But be pushed around by some puppet of Etheridge's? That wasn't going to happen. I sat back down behind my desk and picked up the phone. "Thank you for holding. This is Dr. Bergeron."

"Alison? This is Mac."

I had been expecting that the caller was a

student who had yet to arrive at school but who had a question about the curriculum. Never in my wildest dreams did I think I'd be having more contact with the county medical examiner. It had been my fervent hope and wish that I would never hear from him again, despite the fact that I found him charming. "Hello, Mac. What can I do for you?" A call from the ME never signaled good news, in my experience.

"This is highly irregular, to say the least," he started. "But what the hell? I'm already in a pile of shit, thanks to you and your sleuthing skills." He said it in the kindest way possible and I could picture the rueful smile on his face. "You can't share this with anyone. Got it?"

He sounded serious. "Got it."

"Here's the thing. Your friend Carter?"

"Not my friend."

"Just a figure of speech. Don't get your panties in a wad." He chuckled, presumably thinking about my panties and the uncomfortable wedgie that would result from them being in a wad. "Did you know that he had early-stage ALS?"

"ALS?"

"Lou Gehrig's disease. It's a degenerative disorder. Because we had missed the poisoning in the initial autopsy, I decided to go back and test the remaining tissue for every possible outcome. And I got ALS."

"I know what ALS is," I said.

"So you know that it is most probably fatal. And that before it is fatal, it's an extremely debilitating disease."

I did know that. I didn't know a lot about the disease, but I did know that it was one that caused much pain and discomfort before it took your life. "Why are you telling me this?"

He laughed. "Why? Because it's germane to the case. And nobody else who's involved seems to give a good goddamn about this new development, certainly not the village police for one. You seem more interested in what happened to Carter Wilmott than anyone else. I wanted to test a theory on you. Do you think that Wilmott could have poisoned himself? You know, to avoid what was ahead?"

I gave that some thought. I guessed it was possible, but probable? Not likely. I told Mac what I thought.

"I guess you're right. Although I wasn't a huge fan of Ginny Miller, I just didn't see 'killer' written on her face. Maybe I'm getting long in the tooth. Maybe I'm losing my edge," he said sadly.

"I don't think you are, Mac. It's just hard

to imagine anyone who saves lives for a living taking someone else's."

"True enough, Alison. When all was said and done, though, he was a goner, plain and simple. Despite everything that transpired. And that's just sad to me."

I bid him good-bye and hung up the phone. Maybe that had been her motive all along: she just didn't want Carter to suffer and had slowly poisoned him in the most humane way possible to spare him what lay ahead for him.

It didn't matter, ultimately. Two people were dead, and whether one of them had met his maker because the other had good, albeit twisted, intentions was no longer an issue.

Twenty-Nine

Queen and Kevin had whipped up a delicious dinner of linguine with clam sauce and it was waiting for me when I arrived home. The entire way home I had thought about Ginny's suicide and then Carter's terminal illness. It made me wonder, though. Was Carter's debilitating condition, as evidenced in the blog photos, from the poisoning or his disease? I eventually decided that I no longer cared, particularly if, like Mac said, no one else did. The case was closed and I could move on with things.

Like deciding how, where, and when I would be married.

I sat down at the dining room table with Kevin and Queen and dug into the linguine. "Hey, this is good! Who made this?"

Kevin, whose head was bowed over his plate in a silent grace, looked up. "It was a joint effort." He unfolded his napkin and put it on his plate. "And don't so sound surprised."

"I'm not," I said. "It's just that it tastes way better than anything I could make."

Queen sat in silence, picking at her dinner. Although we hadn't spent a lot of time together, even I was perceptive enough to discern that something was wrong. I asked her if there was something she wanted to talk about.

Kevin gave her a meaningful look but continued eating his dinner.

"What?" I asked. "What's going on?"

"I'm going to move back home," she said.

That didn't seem like bad news to me but I played along. "Back to your parents' home?" Without makeup, she looked young enough to still live at her childhood home so I assumed that she didn't have her own place. I also knew that you would have to work a lot of Hooters shifts to pay for your own apartment in this area.

"No, with my husband."

"You have a husband?" I blurted out, a piece of pasta leaving my mouth.

"And a dog," she added.

"A husband and a dog?" I asked. "Then why are you staying here?" I realized before the words were out of my mouth that that was a question that didn't need to be asked. If she could have stayed with her husband

(and her dog), she would have. She had to get out of her home for some reason, and I guessed that if she felt that she had to get out, the reason must have been pretty darn good. Kevin shot me a look that instructed me to shut up. I did so by forking some more linguine into my mouth. Trixie settled at my feet hoping for more pasta to fly from my mouth directly into hers.

Queen looked down, tracing the pattern on my everyday dishes with the point of her knife. "Things weren't so good there." She looked at Kevin. "But I talked to Father McManus and I decided that I need to go back."

I put my fork down. " 'Weren't so good' how?" When she didn't answer, I looked at Kevin. " 'Weren't so good' how?"

"That's for Queen to discuss with you. I can't say," Kevin said. Sometimes it really sucks having a priest for a friend; his vow of confidentiality usually gets in the way of providing necessary information.

Queen took a long drink from her wine-glass. "Sometimes Jake wasn't very nice to me . . ." she started.

Kevin threw a glance toward Queen's upper arm, and I noticed the blue-black marks of a handprint that stood out in bas relief against her cocoa-colored skin, which somehow I had missed before. Even if I had noticed, I probably would have attributed her bruises to her strenuous and dangerous work as a private investigator charged with kicking cheater ass. The long-sleeved sweat-shirt she had worn on the hot August night earlier should have been a dead giveaway, but as we've established, sometimes I'm dense. Without saying a word, Kevin told me exactly what I needed to know: this young woman was a victim of abuse and needed a place to stay. Max could have been more descriptive in her explanation of why she was leaving Queen here, but had chosen to remain mute on the topic. I hadn't needed to know everything, but just an idea of why she was homeless would have been helpful. Plus, how was I to know that the abuser wasn't out there looking for her and following her nightly to my humble abode? Just another thing to talk to Max about once I got through wringing her neck.

"Then you're not going back there," I interjected. "You'll stay here until you can get on your feet."

"I can't do that," she said. "I've overstayed my welcome already. And Jake's a really nice guy. He's just under a lot of stress."

Kevin was nervously tapping his knife against his plate and I reached across the table to silence him. Queen hadn't really revealed anything with her description of Jake but I had been around the block a few times; she didn't have to. She was living with an abuser and couldn't go back. That much was clear. "Listen, Queen," I said. "If I've learned one thing in my life, it's that men who don't handle stress well act out in a bunch of different ways. And they don't change. You need to move out until Jake gets some help."

"I have nowhere to go," she said, her eyes filling with tears. Trixie whimpered in sympathy.

It only took me a minute to arrive at the decision. "Then you'll stay here."

She shook her head sadly. "You know I can't. You live by yourself. You don't need me here. It was already getting tight with just me, and now you have one more person," she said and looked at Kevin. "Sorry, Father," she whispered. "There's no way we can make this work. Father needs the room more than I do."

She was right. I didn't know how long Kevin was going to stay and my allegiance was to him. And I wasn't in a position to put an addition on my house for displaced Hooters waitresses and AWOL priests. But I also knew that I wasn't letting her go back to stressed-out Jake and whatever he was capable of. There was just no way that was going to happen. I stared at the white wine swirling around in my glass and contemplated the situation. It only took me a second to figure out what I was going to do.

"I'll be back," I said, and pushed my chair away from the table. I stopped in the front hallway and pulled the big telephone book from the shelf in the closet, flipping until I found the number I was looking for. I recited the last four digits to myself as I climbed the stairs to my bedroom, the other digits being consistent for all local numbers. Once in my room, I dialed the number and settled back on my pillows while waiting for Lydia Wilmott to answer.

She was surprised to hear from me. "And I'm surprised to be calling you. But I need your help. Were you serious about the things that WIMP can do to help women in need of assistance in leaving abusers?"

"Of course I was," she said, sounding indignant. Apparently, my not accepting her help had been a slight and a blemish on our nonexistent relationship.

"Here's the thing," I said, and I outlined the situation with Queen. At the end of my recitation of the facts, Lydia was quiet, which led me to believe that perhaps she wasn't on board with what I had outlined. I knew she had a lot of money, so even if Queen didn't go through the whole WIMP thing, I figured I could blackmail Lydia into paying for her new apartment for at least a few months until she got on her feet. "Listen, you've two choices. One, you help me, no questions asked. Or two, I go to the police and finger Clark for assault and battery. Oh, and kidnapping," I added. "Don't forget the kidnapping."

That got her attention. "Of course I want to help your *friend,* Alison. I was just formulating a plan in my head," she said. Liar.

"And don't think this is a veiled request to help me, Lydia. I am not now, nor was I ever, an abused woman. This is for a friend who is young and really at a loss as to how to disengage from her situation."

"Fine."

"Good. Where do you want to meet?"

You could have blown me over with a feather when Lydia suggested Beans, Beans. She explained her choice. "Nobody will expect to see me there and anybody who does see me there will probably leave once I get there. I'm getting tired of the staring, Alison."

I hadn't been there in a few days and I was feeling guilty. I didn't think Lydia would ever want to go back there, but who was I to question her judgment? I thought of Greg and his doughy "guns" and decided that it was as good a place as any, as long as Lydia was comfortable with it. I went back downstairs and sat at the table. Kevin and Queen were still picking at their food. "We've got a plan," I said to Queen, and told her that come hell or high water, we were going to Beans, Beans tomorrow at five, her shift at Hooters or her filming of Dicks with Tits be damned.

She gave it a moment's thought. "Fortunately, I'm free," she said.

"Good," I said. "We'll get together tomorrow and work this whole thing out." I pointed my fork at her to get her full attention. "But listen to me. Executing this plan requires that you follow my directions. Do that and everything will be just fine." She blanched, knowing that that meant leaving her old life behind. "I'm not kidding, Queen. If Jake is as 'stressed out' as you claim, he's not going to be happy that you've left. But you need to get out. And get up again," I said, reciting WIMP's credo. Kevin looked at me as if I were crazy and I guess I was. "Now, who wants some more wine?"

THIRTY

I had reminded Queen about our meeting before I left for work in the morning just to be clear that this was an appointment she shouldn't miss. I also instructed her to leave the drag queen look at home but I wasn't sure she was going to follow my instructions. So I was pleasantly surprised when she walked through the door of Beans, Beans dressed in a denim skirt and a peasant top, small gold hoops in her ears. Her hair was pulled back in a ponytail and she had the freshly scrubbed look of a college coed rather than the slutty appearance of a waitress who exposed her cleavage for money. Apparently, some of her Hooters colleagues had gone to her apartment when Jake wasn't home and packed a few things for her, knowing that she wasn't returning there any time soon. Greg was happy to see us both, whispering to me that business had not been great since the incident of more than a week before, a fact that came as no surprise to me. He gave me a huge hug and offered me anything I wanted, on the house.

"That's not necessary, Greg," I said, pulling out a wrought-iron café chair and taking a seat across from Greg. I gave him our order: a black coffee for me and a café au lait for Queen. "And two muffins," I said. I was not immune to the siren song of predinner hunger pangs.

"Haven't seen you in a couple of days," Greg said, giving me a mirthless smile. He wiped his hands repeatedly on the long apron that was tied at his waist.

"I know. I've been busy with school. We're working seven days a week to get ready for the first day of classes," I explained. I looked around the store and saw that Queen and I were the only customers, an interesting fact given that Beans, Beans was the go-to place in town for the after-school crowd. I knew that Greg was right; business was down and Carter's death had everything to do with that. I introduced Queen to Greg. "Hey, did you hear the latest?" I asked.

He shrugged. "Depends what 'latest' you're talking about."

I lowered my voice even though there was nobody else in the coffee shop. "Carter Wilmott. Poisoned."

He didn't look surprised. "Yeah, I read that in the paper. What a shame."

"It was," I said. "But between that, and the exploding car, and the fight with George Miller, I'm starting to wonder exactly how many ways that guy was supposed to die."

"Good point." Greg shifted from one foot to the other. "Sounds like he was going to go that day one way or another."

"Heard anything new about the explosion or who might have caused it?" I asked.

Greg looked away quickly. "Not a word. You're right, though. He was destined to die that day."

I nodded. I kept the information about the ALS to myself. That was for public consumption when Mac and his cohorts decided that it was.

"I should warn you that the other person we're meeting is Lydia Wilmott," I said. I held my hands up. "Not my fault. She wanted to meet here."

Greg walked back to the counter area and prepared our drinks. After he came back and served me my coffee, he turned and gingerly placed Queen's café au lait in front of her. "Anything else?" he asked.

Queen reached out and grabbed Greg's arm and turned the wrist toward her. I leaned over and saw what she was looking at: a tattoo that said "USMC" and had a ring of stars surrounding what looked like a bird carrying an anchor. I didn't know where he had had it done, but I thought that the artist must have been loaded when he took the tattoo needle to the inside of Greg's wrist. It was possibly the worst tattoo I had ever seen, and working on a college campus, I see a lot of ink. "Are you in the marines, sir?"

Greg smiled. "I was."

"My dad, too," Queen said. "He's doing another eighteen months in the Middle East right now."

"God bless him," Greg said. "May he come home safe." He closed his eyes and offered a silent prayer, presumably to his homeboy, Jesus.

"Thank you." She blew on her coffee. "My mother ships out from Camp LeJeune in another week, too."

Greg looked chagrined. "That's a lot for a young girl like you to handle."

Queen shrugged. "It's okay. I grew up in the military so I'm used to it. They'll be back," she said brightly.

There was a lot more to Queen's story than met the eye. I looked toward the front door to see if I could spot Lydia, but the sidewalk in front of the store was empty.

Queen and Greg were still talking about the "Corps" and the lives they had led, he as a member and she as a child of marines. Before Greg walked back to the counter, Queen asked him what his favorite thing about the Corps was.

"Blowing things up," he said, laughing as he sauntered back to the counter to wait on the sole customer who had walked through the doors since we had arrived.

I froze in my chair, staring down into my coffee cup. But I didn't have time to work through all of the possibilities in my mind, now that I knew Greg was a marine in addition to a guy who liked to blow things up, before Lydia strolled in, the scent of some overpowering perfume announcing her arrival. She threw herself into a chair at our table as if she had lost control of her legs prior to her sitting down; she placed her giant, suitcaselike handbag on top of the table. I pushed the patent leather bag aside to make room for our muffins, which Greg deposited while giving Lydia a polite nod.

Lydia didn't take off her sunglasses, even after I made the introductions, so I couldn't tell what she was thinking, if anything. However, if I had to guess, Lydia knew exactly what I wanted and when, and my presence at this conversation wasn't needed.

I had given her just enough information on the phone to make clear what her role in this process was. I decided that I was on a "need to know" basis with Queen so I excused myself and went over to the counter to talk to Greg while the two women made plans to start Queen on a new path of self-sufficiency.

Greg had his head in the muffin case, assessing the freshness of what was in there. "The banana are still good," I said, taking a piece off the muffin I had bought and tasting it.

"Yeah, they're moist. They stay for a while." He pulled out a tray with lemon-poppy-seed muffins on it. "These always go first," he said, wrapping them in plastic. His day was almost over and it was time to begin closing down the shop. He handed me some plastic-wrapped corn muffins. "These are almost done. Want to take them home? You can toast them for breakfast and they'll still be good."

I was feeding two additional people now so I accepted the muffins. "Thanks."

He handed me a few more muffins in a paper bag. "Here. I hate to see food go to waste."

"I hope we're not keeping you," I said, accepting the bag.

"Nah," he said, pulling a large piece of Saran Wrap from the roll on the counter and placing it over the muffins he was going to try to sell the following day. "You take all the time you need."

I leaned on the counter and read the various advertisements and postcards that patrons had placed under the glass. "So you blew up things in the marines, huh?"

Greg stopped wiping the inside of the muffin case and looked at me through the glass. "Sometimes."

"Huh," I said, picking off pieces of my muffin.

Greg came out from behind the muffin case and stood up, looking down at me. His round chubby face, usually exhibiting a serene calm, looked just a wee bit tense. "Why do you find that interesting?" he asked.

"Oh, no reason," I said, the tone of my voice completely unconvincing, if I had to admit it.

Greg rested his forearms on the counter and leaned toward me. "I know what you're thinking, but you're way off," he said, a small smile on his lips.

"What am I thinking?" I asked.

He smiled wider. "Oh, I don't know. Maybe that Carter's car blowing up had something to do with me?"

I put my hands up in a gesture of surrender and started laughing. "Okay, you got me," I said. The exchange between the two of us had a modicum of tension to it so I tried to diffuse it a little with some humor. "That's *exactly* what I was thinking," I said, laughing harder.

Greg joined in with some loud guffaws, causing Lydia and Queen to turn our way to find out what was so funny. "That's rich!" he said.

"I know!" I said, still going along with the idea that this was just a preposterous conclusion to come to, even though everything pointed in the same direction. The nasty blog posts, the animosity between the two men, the vociferous "Coffee Lover" who commented on Carter's post and who may or may not have been Greg, the exploding car that certainly would have killed Carter had he not met his untimely demise right where I was currently standing. It was alternately completely plausible and completely ridiculous, considering who Greg was and what he stood for: peace, love, and understanding. I grabbed my midsection and laughed harder until I couldn't breathe. Was this what I had become? A suspicious meddler who saw everyone as a suspect, despite my history with them? I looked up at Greg and he was still chuckling a little bit while he was cleaning out his large coffee urn, muttering to himself about how "you people are crazy."

I finished my muffin and threw the wrapper in the silver bullet-shaped trash bin and walked back over to the table, where Lydia and Queen were finishing up their conversation. Lydia looked at me, her eyes still hidden behind the big black sunglasses.

"We're all set here, Alison," she said and stood. She took Queen's hand and promised her that the whole thing would be worked out within twenty-four hours.

I walked ahead with Lydia while Queen cleaned up the table. "Thank you, Lydia."

"You're welcome," she said. "I'm glad you called me."

"You didn't sound glad when you heard it was me."

She fingered the diamond necklace around her neck. "That's water under the bridge. I'm sorry that we misinterpreted your situation. My apologies on behalf of the group."

"Apology accepted." I held the door open for her. "I'm just glad that something good has come from this whole mess."

Although I couldn't see her eyes, I suspected that Lydia was crying. "Me, too," she said, and walked down the street toward the river.

THIRTY-ONE

I sent Queen back to the house armed with the big bag of muffins that Greg had given me. She and Lydia had a plan whereby she would stay in Lydia's guesthouse on the magnificent acreage of the Wilmott estate until they could find a suitable apartment for her. Hooters was in White Plains and John Jay was in the city, so Queen residing on Lydia's property was the perfect in-between point.

I took a spot on the opposite side of the street from Beans, Beans and waited for Greg to finish closing up. I had watched Lydia walk all the way to the river, and suspected that she had gone to the boat; her house was in the opposite direction, and I could still see her car, a silver Volvo station wagon, parked a few spots up from Greg's shop. Although the sun had begun its descent over the Palisades across the river, it was still muggy enough to cause my blouse to stick to my back, quite uncomfortably. I was under the awning of a boutique and, hopefully, not in sight of Greg from his vantage point in Beans, Beans.

Although I had played along with the "aren't we having fun?" conversation in which I basically accused Greg of trying to get rid of Carter by blowing him up and he denied it, I was still thinking about it. Because who better than someone who liked to blow things up blowing up their archenemy, aka Blogenstein, as Max liked to refer to him? But was it so obvious as to not hold any water? I decided that I wanted to see where this led, and although spending a little time shadowing Greg might not tell me anything, it also wouldn't make me late for dinner, so I had nothing to lose.

Greg was a townie and lived in the direction of Lydia's house, that is, away from the river. So I was shocked when he left the shop with a small bag under his arm and started for the river, just as Lydia had a few minutes earlier. I waited until he was almost out of sight before getting up from the bench and starting after him, staying on my side of the street. There was no way I was going to lose him unless he jumped in a cab, but cabs meandering down sleepy village streets on warm summer nights are fortunately in short supply.

Things got a bit more complicated when he started for the bridge that arched over the train tracks. I would have to follow directly behind him rather than from a safe distance across the street and I wondered how this was going to work out. I decided that if he saw me, I would lay blame on the beautiful night and my desire to spend some time at the river. It wasn't completely outside the realm of possibility, yet in case it hasn't been established thus far, I am a terrible liar. Which is why I try not to do it with any regularity.

We continued across the bridge, me a safe distance behind Greg. It was a little after six and there was still plenty of sunlight left in the day and dusk was at least two hours off. He finished his journey across the bridge and took a seat on one of the benches on the train station platform. I decided then and there that I wasn't going to follow him into New York City or up north toward Poughkeepsie, depending on which train he was waiting for. I stole into the ticket office and looked at the schedule, deciding that he was waiting for a New York City–bound train, one of which was on its way into the station in less than a minute. I watched him from the ticket window office, a man deep in reverie on a balmy night with seemingly not a care in the world.

The train screeched into the station and several rush-hour passengers disembarked, while a few got on to head south into New York City. Greg was not one of them. When the train had left the station, he was still sitting on the park bench, enjoying the view, the plastic bag in his hand.

I observed this curious behavior for another hour, while trains came and went, and when the sun had finally set completely over the mountains on the other side of the river, he got up. I left the ticket office and followed behind him, glad that it was dark and that he probably wouldn't be able to tell that I had been tailing him for the better part of two hours. He made his way down toward the river and the boat slips; I was close enough now to hear him whistling what sounded like "Bridge Over Troubled Water," by Simon and Garfunkel. He walked along the dock and finally arrived at his destination, which was surprising, to say the least.

He boarded *The Lydia*.

Not at all what I was expecting, but then again, not sure what I was expecting. I stood on the dock, watching the boat list to and fro, and waited for him to come out.

While the darkness had brought a drop in temperature, it also brought mosquitoes. Big, giant, nasty, bloodsucking mosquitoes. And I don't know what it is, but I'm one of those people to whom mosquitoes gravitate. Crawford could be sitting outside wearing a fructose bodysuit and he wouldn't get one bite. I, on the other hand, am descended upon like an open container of raspberry jelly at a picnic. As soon as I felt the first sting, I knew I was in trouble, but I had invested too much time in this surveillance operation to give up. I was going to see what was happening on board *The Lydia* if it was the last thing I did. Which, I was afraid to admit, it might have been, if my internal radar was any indication.

I couldn't not find out, though. It was too tempting, and too bizarre. The Greg that I had known all of these years as the affable coffee shop owner was different today. And that made me curious.

I had almost reached the boat when the door to the sleeping quarters opened and Lydia emerged. She took off her sunglasses when she reached the deck, realizing that she no longer needed them. It was pitch-black on the water, with only the lights from town and the small dock lights illuminating her way as she stepped off the boat. I jumped onto a boat closer to the end of the dock, praying that no one else was on board, and got on my stomach so she wouldn't see me, listening to her high-heeled sandals making a clicking sound on the wood as she got closer and then hit the pavement, making her way back up toward town. When I no longer heard the sound of her footsteps, I got up and returned to the dock, making my way toward *The Lydia.*

The boat was running, its engine making a loud clicking sound in idle mode. Greg appeared on the deck just as I stepped onto the boat, scaring both of us. He grabbed his chest. "Dude!"

"Oh, Greg, you scared me," I said, acting a little bit. Obviously I knew he was on the boat, but I had no idea that he would appear at that exact moment and scare the bejesus out of me. Surprised? Yes. Scared? No.

He looked around as if searching for someone else. "What are you doing here?" He crossed his arms over his chest. "I don't see you for over a week and then I see you two times in the same day. What are the chances of that happening?" His demeanor was old Greg: friendly, a little loopy, and nonthreatening. Maybe I had exaggerated the whole exchange in the coffee shop to be more sinister and loaded with innuendo?

He had a large screwdriver in his hand and I kept my eyes on it. "What are you doing on Lydia's boat?" I asked.

He held the screwdriver up and waved it in my direction. "Repairs."

"What kind of repairs?"

"What do you know about boats?"

"Why?"

"Because you'd have to have some knowledge of boats to understand exactly what I'm doing," he said. Although he was wearing a tool belt and could have stored the screwdriver in one of its handy pockets, he kept it in his hand.

"Why did you wait until dark to come on the boat?"

"Because Lydia asked me to wait. She wanted to spend some time here. It's the only place she can go to get away from everything. But the engine needs work and I came to fix it." He held up the screwdriver again. "What are you doing here, by the way?"

"Me?" I asked.

He pointed the screwdriver at me again. "Yeah. You." Although the screwdriver gave me pause, he was the same old goofy Greg right down to his old Birkenstock sandals, which he wore with white socks.

I decided not to go with my first choice: I think you wanted to blow Carter Wilmott up and that you had means, motive, and opportunity. I thought that might sound a tad impolite. So I went with my second choice. “Just out for a stroll.”

“On the dock?”

“Uh, yeah,” I said, backing up toward the edge of the boat, taking in the appointments of each boat tethered to a slip. None of them, as far as I could see, had a deep gash in their seats, like *The Lydia* did. I felt vaguely remorseful for bringing Trixie on the boat the week before.

Greg smiled. “Were you always playing Nancy Drew? Even as a kid?”

I laughed. “No. This is a recent development.”

“I can’t believe you thought that I would blow Carter up.”

I wasn’t sure where this was heading, so I played it casual. I waved my hand dismissively. “Oh, sorry, Greg. I don’t know which end is up anymore.”

He sank into one of the tufted benches, and put the screwdriver on the floor of the boat. “Me, neither,” he said, and put his head into his hands. “Having a guy die in your store is not the best thing for business, in case you couldn’t guess.” His voice was muffled. "I don't know what I'll do if I lose the store."

"You won't lose the store!" I said, now feeling guilty for having suspected him of murder. I rushed over and sat beside him, my arm on his back. The plastic bag was next to me and I put a hand on it to ascertain its contents. Not too mysterious — they were more of the almost-stale muffins that he had offered me from the case in the store. "It will take a couple of weeks to come back but —"

At this, he moaned.

"Or maybe not! Maybe people will start coming back sooner." I didn't think so, but it was worth a try, if just to get this hulking bear of a man to stop sobbing. "Maybe you should have some kind of event or something."

He wiped his hands across his face. "Maybe. What were you thinking?"

I wasn't really thinking anything so I came up with a couple of weak suggestions. "Maybe you could have Mrs. Brown's tap class come in and do a show?"

He looked at me as if this were the worst suggestion I could possibly have made. Mrs. Brown's tap class consisted of three octogenarians who insisted on wearing spandex, despite their advanced age and less-than-supple skin.

"Or have an art show," I said. "We've got tons of artists in the village just looking for a place to exhibit their art."

He looked like he was considering that. "I'll think about it." He sighed heavily. "First, I had Carter's horrible blog saying things about me and the store and then the bastard goes and dies there." He picked at a hole in his jeans. "The guy really wanted to see me fail."

"He was just a mean, angry guy, Greg," I said. "Everyone knows you have the best coffee in town." Except for Dunkin' Donuts, I thought, but I kept that to myself. Now I really had to go to Beans, Beans on a regular basis if only to single-handedly keep the guy in business and atone for my lies about his not-very-delicious coffee.

Greg looked up at the starlit sky and took a deep breath, changing the subject from failing coffee shops to the splendor of our environment. "I love being out here. I'm glad you take advantage of it, too." He looked back at me, his face calm and serene. "Not too many people stop to smell the roses. Know what I mean?"

I relaxed a little. We were on the same conversational path that we had been down a thousand times at Beans, Beans and it felt like old times before the two of us had seen a man die, and a car blow up, and a woman jump off a bridge. "I know what you mean. Life gets a little hairy." I swept my arm out, taking in the view. "And look at this view. How could you not walk around down here?"

Greg walked up a few steps to the steering wheel and fiddled with something on the control panel. The clicking of the engine morphed into a smooth rumble. "Isn't this a gorgeous boat?"

I moved back over to the bench that Trixie had ruined with her sharp nails, covering the wound in the seat with my butt. "It certainly is."

"I've got an idea," Greg said, and powered up the boat. The roar of the engine startled me and I jumped up from the torn seat.

"What are you doing?"

"Taking you," he said, pointing at me, "for a ride."

"No, thank you," I said, trying not to sound panicked, while opening up all of the bench seats to look for a life preserver. I found some twine, a deflated beach ball, and a few empty beer cans, but no flotation devices. I lurched forward a little bit as Greg eased the boat out of its slip and headed toward the middle of the river.

He turned around. "What's the matter? It's a gorgeous night."

"I'm sure Lydia doesn't want you sailing this thing, does she?"

"Of course she does!" he bellowed. "That's another reason she hired me. Nobody would ever take this baby out if it wasn't for me."

I headed down into the sleeping quarters, continuing my quest for a life preserver. In the room were two twin-sized beds with beautiful quilts, nautically themed, on top of them. In between the beds was a deep chest on top of which sat an alarm clock and some sailing magazines. I pulled open the drawer on the front of the chest and riffled around in it for something to keep me afloat in the unlikely event that we capsized. My terror at being on the water was unmatched by anything else; not being able to swim had put me in many a precarious position, not limited to an almost drowning at the Jersey Shore when I was sixteen. Although I had managed to get myself out of the river when Ginny had pushed me in, I wasn't sure that I'd be able to save myself if I happened to fall in the middle of the river, where the depths were far greater. I dug around in the cabinet, coming up with a few packages of M&M's

— which I promptly stuck in my pocket for later — and an envelope out of which fell the most disturbing pictures of the relationship between Ginny Miller and Carter Wilmott that I could possibly see.

"What are you doing down there?" I heard Greg bellow from above me.

"Nothing!" I bellowed back, throwing the envelope across the room as if it were a hot iron that I had picked up in error. The pictures flew from the envelope and scattered across every flat surface. I sat on the bed and put my head between my legs. Between my panic at being brought out to the middle of the river and seeing what could only be described as extremely unpleasant amateur shots of a sexual nature, I was feeling queasy. The boat continued its steady path toward the deeper part of the river, a competent Greg at the helm.

If Ginny Miller had thought that the photos that Carter had posted on his Web site were incriminating and unflattering, they had nothing on this set of prints. Seems that *The Lydia* did more than sail; the boat also provided the trysting spot for Carter and Ginny, whose naked body was prominently featured in every single photo.

I don't know how long I sat but at some point during that time, I realized that there was only one reason that Ginny Miller had been on *The Lydia* and it was to find those pictures, something that she was unable to accomplish before her death. She had lied to me about her original intent but that didn't matter. She had found the arsenic . . . or had she? Had the arsenic already been in her possession? One thing I did know was that George Miller was never going to see those pictures if I had anything to say about it. I picked them all up and shoved them in the back of my waistband, thinking that we would have a bonfire later this evening when I was home and in the pleasant company of Kevin and Queen.

Greg appeared in the doorway of the cabin just as I had finished shoving the pictures into my underwear. "What are you doing?"

"I'm looking for a life preserver," I said. And that was the truth. I just hadn't been successful in my quest and I had come across a set of photographs that would require me to gouge my eyes out when I returned home.

He opened a door in the floor that I hadn't noticed and pulled out a bright orange flotation device. He tossed it to me. "Why do you want a life preserver? Planning on going for a swim?"

I grabbed the life preserver and held it in

my hand. "I can't swim."

"Dude! Really?"

Why does this shock everyone so much? So I can't swim. It's not a skill that's required on a regular basis and it certainly is one that you can avoid having to do if you're smart and prepare ahead. I got a little indignant. "No. I can't swim," I said, starting for the stairs. I pulled the life preserver over my head. "You got a problem with that?"

Greg followed me back up to the main deck. "No. It's just surprising. You look like someone who'd be able to swim."

"And what does someone who'd be able to swim look like?"

"Like you. Tall. In pretty good shape." He walked back up to the steering wheel. "Broad shoulders."

"Let's end this conversation before I have to kill you," I said. "Can we go back now? I don't want to go for a ride."

"This is really freaking you out?"

"Yes. It's really freaking me out. Please, can we go back?"

He fiddled with some dials on the dashboard and turned around. "You got it." He smiled, something that he had done a lot since I had boarded the boat and which had put me at ease. "Sheesh — you see a guy die of arsenic poisoning in my shop and you don't freak out, but we go for a little boat ride and you become a complete mental case."

"Wait," I said before I could think. "Arsenic?"

"Yeah," Greg said casually.

A pregnant beat hung heavy in the air, both of us realizing at the same time that there had been no mention in the paper about exactly what kind of poison had been used to kill Carter. Greg looked down at me, and seemed to read my mind, which wasn't hard; I don't have much of a poker face. "Hey, let's continue the ride," he said cheerily.

My fencing skills were going to come in really handy now, I thought, as I watched the twinkling lights of the village fade. As were my scrapbooking abilities. That was another class that I had been subjected to by my mother, her hope being that I would meet other nice nerdy girls with similar interests. I looked over the side of the boat and stared into the murky depths of the Hudson, trying to judge exactly how far we were from shore and how deep the water was. I pulled the straps of the life preserver around my body and attempted to tighten them. No luck. It was so dark that I couldn't see what I was doing, and it became immediately apparent that whoever had worn it prior to me had the circumference of a three-year-old. The straps wouldn't come all the way around and they wouldn't reach the buckles in which they needed to be inserted.

From his perch, I heard Greg muttering. "Gosh, dude, I wish you hadn't followed me."

"You poisoned him," I said. I continued to fiddle with the straps, my fingers shaking.

Greg looked at me, still in front of the steering wheel, sad.

"God, Greg! What were you thinking?" I asked. I hugged the life preserver, my arms wrapped tightly across its puffed front.

"That guy ruined me!" he said, taking a step away from the steering wheel and closer to me. "Have you read any of the shit he posted on his blog? Every week, the same thing. And still he had the nerve to come into Beans, Beans every day! Like nothing had ever happened between us. It was all I could do not to kill him with my bare hands."

"So you poisoned him."

"So I poisoned him! I didn't mean to kill him," he protested. "I just wanted to make him sick. To keep him away."

"If that's the case, Greg, he'd be writing about how Beans, Beans made him sick. And you'd still be out of business." I thought it necessary to point that out. That turned out to be a giant miscalculation on my part. Greg exploded.

"Do you know how long it took me to save up enough money to open that place? It might seem like a shit hole to you, but to me, it's everything! And because of that bastard, I've lost everything! I can't pay my rent, I can't pay my vendors . . ." He looked at me closely, his face grim. "And now, dude, I can't serve you coffee."

Which, to me, was code for "And now, dude, I have to kill you," because the look of sadness on Greg's face just barely masked the rage beneath. He stepped all the way down the stairs and in one deft, strong motion pulled the life preserver over my head, tossing it to the other end of the boat.

"It all makes sense now. The nasty blog posts, the comments from Coffee Lover . . . Greg, you need to turn yourself in."

He stopped walking toward me, a few feet separating us. "You know, I'd heard things about you. That you were nosy. Even a little crazy. Too smart for your own good. But I didn't believe them because I've always liked you, Alison." He frowned. "But now I'm not so sure. I'm disappointed, dude."

"Yeah, me, too," I said. "I never pegged you for someone who could kill."

"I'm not," he said.

"Yeah, well, what about the poisoning?" I asked. I swatted at a mosquito who was dining on my cheek.

"I already told you. I never meant to kill him."

I didn't know whether to believe him or not. He certainly seemed sincere but Lord knows I've been wrong before, reading a situation completely incorrectly and finding myself in a heap of trouble. I had known Greg in a casual capacity for several years and had never gotten the vibe that he was anything but an aging hippie who made terrible coffee and who didn't have great business sense, based on some of his promotional activities. The Prostate Awareness Month promotion had been a huge disaster, what with its promise of providing men over fifty free blood tests and a free cup of coffee to make sure their PSA levels weren't too high. Overzealous phlebotomists had lined the streets trying to entice older gentlemen into the store. I hope he had learned, like I did, that men didn't want to think about their prostates when a cup of coffee was all they desired.

"How many ways can a man die?" I asked. I was thinking out loud. "Carter Wilmott had a lot of strikes against him and he was going to die one way or the other. He had a terminal illness —"

"He did?"

I nodded. "And then there was the car that was destined to blow up, coupled with the fight," I said, making my way closer to Greg as I began to exit the vessel. "And finally, the poisoning."

Even in the faded light, I saw Greg's face change and it was then that I knew what was going to happen next.

Thirty-Two

Dying turned out to be not quite as dramatic as I would have thought.

Greg, a lumbering six foot five — and, if I had to guess, a good two hundred and eighty pounds — would have been the perfect person to save me if my house was on fire. He threw me over his shoulder, obviously accustomed to executing this move in far more dangerous and desperate situations, situations that required immediate and courageous action. But in this case, his intent was not quite so courageous, and as he attempted to hoist me over the side of the boat, me screaming bloody murder the entire time, he was muttering what sounded like some kind of prayer of contrition. In Hebrew, no less. Either that, or he was counting the Hebrew alphabet until he could throw me overboard. I kicked him and clawed at his face, not really making any headway in harming him before he tossed me overboard. He finally released me and I only had about three seconds to hold my breath before I realized that this was the end and that I was powerless to stop it.

I entered the water and now knew what it meant to hit something like "a ton of bricks." My descent wasn't pretty or especially graceful. I didn't know what hurt worse: the feeling in my chest from doing a complete belly flop or the icy sting on my skin from water that should have been a lot warmer considering it was the end of the summer. Either way, it was damn uncomfortable, so uncomfortable, in fact, that I didn't even register that I was drowning.

I sank deep beneath the surface of the water, watching the twinkling lights of the village and the dock become less defined and take on a golden glow the lower I went in the brown water. As I sank, I became aware that we weren't as far from shore as I would have thought and, for some reason, this gave me comfort. Would my lifeless body be found sooner as a result? The water was deeper than I had imagined it would be and I sank like a stone, trying not to flail too much and exert too much energy. My dress pants, which had felt like the appropriate weight for wear on a summer day, were now heavy and weighing me down, along with the light linen shirt that I had donned that morning. My shoes, lovely black pumps, were gone, having fallen off somewhere between being flung into the river and my rapid descent. They were lost to the watery depths of the Hudson, never to be seen again.

The pictures of Ginny Miller and Carter Wilmott, in flagrante delicto, floated out from my waistband and away from me, lost forever to the dark depths of the Hudson River. In all probability, George Miller would never learn of Ginny's infidelity. Too bad Ginny and I both had to die in order to protect her secret.

As I continued to sink, I observed Greg's blurry face looking down at me from above, obviously not concerned at all that I was going to drown. After a few seconds, he turned and walked away, and it was then that I began to panic. The flailing began as I tried to hold my breath, even as I knew my lungs were close to bursting.

I thought about my mother, and if I hadn't already been completely soaked, I would have begun to cry. A deep sadness welled up in me as I thought about how I had been manipulated by Ginny into helping her, not really knowing if she had attended to my mother during her illness or not. Maybe she had. Or maybe she had just used that information, easy enough to find out if one had access to hospital records and online obituaries, to make me feel sympathetic toward her. I had gone along with the whole thing, using my heart instead of my head, a sure recipe for disaster, particularly in this instance. My mother's beautiful face appeared in front of me, the picture of health. I relaxed, filled with a kind of peace that I had never experienced in my life. The flailing stopped and I allowed myself to drift along in the dark waters of the river, not feeling the cold, not feeling the pain. I continued my slow descent to the bottom of the river.

My happiest memories of my mother flooded my mind — the summers we spent in Baie Ste. Paul together visiting family; the day she let me drive the car by myself the first time; the time she brought home my puppy, Coco, and presented her to me on my birthday. How she used to say *"je t'aime . . . je t'aime . . . je t'aime . . ."* exactly three times as she kissed my forehead every night before I went to sleep. And how, at the end, she was more concerned about me than she was about herself. I wondered if this was how she felt when her time was short, wrapped in the warm embrace of a death that came too soon and not soon enough.

She offered me her hand.

"Just relax and stay still. I'll help you," I heard just before blacking out.

Thirty-Three

Throwing up river water is so incredibly vile that words cannot describe it.

I awoke to find Queen practically kneeling on my chest, her hands crossed one over the other, pumping strenuously. I struggled to get up but only succeeded in retching all over the dock and myself.

"Stay down," she said, taking her hands off my chest and moving them to my shoulders.

I did what she said and hoped that by remaining prone on the dock, I wouldn't have to throw up any more water. In the distance, I heard sirens.

"Where's Greg?" I asked.

Queen smiled and hooked a thumb over her shoulder. "He's on the boat," she said. She wiped a clump of hair away from my forehead. "Don't worry about him."

In the distance, I could hear a low growl followed by a few short angry barks. I stayed flat on my back for a few minutes and listened to what was taking place around me. I closed my eyes and drifted off.

When I came to again, I was in a darkened hospital room. The décor of the rooms hadn't changed that much since my mother had taken her last breaths here. At the end of the bed, I could see Crawford's lanky frame, outlined in the glow from the fluorescent night-light that was lit beneath the shelf that housed the television. I let out a little croak and got his attention.

I grabbed my throat. "My throat hurts."

He came over and sat on the edge of the bed, leaning over to kiss my head. "When were you going to tell me that you can't swim?"

"Never, if I could help it," I said. I coughed, clearing whatever it was that was preventing me from speaking clearly.

He gave me his patented "sad face," the one that's reserved for next of kin. "We're going to have to fix that."

"Let me guess," I said, my voice getting stronger. "You swam for your high school team in addition to being the star center of the basketball team."

"Not quite," he said. "But I do know how to swim."

"Good for you." I sat up a little straighter

in the bed. "I can't ice-skate, either."

"Me, neither."

"Good. Finally, something we have in common," I said. I leaned forward to pick up a cup of ice water on the tray next to the bed and took a long sip. "What happened?"

"Your friend Greg poisoned Carter Wilmott," Crawford said. Alerted by Queen, the other members of the village boating association, or whatever they called themselves, had detained Greg until the police had arrived. He was already in custody, and judging from the information Crawford had, spilling his guts.

"I got that impression when he confessed and subsequently threw me overboard."

"He was putting arsenic in his coffee, slowly poisoning him over time. Not sure how long this had been going on, but long enough to kill the poor bastard." He rubbed his hands over his eyes.

"So he didn't want to blow him up?" I wondered aloud if the explosive device was an insurance policy that Greg had also masterminded to make sure the job was done thoroughly.

He shook his head. "Nope. And he didn't want to poison him to death, either. According to what I heard, he only wanted to make Carter sick, not kill him. Apparently he went a little overboard on the arsenic, which slowly built up in Carter's system. I didn't get much information from Detective Madden other than what I just told you." He smiled. "I don't know why but that lady just doesn't like me."

"How did I get out of the water?"

He let out a belly laugh. "You're never going to believe this part."

"Try me."

"Queen."

"My Queen? Hooters waitress cum private investigator? My roommate, Queen?"

Crawford explained that Queen had followed me while I was following Greg. Ostensibly, she had been walking Trixie. But she had been around me long enough and had gotten enough information about me from Kevin to know that I'm a giant nosey parker and that when I didn't want to come home, something was up. Being a good private investigator, she wanted in on the action. She went home and got Trixie, then stayed just far enough behind me so that I didn't know she was following me but close enough to know that I was in trouble when I hit the water.

In addition to being a great waitress and a very astute sleuth, Queen Martinez had been captain of her swim team at Our Lady of Lourdes High School and had supplemented her high school income by working as a lifeguard at a tony hotel in New York City during her summers off. Queen Martinez, it would seem, had lousy taste in men but a varied and interesting résumé that was going to serve her well, I imagined, as her life progressed. One thing was for sure: she would always be able to support herself with that kind of skill set.

She had commandeered a boat at the dock from a young guy who was cleaning the decks. They had followed us out, and when it appeared that my life was in danger and that I obviously couldn't swim, she jumped in and saved me. I thought about the voice that I had heard right before I passed out and wondered whose it had been: my mother's or Queen's?

"I don't have to give her free room and board for the rest of her life because she saved mine, do I?" I asked.

Crawford took my face in his hands and smiled. "I don't think so." He planted a kiss on my lips. "Yum. River water."

I took a deep breath and felt the pain of a classic belly flop. "Is my not being able to swim a deal breaker?" I finished the water in my cup and handed it back to him.

"A deal breaker?"

"Yeah. Are we still 'on'?" I asked.

"Yeah. We're still on," he said. "Is that a yes?"

I smiled and closed my eyes, exhausted. "It's a yes."

"Is that what you want?" he asked, just to be sure.

I smiled and nodded. Yes, that's what I wanted. I drifted off to sleep thinking that everything I've ever wanted, I already had.

Thirty-Four

Queen moved out of my house and into the guesthouse on the Wilmott property on the Saturday before the Labor Day weekend. Kevin moved in with his brother Jack, he of the spectacular teeth and most excellent kisses (not that I remembered). I still didn't know what was going on with Kevin, specifically, and he wasn't offering up any new information. So I just let it be. When the time was right, he would let me in on the big secret. Until then, we had an unspoken agreement that we would still be friends, but that I wouldn't ask any questions.

I was returning to school full-time on the Tuesday after the holiday weekend and was relieved to have my house back to myself, just me and Trixie and Crawford, when we could get him. People were getting murdered left and right in his precinct, and he was busy.

Since my unfortunate dip in the Hudson,

I had learned a few things. Greg was standing by his original assertion that he only wanted to make Carter sick, not kill him. But kill him he did. Carter, despite his rantings about Greg and Beans, Beans on his blog, was a regular at the coffee shop, ballsy bastard that he was, so it seemed that he was getting a steady diet of French roast with a healthy serving of arsenic every time he frequented the shop. Mac the Knife was sticking to his cause of death as poisoning, and Greg was going away for a long time. Mac had also called me to find out if Crawford and I could come over for dinner after the semester started. Reezie was making beef Stroganoff.

There was a troubling aspect to the whole story, however, and that was that nobody really knew whether or not Greg was poisoning Carter's coffee specifically or just poisoning the whole entire lot of us. I thought back to how sick I had felt and how my health had improved once I stopped frequenting Greg's. Several other patrons reported feeling sick as well, but the district attorney couldn't decide if it was a case of mass hysteria or the truth. Enough time had passed that there was no way to know from any blood tests or such whether or not we had started on a dark journey just by drinking Greg's crappy, and poisonous, brew. I had watched Greg clean out the coffee urn the night that I had followed him to the river and he was pretty thorough so it was unlikely that we'd ever find out what the true story was.

All I knew was that I was grinding my own beans from now on.

As to who had wanted to blow Carter to smithereens, no one knew. I thought back to Tony and his Korean War exploits but decided that I would keep them to myself. The list of potential suspects was so extensive that I expected that Detective Madden would be busy for a long, long time.

Kathy and Jane popped in on Saturday to check on me and to say good-bye to Kevin and Queen, who interestingly, and not surprisingly, had become more a part of the neighborhood in the several days they had lived with me than I had in the many years I had resided there. They were disappointed to find out that both were gone, but they were glad they would see Queen in town, given the proximity of her new dwelling to our neighborhood.

I was out back, playing tug-of-war with Trixie, when they came up the driveway. They wrapped their arms around me at the same time and Trixie joined in, the warmest group hug that I had ever experienced. When we separated, Jane held me at arm's length.

"You don't look any worse for wear," she said. "And listen, we're going to teach you to swim."

Kathy did a dry-land American crawl. "Really. How do you get this far in life and not know how to swim?"

I shrugged. "Don't know. But I can fence. And I can make a wicked scrapbook."

Kathy snorted. "And that's going to help you a lot. Seriously, sister, we've got to get you into the pool."

"Deal," I said, starting for the house. "And I'll teach you how to order off a French menu without sounding like a foreigner. That'll come in handy if the two of you ever get to Paris."

"You're on. Paris has always been a dream of mine," Kathy said.

We took seats around my patio table, Trixie resting at my feet, thankful that it was just the two of us again. Although she got walked more than she ever had while we had Queen and Kevin around, when it came down to it, she wanted to be with me and me alone. She wasn't all that enthusiastic about house guests, with the exception of Crawford. And that's only because he fed her steak when he thought I wasn't looking. I knew what went on; I just pretended not to notice.

I served Kathy and Jane some wine and made a plate of cheese and crackers to nosh on while we visited. We finished one bottle of sauvignon blanc and started a bottle of Sancerre. After a couple of glasses of wine, I finally got the courage to ask Kathy and Jane the question that had been niggling at me since we had last been together.

"Why are you so negative about Lydia Wilmott?" I asked Kathy.

Jane shot her a look that transmitted her discomfort with this conversation. Kathy ignored her, emboldened by the white wine or tired of staying silent on the subject.

Kathy looked at Jane. "You know I'm conflicted about this," she said to her. Jane looked down. "If it wasn't for Lydia and her crackpot ideas, we wouldn't be together." Kathy turned to me. "It's like this. Lydia did the same number on Jane as she did on you, thinking that Jane's complaints about her ex, Stu, were veiled hints at abuse. She's the one that convinced Jane to get out of the marriage, thinking that Jane's well-being was at stake. But Jane wasn't abused. She was gay. And Lydia misread the entire situation, just like she did with you, and created all of this conflict where there was none."

Jane was silent, staring into her wineglass.

"You just didn't know who you were when you married him," Kathy said softly, putting a hand on Jane's knee. It sounded as if they had had this conversation many times before and it wasn't a pleasant one. "I like Stu. He's a good guy. Actually, he's a great guy. He just had the unfortunate luck to marry a gay woman who befriended a woman who did everything in her power to make him seem like a really bad guy." Kathy squeezed Jane's hand. "Listen, if I were straight, I would have fallen for the guy. He's handsome, he's smart, and he makes a lot of money," she said, laughing at the last part of her description. "But he's not an abuser. And Lydia caused a lot of trouble for him unnecessarily, making him have to deny something that he never did." She looked at me intently. "Stu's my friend, believe it or not. We have a weekly tennis game. I don't think I can forgive her for trying to ruin his reputation."

Kathy was very invested in Stu's reputation and it was obviously a subject she felt passionately about. I changed the subject to the rescheduling of Jimmy Crawford's pool party and got their input on the appropriate dress for the meet and greet with all of the Crawfords, which would happen eventually. Jane — who suggested that I wear a sundress — was more helpful than Kathy, who suggested wearing a bathing suit under a terry-cloth cover-up.

"Thank you," I said. "You have been little to no help at all. First of all, I don't own a sundress, and second, I would no sooner be caught dead in a terry-cloth cover-up than a tube top. But thank you for your input."

They left after the second bottle of wine was finished and all that was left of the cheese and cracker platter was the rind of the Jarlsberg that I had served. I cleaned up and, seeing that it was just a little before five, decided that I would go over to Lydia's to thank her for setting Queen up in what was a very nice guesthouse with a hint of a river view outside of the bedroom window.

Let bygones be bygones.

I drove over to the Wilmotts and bypassed the house, opting to park in front of Queen's little guest cottage so I could check in with her to see if she needed anything. She was already in possession of the futon from my guest room, until she was able to buy a bed, and a set of old china from my mother's family that I didn't think I'd ever part with but whose pattern I hated nonetheless. I figured my mother wouldn't mind; giving the china to Queen was what my colleague Rabbi Schneckstein would call a "mitzvah." The house was a miniature replica of the big Wilmott Colonial, down to the boxes filled with flowers that hung in front of the leaded windows. Queen opened the door. When she saw me, she grabbed me by the arm and pulled me into the small living room.

I objected loudly to being manhandled and she put her hand over my mouth. "Be quiet," she said. "Hear me out."

With the exception of Crawford, I wasn't used to looking up at someone. But I looked up into her dark eyes and did what she asked: I heard her out.

THIRTY-FIVE

I don't lie.

But I'm really good at keeping secrets.

Heck, I've got a head full of secrets and, most times, I can forget about them and live in a world where none of the details of those secrets ever happened or would ever come to light. Remember, Max is my best friend — my sister, really — and has been for a very long time. If I didn't keep many of the facets of her interesting and complicated life a secret, she'd be in a heap of trouble with a lot of people. My secret-keeping began when we were first friends, back at St. Thomas, back when I was an impressionable kid who toed the line but was in thrall to my new friend, one who lived life on the edge.

To me, keeping a secret is way different than out-and-out lying, but it was a slippery moral slope and I knew that.

Max's inability to walk the straight and

narrow path and her clinging to her patented brand of extraordinarily bad judgment started long before we were adults, which will come as no surprise to anyone. Fueled by liquor, her judgment goes from extraordinarily bad to unconscionable and that's how I found myself stuffing her alcohol-soaked body into a closet one December night at St. Thomas when we were both still teenagers, me concocting an alibi for her as she slept off one of the worst drunks I had ever witnessed.

The police were not amused. Nor was the Guatemalan cab driver who wailed about his *cabina* over and over until Sister Marguerite Durand — aka Sister Billy Martin for her striking resemblance to the Yankees manager of the 1970s — was roused from her holy slumber on the fourth floor and came down to the first floor to see what all of the commotion was about. The commotion concerned the driver, who had left his cab running as he ran into the building to use the men's room on the first floor, and his missing vehicle. As the resident assistant on duty, I was doing my best to take charge of the situation but was doing a fair to middling job at best.

The last time I had trembled like that was when I had food poisoning and a hundred and four fever. I prayed that Max, in the coat closet right inside the front door of the building, didn't wake up before Sister Marguerite, the two cops, and the cab driver vacated the premises. I guess I might have noticed that one of the police officers was young, handsome, and tall, wearing a clean white undershirt that peeked appealingly from the top of his unbuttoned uniform shirt. I know for sure that I did notice the gold band glinting on the ring finger of his left hand, thinking that he was too young to be married. He was sent to find the cab, which he did with alarming alacrity. Turns out our cab thief, one Maxine Siobhan Rayfield, hadn't driven it very far; it was found, running with all of its doors locked, about five hundred feet from the circular driveway in front of the dorm but as close to the river as one could get with a motor vehicle without getting it wet. The officer, whose name I never got, had jimmied the lock on the driver-side door and driven the car back to the dorm. He was the closest thing to a superhero I had ever encountered.

Sister Marguerite looked at me as the cabdriver described the young woman whom he had picked up in front of Maloney's on Broadway: short, thin, dark haired, dressed all in black. Drunk as a skunk. Sister looked as though she were ready to blurt out Max's name, but something about my expression stopped her. Maybe it was the recognition that if Max was fingered and subsequently expelled (or worse), I would be lost; my father had died suddenly the summer before of a massive heart attack at the age of forty-four and Sister Marguerite knew that I was hanging on by the thinnest of emotional threads. Maybe it was the idea that Max's stunt would cast aspersions on our fine institution of higher, Catholic-style learning. Maybe it was the dawning realization that she herself would be in deep shit for not keeping a closer eye on things. Whatever it was, she stopped and disavowed any knowledge of the little deranged pixie who, if found, would be charged with a felony. She paid the cabdriver the fare from petty cash with an extra twenty for his trouble, apologized profusely for wasting everyone's time, and told the police officers and the cabdriver that she would pray for their safety every day for the rest of her life at evening vespers. She never did bring up the incident again but it was clear that she wasn't pleased and that she would look for any transgression to boot Max's skinny little ass from the dorm and, eventually, St. Thomas.

It was an incident that I had buried deep in my unconscious until Crawford had brought it up at dinner the week before. I was ashamed that I had been part of the incident, and that all these years later, I was still lying to protect my delinquent friend. He sometimes asked me why I was still friends with her and all I could say was that I loved Max. She had seen me through some very dark days and I was forever in her debt, as she was in mine. In her own way, she takes care of me. We don't always see eye to eye but we share a history. I am an only child and both of my parents are dead, having died long before they should have. Before I met Crawford, Max was all I had.

I understand undying love, even the platonic kind. I understand going to the ends of the earth for someone you love, even when they disappoint you or even when they betray you. I understand doing things that go against your very core so that they don't suffer for their transgressions or for the things that they don't even bring on themselves. I understand all of that.

So I understood why Lydia Wilmott wanted her husband to die.

Queen had already figured out who had put the explosive device on Carter's car engine. She had been in the guesthouse less than twenty-four hours and had solved the mystery of who else wanted Carter dead, but that's what happens when you're dealing with amateur criminals. They talk too much, and leave too many clues. You just have to be looking in the right place at the sort of right time, and you'll know everything that went into the commission of the crime.

Queen had been looking for a hedge clipper in the shed so that she could trim the boxwood that grew around the front door of the guest house. She never did find the hedge clipper, but she did find a cache of explosives and some copper wiring, and some kind of electrical setup that would serve as the igniter, or so she surmised. It was all there, right next to a bag of fertilizer and three half-empty cans of paint, the same paint that had been applied to the outside of Queen's doll-like new residence.

Unlike me, who gets all of her information through idle gossip or snooping, Queen does research. She went through her list of fellow Hooters waitresses until she came up with someone who had done a stint in Iraq and knew a thing or two about explosives. She told her coworker what she had found and her suspicions were confirmed. Just like eggs, flour, and butter sitting on a counter indicate that baking will commence, copper wiring, electronics, and fertilizer can mean only one thing. A bomb is in the works.

Armed with that information, I headed up to Lydia's, where I found her at the same counter at which I had originally encountered her, her hands deep in the sudsy water in the sink, washing out a wineglass. The sun setting over the Hudson cast a golden glow over the kitchen and I took a minute to admire the view.

"He wasn't healthy as a horse at his last physical," I said. "That's what your sister told me the first time I came here. I've been wondering why she offered up that information so readily and without provocation."

Lydia looked up and regarded me with her dark eyes. I was momentarily distracted by the hunk of diamonds around her neck. "What are you talking about? And how did you get in here?"

"ALS. Lou Gehrig's disease." I pointed to the front door. "And I walked in through the front door."

Her usually impassive gaze turned sad. She didn't ask me how I knew about Carter's diagnosis. "What do you know about terminal illness, Alison?"

"More than you'd think."

"Have you ever seen anyone die after a

long illness?"

I swallowed hard, forcing the emotion back down into my gut. My sadness about the loss of both my parents, but especially my mother, was like a wound in my heart that opened occasionally and brought with it great pain and suffering before it closed over again. It was always there and never healed completely or for very long. It just lay dormant until something reminded me of it and how much it hurt. "Sadly, yes."

"So then you know." She placed the wineglass that she had been washing on the drain board next to the sink, wiping her hands on a dish towel. "It's not pleasant."

"That's an understatement."

"I would never want anyone to suffer like Carter's father had." She saw the look on my face. "Yes, Carter's father died of ALS, as well. We know how it goes and it's not pleasant," she repeated.

"So you were going to blow him up."

The blank expression returned.

"The explosives," I said, showing her a little piece of copper wiring. "This." I thought back to the day at Beans, Beans, and how Lydia had asked for the car keys. And how she had started the car from a safe distance with the remote access feature.

She glanced at the copper wiring briefly.

"Interesting." She put her hands together as if in prayer. "I hope Queen is comfortable."

I was silent. If she wanted my thanks, she wasn't going to get it.

"I'm not sure why, but I loved him more than you'll ever know, Alison."

"Enough to kill him?"

"Enough to know that I never wanted to see him suffer as much as that disease would have made him suffer."

And with that one statement, I had my answer. Lydia stared at me and I stared back at her, neither one of us really seeing the other. I didn't know if she was telling me the truth; for all I knew, she wanted to blow him up to punish him for his various and numerous transgressions. Or she really did love him as much as she claimed. All I knew was that if I could have saved my mother the suffering that she had endured, I would have. The thought had crossed my mind on more than one excruciating night that it would take nothing to smother her and put her out of her misery and hasten the peace that she was due. I had always felt that I had failed her by letting her suffer all those many days and nights until she had reached her inevitable end.

"He had a lot of enemies," she stated flatly. "Any one of them could have set up that bomb and the timer to explode when Carter started the car." She looked out at the river. "Any one of them. They would have wanted him to die violently." She looked back at me. "Don't you think?"

I snapped out of my reverie and looked at Lydia, seeing her for what she was: a betrayed yet grief-stricken woman. Her story was certainly plausible because, yes, Carter had a lot of enemies. And most of them would have wanted him to meet a violent and untimely end. She had crafted a very believable explanation in the event that she was found out by someone other than me and Queen. I believed her; I wasn't sure why. My own unrelenting grief over the loss of my mother clouded my judgment, but I walked from the Wilmott house, secure in the knowledge that, like the identity of who had stolen Mr. Posso's *cabina,* the identity of the person who had rigged Carter Wilmott's car to explode would remain my secret alone.

Because I understand that kind of love.

Once back in my house, I took a deep breath and felt the wound that was my sorrow close over one more time.

But it would open again. It always did.

Thirty-Six

I found myself sitting in front of the Millers' tidy abode just a few minutes later. I wasn't sure what had brought me there. Maybe it was to offer a silent apology to George Miller for suspecting him of murder these past days or maybe it was to see how he was doing. Everyone had suspected him of murder, so I couldn't take on that guilt all by myself. And I didn't know him, so why would I care how he was doing?

The Subaru Outback that had belonged to Ginny, the car that she had used to follow me and Crawford on the day that Carter had died, was parked in front of the house with a homemade FOR SALE sign stuck inside the windshield on the dashboard. BEST OFFER, it said. The car was a little banged up, and had a few miles on it, just like its previous owner, and I wasn't sure how much money George would actually get for it, but it was clear that he wanted it gone. Beyond the car and down the driveway, I could see George Miller crouched beside a motorcycle, a toolbox beside him. Before I lost my nerve, I walked down the driveway toward him, a man with a lined and florid face that telegraphed sadness and a slight bit of menace, if I was being completely honest with myself.

I imagined Crawford's reaction when I told him what I had done, deciding then and there that he would never know. Why give him another illustration of my poor judgment and lack of common sense?

George stood slowly as I approached, pulling a handkerchief out of his back pocket and wiping his brow. He folded it neatly and put it back into his pocket. Introductions weren't really necessary, but he held out his hand anyway. "George Miller."

"Alison Bergeron." I shifted from one foot to the other. "I'm very sorry about your wife. About Ginny."

"I know what my wife's name was," he said, not unkindly. A brief smile passed over his face. "And I'm sorry about what happened to you. I never meant to hurt anyone."

"Thank you," I said. I touched my eye briefly and was relieved to find that it no longer hurt. That was the thing about physical pain: it goes away. The emotional kind just lingers and that's what makes it so hard to transcend. I thought about this as I stared into George Miller's craggy face. I would never know how deep his pain went, but judging by his eyes, it had no end.

"You interested in the car?" he asked. "I saw you looking at it."

"No," I said. "I was just thinking about how Ginny chased me in that car on the day that Carter died."

"She made it her business to make sure that I didn't get convicted." He ran a hand over the glossy leather motorcycle seat. "I'm lucky she was so devoted."

I knew why I had come. "Why did she kill herself, George?" I asked. "I mean, I have my suspicions but it's been bugging me. Why take her own life?"

He looked around, seemingly deciding how much he wanted to share with me. Finally, I guess he decided that there were no more secrets to keep and he just let it out. "The affair. With that scum, Wilmott." The menace that I detected drained out of him and all that was left was a grief-stricken husk. He was a big, powerful man who couldn't hold it in anymore. "She couldn't live with herself. Once I got out and it was clear that I had nothing to do with his death, she was done."

"But you didn't know."

"Not until right before she died. I don't know why but she told me." Again, the rueful laugh. "I never would have found out if she hadn't let her guilty conscience get in the way." The last part he muttered under his breath, but it sounded to me like "stupid broad." "Wait here," he said, and disappeared into the house. When he returned, he held out an envelope. "Here. Take this. It's addressed to you." A single tear dripped down the side of his nose.

I took the small white envelope from his hand, still sealed, and looked down at it. My name was on the front. "What is this?"

George shrugged and, with that effort, folded in on himself. "I don't know," he said, beginning to sob. "All I know is that it was with the suicide note that she left me. And it's addressed to you. You're Bergeron, right?"

"I'm Bergeron," I said, now figuring out why Ginny always referred to me by my last name. It was obviously a habit she had picked up from her rough-hewn husband.

As I turned to walk away, Ginny Miller's note in my hands, I heard him say one last thing that I hoped would be the last I would ever have to hear him say unless it related to garbage pickup.

"I would have forgiven her, you know."

According to the note she left me, which I read in my car in front of the Millers' house, Ginny didn't think he would have.

And according to the note, Ginny was terrified of George finding out, and clearing his good name was the only way she could atone for her sins.

According to the note, which had been left under George's pillow, Ginny Miller had been deathly afraid of George, a fact that surprised me more than anything else I had learned in the past week. I figured it would be the other way around, having gotten to know Ginny as well as I had.

And according to this note — which I wished I had never seen — not only had Ginny Miller never cared for my mother, she had never even met her. She had only found out about my beloved mother, Giselle, and her death through a memorial note that I published in the local paper every year on the anniversary, in which I expressed my love for my mother and my profound sadness at her passing. After that, it wasn't hard to figure out that she had been treated at Phelps while Ginny was working there, even though Ginny was working in maternity at the time and had never even considered oncology as a profession. It was all there in Ginny's handwriting, the words seared into my brain.

She asked for my forgiveness, but I wasn't in a very forgiving mood. And the only person who could help me reach full forgiveness was still not talking about his alleged transgressions and was still very angry at those who accused him of things he would never dream of doing.

I tore the note up into what seemed like a thousand little pieces, and as I drove away, scattered them on the Millers' street. I had been emotionally blackmailed into helping a woman exonerate her pig of a husband, and if that wasn't the stupidest thing I had ever done, I wasn't sure what was.

The only place I could think to go was a short drive away and flanked by the highway on both sides. This was the place that was supposedly Babe Ruth's final resting place, as well as that of Miles Davis, so to say that its residents were quite an illustrious and talented group would be an understatement.

My mother's grave was under a giant oak toward the center of the cemetery, and even though the day was hot and humid, I was chilled by the time I got there. I wrapped my arms around myself as I knelt before the stone, just to the left of my father's, and wiped away a year of grime that had collected in the etched letters that showed her name: Giselle Bergeron.

"I'm getting married, Mom," I said as if she were standing right in front of me; the tombstone was just her stand-in. "You'd love him. He's nice, he's smart, and best of all, he's tall!" I imagined her beautiful smile and her melodic laugh; she always told me that I was the funniest person she knew but it wasn't until after she died that I realized that that was a compliment and not a criticism. "And he loves me. I'm not sure why, but he does." I stared at the words on the stone until the letters blurred together. "I'm going to see if just letting myself be happy for a while works out." I laughed. "I know! I'm maturing finally. You always hoped that would happen." I looked around but I was the only person in this section of the cemetery. The trees were still in the mucky humid air. "He would have loved you just as much as I did. Just as much as I do." I put a hand on the stone which sat beneath an angel that had watched over my mother since she had arrived here. I reached up and touched the toes of the angel, something I did every year while I made a wish for the coming year. I don't know when that had started but it was something I continued to do.

It was on the toes of this angel that I had wished for Crawford, although I hadn't known his name at the time.

In my heart, I knew that wishing on the angel was a little silly. I also knew that stonecutters worked from the same molds and that there were probably a thousand angels in this cemetery and even on Catholic college campuses everywhere that looked just like this one. But when I looked up and discovered that this angel was exactly the same as the one that had been stolen from school, right down to the chipped wing tip, I knew that it was more than a coincidence.

"See you next year, Mom."

Thirty-Seven

I stretched my body on top of Crawford's, feeling the cool air from the air conditioner in my bedroom wash over my bare skin. I kissed him. "You know, we met once before. A long time ago."

His hand, the one that he was running down my spine, stopped, settling on my hip. "What?"

"We met. At St. Thomas."

"We did?"

I'm really good at breaking the mood. I rolled off him and pulled the duvet cover up over my chest. I was glad the room was dark because I didn't want to see the look on his face after I confessed what I knew. "Remember that story you told me about the stolen cab?"

He was silent as he put all of the pieces together. Slowly, it dawned on him. "You were the RA."

"Yep."

He rolled over on his side, propping himself up on his elbow. "And when were you going to tell me this?"

"I just figured it out. When you mentioned it at dinner. It all came back to me."

"You lied to me," he said, but I could detect, even in the dark, the smile on his lips. He could hardly believe that I had kept it from him for the last several weeks but found the humor in the situation, as well.

"I had decided a long time ago that I was going to take that piece of information to my grave," I said. I had also decided that if I was going to keep Lydia Wilmott's secret, I had to let another one out. Otherwise, I decided, I might explode. I didn't tell him that, however. Max's secret seemed like the most innocuous one to reveal under the circumstances. "Do you remember anything about that RA?"

"I remember that she looked like she was going to throw up," he said. "I remember that she was tall. And I remember that she kept staring at my undershirt." He traced a heart on my shoulder. "And I remember that the nun looked like Billy Martin."

I took his hand in the dark. "Max was in the closet right next to where we were talking."

He started laughing. "You must have

thought you were going to die."

"That about sums it up."

He chuckled again. "Why the hell are you friends with her again?"

"Because I love her," I said. "Remember? When you love someone, you don't want to see her suffer. Know what I mean?"

He knew exactly what I meant. He didn't subject me to the Crawford cross fire, and I didn't subject him to any more of my dithering. I had stopped my excessive overthinking on the subject and he had let go of the fact that his family needed to have any say in the subject of his happiness.

We boarded a plane the Friday of Labor Day weekend at Kennedy Airport, our destination Hamilton, Bermuda, and the Elbow Beach Resort, armed with a couple of bathing suits, a marriage license, a simple off-white dress for me, and little else. We even left Max and Fred behind, knowing that what we were going to do didn't need anyone else in attendance.

As I lay beside Crawford in bed, the ocean visible beyond the balcony of our hotel room, I realized that the wound, which I thought would always be a part of me, had closed for good.

ABOUT THE AUTHOR

Maggie Barbieri's father was a member of the NYPD, and his stories provide much of the background for her novels. This is her fifth Murder 101 mystery; Kristin Davis of *Sex in the City* has optioned the series for television. Maggie lives in Westchester County, New York.

We hope you have enjoyed this Large Print book. Other Thorndike, Wheeler, Kennebec, and Chivers Press Large Print books are available at your library or directly from the publishers.

For information about current and upcoming titles, please call or write, without obligation, to:

Publisher
Thorndike Press
295 Kennedy Memorial Drive
Waterville, ME 04901
Tel. (800) 223-1244

or visit our Web site at:

http://gale.cengage.com/thorndike

OR

Chivers Large Print
published by AudioGO Ltd
St James House, The Square
Lower Bristol Road
Bath BA2 3SB
England
Tel. +44(0) 800 136919
email: info@audiogo.co.uk
www.audiogo.co.uk

All our Large Print titles are designed for easy reading, and all our books are made to last.